Buried Stuff

Also by Sharon Fiffer
in Large Print:

The Wrong Stuff

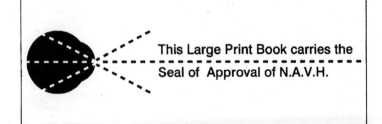

This Large Print Book carries the
Seal of Approval of N.A.V.H.

Buried Stuff

Sharon Fiffer

Thorndike Press • Waterville, Maine

Published in 2005 by arrangement with
St. Martin's Press, LLC.

Thorndike Press® Large Print Americana.

The tree indicium is a trademark of Thorndike Press.

The text of this Large Print edition is unabridged.
Other aspects of the book may vary from the original edition.

Set in 16 pt. Plantin by Minnie B. Raven.

Printed in the United States on permanent paper.

Library of Congress Cataloging-in-Publication Data

Fiffer, Sharon Sloan, 1951–
    Buried stuff / Sharon Fiffer.
        p. cm.
    ISBN 0-7862-7173-6 (lg. print : hc : alk. paper)
    1. Wheel, Jane (Fictitious character) — Fiction.
  2. Women detectives — Illinois — Chicago — Fiction.
  3. Antique dealers — Fiction. 4. Chicago (Ill.) — Fiction.
  5. Suburban life — Fiction. 6. Large type books. I. Title.
PS3606.I37B85 2005
  813'.54—dc22   2004062047

Steve —
just when things seem impossible,
you remind me of everything
that can be accomplished.

As the Founder/CEO of NAVH, the only national health agency solely devoted to those who, although not totally blind, have an eye disease which could lead to serious visual impairment, I am pleased to recognize Thorndike Press* as one of the leading publishers in the large print field.

Founded in 1954 in San Francisco to prepare large print textbooks for partially seeing children, NAVH became the pioneer and standard setting agency in the preparation of large type.

Today, those publishers who meet our standards carry the prestigious "Seal of Approval" indicating high quality large print. We are delighted that Thorndike Press is one of the publishers whose titles meet these standards. We are also pleased to recognize the significant contribution Thorndike Press is making in this important and growing field.

Lorraine H. Marchi, L.H.D.
Founder/CEO
NAVH

* Thorndike Press encompasses the following imprints: Thorndike, Wheeler, Walker and Large Print Press.

Acknowledgments

Thank you to the following people who provided medical expertise, gun information, general research, and friendship — not necessarily in that order: Judy Groothuis, Dennis Groothuis, James Hime, Michael Swartz, Lauren Paulsen, Becca Gay, Catherine Rooney, Thom Bishop, and Alan Rosen.

Thank you to my husband, Steve, and children, Kate, Nora, and Rob, who provide me with excellent advice, and who know how to balance good humor with unconditional support.

Thanks to Carly Einstein, Ben Sevier, and everyone at St. Martin's Minotaur, and to Joanne Brownstein and everyone at Brandt and Hochman.

And finally, thank you to Gail Hochman and thank you to Kelley Ragland, who make my professional life fun, interesting, fulfilling, and . . . oh yes . . . possible.

Chapter 1

If Jane Wheel could do it all again, go right back to the first step, square one of the major decision-making junctures of her life, if she could Michael Jackson moonwalk right back to where the metaphysical tines in the figurative fork in the proverbial road were first joined, then divided, would she choose the same path?

Flattened against the side of her garage, doors and windows locked against the outside world, Jane looked over at her husband, Charley — a geology professor who was one part Harrison Ford's Indiana Jones, one part James Stewart's Mr. Smith, and one part Jerry Lewis's Nutty Professor. Any woman in the world would feel lucky, grateful, and desirous watching him now, kneeling over a box and sifting though jagged hunks of rose quartz that the family had collected one summer vacation. If it weren't for the voices outside the garage door, the footsteps Jane could hear on the deck, the approach of strangers coming to reckon with her, she would feel all of those emotions herself — lucky, grateful, desirous. But instead she was scared, panicked, and paralyzed, knowing full well what was about to happen to all of them.

She needed to speak, to cry out, to warn her son. Nick was looking through a bag of books, blowing the dust off the top of the bindings, clapping the pages together hard, sending a shower of fine particles into the air. She might deserve what was about to happen, but Nick did not. He was only thirteen, a good student, a fine athlete, his whole life before him. Jane's heart cracked watching him, innocently smiling up at his father, showing him one of the books he had fished out of the bag.

Jane watched their mouths move, saw their hands gesture, their eyes crinkle in laughter, but it was as if she saw it all from underwater or through a Vaseline-smeared lens. It was all in slow motion, silent. Yes, time had slowed to a crawl; but instead of giving her the time to gather strength and vanquish the enemy, it only forced her to watch what was happening in excruciating detail, powerless to stop the encroaching evil.

On the other side of the garage, also moving in painfully slow and silent motion, was Tim Lowry. He held up a small rug. Jane remembered where she had found it, at a small, brick bungalow on Chicago's Northwest Side. It was hand hooked, a dog with a crooked tail and a smile. Jane remembered calling Tim and describing it as a dog with a human smile. She also remembered Tim, telephone smirking — he could smirk across the wires — telling Jane she must be a true connoisseur if she could tell the difference between a human smile and a canine smile. Then they had argued for more than thirty minutes about whether or not dogs smiled — or whether it was an attribute assigned to them from their human owners, who wanted to see and believe in doggy smiles. Jane wanted to shout at Tim now to look at Rita, panting and whimpering in the corner. Rita was not smiling, but she was grimacing and shaking her doggy head at what was about to happen. *And a dog has to be able to smile in order to grimace,* Jane wanted to tell Tim.

Tim was still silently chuckling, looking at the rug. Jane knew it wasn't well made and the colors were hopelessly faded. The finishing was not done properly, and it was beginning to come apart near the dog's left ear. But Jane loved it for the tiny signature barely decipherable on the backing. *Sarah's first project, made with Grandma Jessie, 1938.* Tim, Jane's best friend since they were both five years old, was shaking his head at the rug, that disdainful smirk on his face. *Look at the signature,* Jane would have cried had she still had the power. *Look on the back. It was Sarah's first project, for god's sake. Who will care for it? Who will protect it?*

Claire Oh smiled back at Tim, taking the rug from him, giving it a shake that was efficient and dismissive at the same time, draped it over the rungs of a ladder, a prize Jane had found at an auction in Wisconsin. A U-Pick orchard was selling out to developers, and Jane had snagged five great "picking" ladders, wide at the bottom for stability, narrowing at the top to reach into the branches of the apple trees. Claire Oh, dressed all wrong for the massacre that was about to take place, in a tailored navy blue suit with matching navy-and-white heels, narrowed her eyes while looking at the rug. She shook her head, as if to signal to the dog that he had nothing to smile about.

Jane had to find her voice, choke out a warning. She had to stop this.

Bruce Oh stood next to her, only two feet away. He looked straight ahead, as if he were steeling himself for something. Maybe he knew, too. Maybe he sensed what she had been unable to say. If she could raise an arm, she might be able to tap his shoulder. He would then read her eyes and know everything she knew. He would know the extent, the depth of what was about to happen. He would stop it. He would help her.

Jane desperately wanted this to be a dream. If she could wake up next to Charley, Nick snoring softly across the hall . . . what would she give for that? All of her hotel silver, the heavy forks and spoons and butter knives that she had found piece by piece? Her Chase cocktail shaker with the butterscotch Bakelite handles? The carton of old writing workbooks dated 1932 that she had found in a moldy box at the convent school? Her sewing boxes? Her giant tins of vintage buttons? No, no, no, and no. What bargain was she willing to make to have this reality be a dream?

How odd this was! All of the people she cared about were in this garage: Charley, Nick, Tim, Bruce and Claire Oh, and even her dog, Rita. Here they were, talking to one another, laughing, totally oblivious to Jane's fear. She could not choke out a syllable that they could hear nor could she understand what they were saying to one another, and yet she could pick up the smallest movement from outside. Of course she was expecting those sounds, those heavy footsteps, those thuglike voices, speculating on what they would do once they got inside. Who could she blame for this except herself? Jane had been warned. Just last night there had been the phone calls.

We're coming, the voices had said. *We know how to get there.* One particularly belligerent man had insisted that he wanted to come immediately. *I want to come tonight,* he had said. *I want to get to you first.*

Jane had hung up on him. She had locked the house and stationed Rita in the garage to bark at any intruders, but now Jane saw that the crowd gathering was too much for her dog. Rita looked at Jane with all the pain and suffering she could muster, as if to say, what have you gotten us all into now?

Tim was walking over to where Jane stood. She saw his lips moving and noticed that he was pointing to his wrist. Was he hurt? Already? No one had gotten through the door yet. What could have happened? Now Tim motioned her away from where she was standing. What was happening? They were all looking at Jane now. Charley was smiling and Nick talking. Claire Oh had pulled herself up to her entire six feet and was looking ready and able to fend off the hordes, and Bruce Oh was breathing deeply and standing perfectly still. Jane tried desperately to focus on what Tim was saying to her.

"Ready, we're ready," he said.

"No, we're not," Jane whispered back.

Jane felt something near her hand. Nick was patting it awkwardly, as if he wanted to comfort her and take it in his own, but knew that he had reached an age where it simply could not be done.

"It'll be all right, Mom," he said. "We're ready."

"No," Jane whispered again, wanting desperately to hold her son and shield his eyes from what was about to happen to her, to them.

"Can we please stop this nonsense?" said Claire Oh, cutting through Jane's anxiety like a knife. She reached her hand behind Jane to push the button that would open the electric garage door.

"It's eight a.m. My ad said eight a.m. If there's one thing I can't stand, it's a garage sale that doesn't start on time."

15

When the door opened, Jane's fears were confirmed. There were at least a hundred people — men and women carrying their own bags and bubble wrap, as Jane herself did when she stood on the other side of the door — shoving one another on her driveway, waiting to rush into where Claire, Tim, Charley, Nick, and Bruce had set up tables and racks of stuff — Jane's stuff — that she had grudgingly, when pushed and prodded — allowed that she might be willing to sell.

Claire Oh, a high-end antiques dealer who normally wouldn't dirty her hands — and still wasn't dirtying them, Jane noted, as she took in the thin, latex medical gloves Claire was wearing — was repaying a favor Jane had done her by running a garage sale for some of Jane's "extras."

Some favor, Jane thought. *I help her get clear of a murder charge, and she comes in to tear out my heart.*

Tim Lowry, not wanting to be left out, had also offered to help, but Jane had her suspicions about the attention he was paying to this sale. Jane knew she had several treasures Tim coveted, and she also knew that as a downstate dealer he didn't want Claire Oh getting first crack at anything valuable that Jane might be willing to part with.

Well, ha! Jane thought. *The laugh was on them both since she wasn't willing to part with anything.*

"Mom, how much for the ladder?" Nick asked.

"Not for sale," Jane said, delighted to find that her voice had returned when she needed it most. "We're just using them for display."

"Janie, you have five of them," said Tim.

"No," Jane said. "I want them all. They come in handy for . . ."

With all the noise and chaos and people pawing through her stuff, why suddenly did all of them get quiet as if waiting to hear what she would come up with as her reason for not selling the ladders?

". . . hanging stuff. I need them for hanging stuff."

"And you are a picker, Mrs. Wheel," said Bruce Oh. "They are the ladders for picking? Seems fitting. Perhaps hanging on the wall in the hallway, on their sides, you know?"

"Bruce? Is that you giving a decorating suggestion?" asked Claire, making change for a man with an armload of books whose titles Jane was desperately trying to read in case there were any she needed to snatch back. "Your idea of a well-decorated house is an empty one, isn't it?" she added.

"Not exactly empty," Oh said, considering his wife's comment. "I like a space to be itself, a space first, before it is . . . claimed. But there are certain objects that cry out, that have their story. These ladders . . ." Oh stopped and felt one of the rungs, sturdy and substantial, the wood burnished and worn in the places where so many feet had climbed. "These ladders have the quality of *wabi-sabi* . . . the worn and the used and the beauty of that use," Oh said. Then he shrugged. It had been a long speech for him to make.

Jane was deeply moved. It was what she believed. Objects had a story, a life, and if one had the eyes to see it, they conveyed their beauty and sense of history, of worth. Jane had so long been a curator of the unwanted that she felt supreme relief that someone else had made such an eloquent explanation of why she needed those ladders.

Jane was breathing a bit easier now that the sale had actually started. If she threw her eyes slightly out of focus, she wouldn't recognize that the stuff being bagged and bundled and shoved into backseats and tossed into trunks was the very stuff she had brought home and crowed over. Not all of it, of course. There had been some impulse buys, a few mistakes, and, as Tim put it so neatly, some "loser trash."

One of the benefits of clearing out some old stuff was making way for other old stuff. Claire Oh had done Jane the great favor of going through closets with her, helping her replace old "new" bedspreads and threadbare quilts with new "old" bedspreads and quilts. The just-in-case-we-have-to-host-a-marauding-army supply of old blankets that Jane hadn't liked when she bought them new on sale when she and Charley were first married were now someone else's treasure. And Claire had convinced her that the vintage chenille spreads Jane had captured years ago for a song before all the cable home shows and flea market parades had made vintage linens the next hot thing should be used on their beds and stored in the linen closets instead of boxed and labeled in the garage. Jane did believe in using her finds, she just didn't always get around to unpacking them. Claire was helping her take baby steps.

But what was that brute Big Elvis, a book guy and rival picker Jane battled with at every big sale, doing here in her garage, actually finding things he wanted? If he wanted them, that meant Jane shouldn't be selling them.

"Sorry, that's not for sale," Jane said, unable to see what was in his hand.

"It was out here, on the table," he said, not missing a step or looking at her. His eyes were in "sweep" mode, taking in everything in the garage; and he wasn't about to allow someone to stop him from finding the best, the rare, and the valuable. The fact that Jane happened to be the owner of the stuff was beside the point. Once that garage sale sign was hung, the owner had better stand back and wait for it to be over.

"Sorry," Jane said louder. "Mistake. It's not for sale."

She wished she knew what *it* was.

"What do you say? Is it for sale?" Big Elvis, his pompadour even higher than normal, arched his eyebrows and looked beyond Jane's left shoulder.

Charley walked up next to Jane, and said firmly, " 'No' always means 'no.' "

"Although in this case, I can't for the life of me . . . ," Charley started to say, as Big Elvis, disgusted, threw down the cigar box he had been carrying. He stomped out of the garage saying loudly that he had never seen a worse collection of junk.

"Thanks, Charley," Jane said.

He was a good husband. *Is a good husband,* Jane corrected herself. What was it about reaching their middle years, as Jane had begun to think of them — much better than labeling them the final half — that made her see things in past tense before she slapped herself into the present? She resolved to get a handle on now — right now.

Take Charley, for instance, and not for granted as she so often had. All of his qualities, his handsome face, his tan, strong forearms — Jane had always been an *arm* girl — his quick intelligence, his thoughtful answers to Nick's questions — all of these made Jane grateful for the man. And in a moment like this, when he came to her rescue without knowing why or what he was rescuing her from, that was an over-the-top moment. She would be present in this moment. Yes, she would, and not notice that someone was walking out of the garage with a boxful of hand-embroidered tea towels. *Breathe,* she told herself.

"Thanks, Charley," Jane said.

"You already said that," Charley said, picking up the cigar box. "What is this anyway?"

The rescued object was an El Producto cigar box. El Producto was alternately lettered in a deep rusty orange and black, and the picture was of a woman who had a most womanly figure dating from those good old days when arms could be soft and hips could be generous. The model's coloring, however, was from the bad old days when hair might be raven black, but Hispanic or Latina beauty was represented by a dark lace blouse, a tight skirt, and a stringed instrument incongruously placed in the most lily-white hands imaginable. Although the extremely white and voluptuous model with vivid red lipstick might date the cigar box to the fifties or early sixties, the two-for-twenty-seven-cents price was probably the most telling clue.

Jane was pointing this out to Charley, who flipped the lid up and down and said, "1967."

"I don't know, that seems a little late," Jane began.

Charley flipped the lid up again, and showed Jane that written across the top of the box in fat turquoise marker was JUNE 1967.

"My dad," said Jane, delighted. This *had* been worth saving. "It's one of my dad's."

Jane's dad, Don, and her mother, Nellie, ran a tavern called the EZ Way Inn in Kankakee, about sixty miles south of Chicago, seventy south of Evanston, where Jane and Charley and Nick lived and were currently fighting off the North Shore garage-sale hordes. Although the tavern was a sleepy neighborhood bar now, it had once been a bustling hot spot where Jane's dad tended bar and Nellie ran the kitchen with a cast-iron skillet and an acid tongue. She had stood at the grill or faced the giant soup pot as the factory workers lined up at the door and shouted their orders.

"Two double hamburgers, onion and pickle, and a vegetable beef, extra crackers," Leroy would yell, then move on to grab a seat at the bar and down two bottles of Pabst during a thirty-minute break from building stoves at Roper across the street.

"I'm charging you for extra crackers," Nellie would yell, flipping burgers, then preparing buns on a paper plate, throwing on the onions and pickles as she listened to the next order.

During the hour-long wave of factory workers that poured into the tiny tavern and clogged the kitchen doorway at the back of the shack, Nellie never stopped her constant motion of stirring, flipping, ladling, and plating orders. She never wrote anything down.

Since there were no bills, customers were on the honor system. After wolfing their food, washing it down with bottles of beer, they told Don what they had had and he collected the money or wrote it down on their lunch tab. They then settled those tabs on Friday when they brought their paychecks over and Don, with cash picked up from the bank earlier in the day, set up the check-cashing station in a back alcove of the bar. The EZ Way Inn might have predated credit cards and ATM machines, but in its heyday, it was as full-service and high-tech as its customers demanded.

The honor system worked, too, in those days. Although Jane did suspect that people might have been more honest then, she knew that the secret to Don and Nellie's high degree of success with their operation lay in the fact that Nellie's hearing was as sharp as her eye for seeing a smudge on a glass that Don had inadequately rinsed behind the bar.

From the kitchen she listened to the boys, as she always referred to them, recite to Don what they had ordered and consumed. If Leroy failed to mention the extra crackers, Nellie would come storming out of the kitchen, lambasting the red-faced Leroy.

"Who do you think pays for those crackers? Don't you think I got to pay somebody? Don't I deserve a dime for what I do?"

The regulars knew that Nellie's bark was worse than her bite. She would never let any of them starve. When Roper began a series of cutbacks and layoffs, long after serving food made any sense or profit, Nellie would still go in with Don at 7:00 a.m. and fire up the grill and chop the vegetables for soup. If Jane, or God forbid, Don, tried to reason with her about the sanity of pouring money into the food operation, Nellie would shout back, "Who's going to feed those boys? They got to eat."

Only after Roper Stove closed its doors for good did Nellie allow her kitchen to go dark. Don plugged in a pizza oven, and they kept the freezer stocked with pepperoni and sausage pies for the boys — now mostly retired stove workers — who might need a snack after playing cards all day or watching a doubleheader. The regular days of homemade soup turned into the occasional pot when Nellie was in the mood, and Nellie's incredible melt-in-the-mouth cubed steak and onions on white bread passed into a kind of folklore that the old-timers shared with their sons when they brought them in for their first legal beer.

This cigar box, this equivalent of Proust's madeleine for Jane, was, or rather had been, part of Don's EZ Way Inn system. Once a cigar box was empty of cigars, in this case, El Producto Blunts at two for twenty-seven cents, it entered into a new life as office equipment. Don wrote the month and year on the box lid and it became the file for beer and whiskey orders or canceled checks or whatever turquoise markers meant in June of 1967. He had a constant supply of cigar boxes, so once he rotated them out of use, Jane snatched them up for her various childhood and teenaged collections.

Gum-ball trinkets, ticket stubs, crayon stubs, shells, stamps, pennies — all had taken their turn as cigar box treasure. This particular one, though, was filled with what looked to Jane like rocks. But, of course, they were more than rocks to Charley.

"Some nice agate, a few hunks of quartz. Pyrite? What's that doing in . . . hey, Nick, look at these arrowheads," said Charley, wandering away with the box.

Jane didn't remember stashing any odds and ends from rock-hunting expeditions in one of her dad's old cigar boxes, but she had stacks of his old empties in the basement and Nick might have taken one for his own stuff. The zealous Claire Oh might have grabbed a few items from the hall closet outside Nick's room. Jane began to scan the tables frantically for some of Nick's carefully stored treasures, his old coins and baseball cards, items even more off-limits than all the other items that, in Jane's mind, were all off-limits.

Jane grabbed a deck of cards, whose backs advertised Butter-Nut Bread with the animated figure, Fred. Jane could still sing the jingle, "Bring home the Butter-Nut Bread, Fred," and as long as she could remember that, she thought she earned the right to keep the deck of cards. She also retrieved an apple corer with a red Bakelite handle as well as a Bakelite-handled cake breaker.

"Those are doubles," Claire said, seeing Jane grab the vintage utensils, "and besides, I put a high tag on them. You'll make money on those."

Jane noted that Claire was charging eight dollars for the corer and ten dollars for the cake breaker, so called because it could be used to separate hunks of angel food more efficiently than a knife could slice through it. Hefty garage-sale prices, especially since Jane had paid only a dime and a quarter for them, respectively, at a rummage sale last fall, but still . . . Yes, she had others, but these had *red* Bakelite handles and red was her favorite. The ones that Claire had left in her kitchen drawer had Butterscotch handles. She didn't want to part with them either.

"Take me out to the ball game, take me out with the crowd. . . ." Hearing the familiar melody, Jane started humming along, then realized that there must be a music box playing. Where had Claire found her music box that played "Take Me Out to the Ball Game"? And was the sweet little music box already in someone's hands; was another picker already shelling out money for it? Would Jane have to buy it back?

Wait. Did Jane have a music box that played "Take Me Out to the Ball Game"?

She focused in on the tune, reached into the pocket of her carpenter apron, and fished out her despised cell phone. Nick. He changed the ring almost daily, which made her hate the thing even more than she did when she had first gotten it. It was supposed to make Nick feel safe. Before becoming a picker a few years ago, Jane had worked long hours in advertising, producing television commercials. Charley, a geology professor and part-time paleontologist, was often in class or unreachable. And there was that little stretch when Jane and Charley lived apart — only a few blocks apart, but apart nonetheless — and Jane had promised Nick that she would always answer her cell phone. She'd sworn that no matter how seductive the rummage at a sale was, she would stop what she was doing and be there for him. It didn't always work out quite like that so Nick got his revenge by changing the ring on the phone almost daily. Every time "Jingle Bells" or "Greensleeves" started playing in the produce section of the grocery store and all the shoppers started slapping purses and pockets, Jane was always the last to know.

Tim and Nick were rocking side to side, singing "buy me some peanuts and Cracker Jack, I don't . . . ," laughing and slapping each other five, when Jane, glaring at both of them, ended the musical accompaniment by pushing the talk button.

Jane could tell right away that the worst morning of her life — okay, maybe not the worst, since she had found a few dead bodies in her day, although strictly speaking, she thought each of those events had taken place after noon — was about to get worse.

"Yeah, you're not driving in your car, are you?"

Jane's mother, Nellie, always started a conversation in the middle, never saying hello and always acting like she was the one being interrupted.

"No, I'm in the garage, I . . . we're . . ."

"Turn off the car. Don't back out while you're talking on the phone, for god's sake. Don, she's backing out of the garage and on the phone . . ."

"No, Mom, I'm standing here, just standing here, talking to you," Jane said. "What's up?"

"You still picking through junk or are you playing police with that Oriental guy?"

"Mom, I'm still a picker, and I'm assisting Detective Oh, who happens to have a Japanese father, on a case by case . . ." Jane stopped. Her mother never asked her what she was doing. Something was wrong. Nellie needed something.

"What's up, Mom?"

"Oh I don't know, your dad has some idea about what's going on out at Neilson's farm, thinks you and Charley can help with it, but I told him it was probably a waste of everybody's time."

Okay, thought Jane, just sort it out like untying a knot. *Keep the threads loose and work them out slowly, one at a time.*

"Fuzzy's here if you want to talk to him," Nellie said.

"No, wait," Jane said, too late. Fuzzy Neilson, an EZ Way Inn customer for as long as Jane could remember, was saying hello.

"That you, Janie?"

"Hi, Fuzzy," said Jane, watching someone carry off a box of Nick's old AYSO (American Youth Soccer Organization) jerseys. She had wanted to save them and make them into a quilt for Nick when he went to college. He was only thirteen. She could learn to quilt by the time he was eighteen, couldn't she?

"Don't get her agitated; she's got the car in reverse," Nellie said in the background. Jane could also hear her father's voice, shushing Nellie, the original unshushable.

"Hate to bother you, Janie, but your mother was bragging about you being able to figure out stuff, and she said your husband knew a lot about rocks, so . . ."

So far Fuzzy wasn't coming in so clear. Jane's mother, Nellie, bragging about her? Jane highly doubted that.

Jane heard a clunk and some heavy swearing. Nellie. Then she could hear Don yelling Fuzzy's name.

"Nellie, let him alone. Call an ambulance. Fuzzy? Fuzzy Wuzzy? C'mon, Fuzz! Get up!"

"Don't think he's breathing," Nellie said. "Dead."

"What's going on?" Jane shouted as loudly as she could into the phone.

Everyone in the garage, sellers and buyers alike, stopped at the sound of Jane's voice. Claire Oh, in the middle of a transaction, stood frozen with a twenty-dollar bill in her hand. Charley, Nick, and Tim looked up from the box of rocks, concerned. Bruce Oh looked Jane in the eye, calm and expressionless as usual, but fully engaged and curious, also as usual.

Jane heard her dad say something ending with the word "dead."

"Sale's over," Jane said firmly. "Everybody out of the garage." She had her finger on the electric door button. "Now."

Shoppers grumbled and groaned. Claire handed back the twenty and pointed the woman who had been waiting to buy three old wooden jigsaw puzzles the way out. Jane pushed the button as the last of the bargain hunters rushed under the closing

32

door. The garage door clunked to the ground at the same instant Jane's phone clicked off.

Fuzzy Neilson, a Roper Stove press room worker, a weekend farmer who supplied Jane's family with fresh tomatoes and peppers all summer long, a kind old man Jane had known all her life, was calling for her help.

Dead?

Fuzzy wasn't, was he?

Chapter 2

"Two hundred and forty-one dollars and fifty cents," Claire said, placing the wrinkled bills firmly on the kitchen table. "We were open for just under fifteen minutes. Can you imagine if . . . ," Claire began, then looked at Jane, pacing the kitchen, punching redial on her phone. She let the rest of the sentence go.

"That's exactly what my lawyer charges when I talk to him on the phone for fifteen minutes," said Tim, poking through the refrigerator. He found a foil-wrapped triangle and held it up. "Anybody have a clue what this once was?"

Nick took the leftover pizza, unwrapped it, zapped it in the microwave, and handed it to his godfather. "It's only from last night. Mom says we can eat it up to three days, four or five if it's vegetarian."

"How did you arrive at that time frame, Ms. Home Ec Dropout?" asked Tim, taking a small, careful bite of pizza.

Jane stopped pacing, looked at Tim, looked around at everyone standing and sitting in her big friendly kitchen, and was glad to see them all — Nick, Charley, Tim, Oh, and Claire — but she couldn't for the life of her think why they were all there expecting her to say something. Her eyes fell on the money Claire had placed on the table.

"What did we sell that made so much?" Jane asked. She still held her cell phone with both hands. She looked from it to Claire to the money.

Before Claire could recite the list of objects that had passed through her hands in the quarter hour of Jane Wheel's *first ever giant garage sale, a picker's delight, tons of vintage and collectibles,* according to the classified ad Claire herself had placed, Charley interrupted.

"I got through," he said, holding the kitchen phone out. "It's ringing."

"You talk, Charley," said Jane. "Ask if . . ."

Jane stopped. Was it because she was confident that Charley would know what to say, could speak to Nellie and Don more efficiently than she could? Yes, absolutely. It was also because she was afraid to hear her mother say that Fuzzy Neilson had dropped dead on the floor of the EZ Way Inn and that the dead body problem that

had dogged Jane for too long was now rubbing off on her parents. If people started
dropping dead around Nellie, what was
next? Would Tim find a body every time
he opened up a hand-painted marriage
chest?

Claire was explaining to Oh why people
were willing to pay money for pieces of a
wrought-iron fence that Jane had dragged
home from the alley. Jane had kept the
most ornate two sections, thinking they
would make a great headboard. If she ever
cleaned them up. If she ever got the hardware to mount them on the wall behind
their bed. If she ever found them again
under the pile of old wooden shutters
where she had stored them. The intricate
ironwork had initials in the two front sections and Jane was a sucker for initials. If
you squinted on these gates, one of the letters could almost be a *J*.

Jane carried the following in her oversize
bag: A leather business-card case monogrammed with *ASF*; two handkerchiefs,
one embroidered with a blue *AUNT BETTY*
and one with the initials *SS*; a vintage com-
pact with the inscription *JESSIE FROM
ALVAH*. When Tim, pawing through her
purse in search of food, questioned all the
initials and names that were not her initials

and names, Jane could only shrug and explain that the names belonged to someone. The objects had someone's identity entwined with their history. Someone had loved them or been loved enough to receive them, and Jane's job was to allow the history to continue.

"Yeah?" Tim had asked her, chomping on the celery sticks he had fished out. "What about your history? What're you entwining with your identity?"

Oh was telling his wife that he understood the *wabi-sabi* of the gates, the beauty of the worn and well used. However, since Mrs. Wheel had found them in the alley, or the Big Store, as she preferred to call it, why did people now pay money for the sections of fence? Couldn't they find their own pieces of — what was the word his wife preferred to garbage? Refuse? No. Salvage. Yes, couldn't people find their own salvage?

Jane saw Charley nod and smile, although she hadn't heard him say anything into the telephone. Not unusual for a conversation with Nellie. Listening was one's primary role or, in Jane's long-running mother-daughter drama, listening and knowing when not to listen.

Charley would not nod and smile if they

were describing Fuzzy's demise. Charley would get that concerned scrunchiness around the eyes, all the weathered creases at the corners forming a network of concern and compassion. Jane began breathing more normally; and as she calmed her fears about a corpse at the feet of Don and Nellie, she got more and more curious about why Fuzzy Neilson had wanted their help.

Fuzzy was a regular at the EZ Way Inn, had been since Jane could remember. As a matter of fact, Jane couldn't think of one new customer at her parents' tavern. Every one was a regular. Fuzzy, Gil, Pete, the two Barneys, Vince, Henry, Junior, Willy, and Aggie had all been sitting around the bar at the EZ Way Inn since Jane's first memories of hoisting herself up on a bar stool and having Nellie tell her to get down and take her coloring book to a table in the adjoining dining room. The dining room was not separated from the barroom by a wall or a door but by a slight rise in the floor, a tip-off that this adjacent room with eight tables and the only pay phone had been built as an afterthought to the real business of the EZ Way Inn. That business was conducted around a large square mass of oak with dim lights hanging from the low ceiling, a brighter light coming from the television perched high on a corner shelf, bearing a sign that reminded all watchers that only Don and Nellie adjusted volume or changed channels.

Nellie told Jane that the bar was no place for children, but she never found it necessary to explain or ironic to observe that Jane spent all of her after-school hours at the EZ Way Inn waiting for Don and Nellie to finish up the business of the day and hand over the reins to the evening bartender, who came in at six.

Nellie was a literal-minded woman. A pragmatist. It was a fact of life that if you owned a bar and happened to also have a kid, the kid might have to be there waiting while you mopped up, counted money, served customers, or finished a card game. It did not mean that said kid could actually sit at the bar. Kids didn't belong in bars. Nellie didn't bother much with explanations and wanted nothing to do with irony. It held no interest for her unless it had something to do with washery or dryery.

So Jane, the kid in question, would take a seat at one of the tables, open her coloring book or pad of paper, spill out the crayons, and begin to practice her art. With every passing day of childhood, it had less to do with applying color to paper and all to do with listening and watching. She might not be able to see the TV in the corner, always tuned to the White Sox by choice, the Cubs by default, but she had the big-screen view of the barroom where Nellie and Don performed their give and take with the customers, Nellie scolding and harassing, Don serving and soothing. Jane's art, it seemed, would be the art of observation.

Tuning the memory channel to Fuzzy, Jane got a clear picture. A tall man with black-framed glasses, a toothy smile, a spikey crew cut, which somehow must have translated into "fuzz" hence "Fuzzy." Nicknames were an odd mix of skewed observation and grammatical adventure. For example, Nellie's sister, Veronica, was tall and thin and a marvelous athlete, a center on the Orange Crush girls' basketball team, and this somehow earned her the nickname "Fat." Jane called her Aunt Fat for twelve years without question, despite the fact that the woman hadn't an ounce of extraneous flesh. The fat part hadn't even raised Jane's eyebrow, but the grammatical construction of using "fat" as a proper noun had always given her pause. Kankakee did strange things to syntax, grammar, and intellectual curiosity.

Anyway, Fuzzy or Fuzz or Fuzzy Wuzzy, had a tall stand of salt-and-pepper hair, an easy laugh, and a gee-whiz kind of expression that Jane found endearing. He worked at Roper, but his real love was farming. He had a place west of town, twenty acres or so that he farmed himself on weekends and hundreds more acres that he leased out to others. Corn and soybeans were the major crops, but Fuzzy's vegetable patch was the love of his life.

August first or fifth or thereabouts, depending on rain, sunshine, and how late the frost had visited during the past spring, Fuzzy would appear in the doorway of Nellie's kitchen. The EZ Way Inn might belong to Don and Nellie, they might share the floor space behind the bar and in the dining room, but the L-shaped alcove behind the bar and in the northwest corner of the tavern held Don's desk and adding machine and was Don's. The kitchen, accessible through an open doorway and down a step from the barroom, as well as through a flimsy screen door from the parking lot via a concrete slab porch, was Nellie's. She allowed Don to help with chopping onions on cubed steak days and wash a few pots and pans while she cleaned the rims of the ketchup bottles and mustard pots, but the space itself remained hers: Nellie's kitchen. And when Fuzzy appeared in her doorway with two newspaper-wrapped orbs in each of his large, meaty hands, holding them out to Nellie with a wide-open grin, it signaled the peak of summer.

Beefsteak tomatoes; redder than the reddest thing you can remember, the tomato nearly bursting out of its skin. A solid slicer, holding its shape and looking like a magazine advertisement, it had a flavor so warm and earthy and sweet that just a wave of the saltshaker took it to culinary heaven. Nellie would sniff it and pinch it and slice it. Don ate his with salt and pepper and a knife and fork, Nellie tasted it plain, nothing to interfere with her pronouncement of whether Fuzzy had bested last year's cream of the crop.

Jane loved it plain, with salt, with pepper, with the juice running down her chin. But best of all, she liked it on two slices of white bread with a smear of mayonnaise. Yes, a sacrilege to some, and as an adult, a cholesterol-laden, food-snob no-no, but at eight years old, tomato and mayonnaise oozing out of both sides of the first bite of the gummy Wonder Bread, it was as close to perfection as the EZ Way Inn experience allowed.

For the adults who called the EZ Way Inn their second home, it might have been an ice-cold bottle of beer pulled from low in the cooler or a frosted mug of whatever Don had on tap that season, but for a kid like Jane and a teetotaler like Nellie, the tomatoes were summer. When Fuzzy arrived, fruit in hand, Nellie's straight line of a grim mouth cracked into a million pieces, wreathed in a hopeful smile.

"They good as last year's, Fuzzy?" Nellie would ask.

"Better," he'd say, nodding and placing them on her wooden counter, offerings to the great Nellster at the altar of EZ Way.

"Reports of Fuzzy's death were, it appears, greatly exaggerated," said Charley, hanging up.

"Shall we?" asked Claire Oh, directing her question about reopening the garage door and cash box more to Tim than to Jane. She had not given up on salvaging the garage sale, even though they had lost much of the prime Saturday morning first-hour crowd. Any early shopper who had come by in these first fifteen minutes and seen the garage door closed would have

43

rushed to the next house. They wouldn't loop back this way until they had gone through their ranked list. Claire, a dealer now, had not picked a garage sale herself for many years, but she remembered the drill. First hour, jammed, a small drop off, then the second wave of shoppers who had marked your sale the second most interesting of the morning. People would roll in like the tide until around 1:00 p.m., then no one would come until fifteen minutes before your closing time, hoping you were dog tired and brain-dead, ready to give away the kitchen sink and all the old, unopened wedding gifts, stained linens, and electronics in questionable working order.

Bruce Oh, sensitive to his wife's promise that she would assist Jane Wheel in clearing out some of her "extras" as a personal thank you for Jane's help in clearing her name and reputation as a dealer, appraiser, and upright citizen in general, noted the horror on Mrs. Wheel's face when she realized that she might not have gotten out of today's sale after all. They were so different, these two women in his life. A bystander might say that they had so much in common, both interested in antiques and the business of collecting. Oh knew, however, that his wife had an eye for the business, the buy and sell. Mrs. Wheel had an eye for the romance, the buy and protect.

"First, before we discuss reopening," Oh said, subtly directing that toward his wife, "may we know what happened to your friend?"

"Fainted," said Charley. "Stress, heat . . . he was out in his garden in the sun all morning. I pieced that together listening to Nellie grill him and Don getting him to drink water."

"Stress?" said Jane. "Fuzzy Neilson used the word 'stress'?"

"My word. His statement went something like, 'I been banged around so much lately, my teeth are rattling,' " said Charley, "or something like that."

Jane tried to picture Don and Nellie and any of their customers succumbing to stress. All the ailments she and her contemporaries suffered — anxiety, carpal tunnel syndrome, stress — would be dismissed by the EZ Way crowd. Whenever Jane complained as a child about any ache or pain, her mother's response had always been the same. *Mom, my leg hurts. Oh yeah? Well, everybody's leg hurts.* Nellie had been a pioneer in tough love.

"What did Fuzzy want, Charley? Or

what did Mom say he wanted?" Jane asked.

"Seems Fuzzy's made an interesting discovery on his land," Charley said, pouring himself coffee and waving the pot around to offer some to the others. "Some weekend gardener was driving around in the country and saw Fuzzy out working in his vegetable patch, admired his corn and tomato plants, and asked for some tips. Fuzzy extolled the virtues of his dirt, and the guy asks to buy some topsoil."

"What guy? Did Nellie give a name?" asked Tim.

"No, why?" asked Charley, rummaging in the refrigerator for half-and-half. When he found a carton, he read the date, sighed, and poured the lumpy mess in the sink.

"I don't know. Seems like a funny thing for any townie to do if they're from Kankakee. Just seems out of character for anyone to be offering money for soil. I can't get them to part with a dime to buy decent flowers, so" — Tim stopped — "Hell, it makes perfect sense, I guess; they'd rather spend money on the dirt. Figures."

Tim mumbled something about Kankakee, and Jane gave him the evil eye.

"If you dislike it so much, move up here.

You can't go around knocking all the people who live there if you're one of them."

"So what's the problem, Dad?" asked Nick. "Money for dirt sounds like a great deal." Nick was still looking through the cigar box that Jane had snagged away from the sale. He was lining up the rocks in front of him at the kitchen table.

"Fuzzy thought so, too. In fact he stuck a sign out by the road advertising topsoil for sale, and when someone came along wanting to buy a big load of it, Fuzzy got out his tractor or tiller or whatever he was using to dig it up and turned up more," said Charley.

"You're being pretty dramatic about this, Charley," Jane said, smiling. What was making her quiet, thoughtful husband so bright-eyed and expansive?

"Well, my dear, it seems you're not the only one who finds bodies strewn about your path. Fuzzy uncovered some skeletal remains."

"A body?" Jane asked.

"Bones, anyway," said Charley. "Might be something. A real find."

Claire, looking out the kitchen window, reminded everyone that people were still arriving for the garage sale.

"Are we closed for good?" she asked. "I'd be happy to go out and handle things while you all discuss . . ." What was it they had been talking about? Claire had been calculating how much money they were losing huddled together in the kitchen when they should have been moving merchandise in the garage. What was the big deal in here again? Oh, yes. ". . . the bones in question," she said.

All eyes went to Jane. She closed her own eyes and pictured the garage, the tables and the racks they had filled with stuff. Most of the dishes and the smalls were pieces she had collected for Miriam in Ohio, then realized that her old dealer friend wouldn't want them, they were too common to be worth shipping out. Or the stuff was *mistake stock:* stuff that looked good from the auction floor, bought on a quick, cheap whim, then unpacked and found to be worth even less than the dollar she had given the cashier. There were also things in the garage she had dragged home from the alley. What was it that made a green ceramic lamp look so great perched on a Dumpster and look so terrible wiped down and set on a table?

"Why were Mrs. Wheel's parents calling on you about this?" asked Oh.

"The police came and determined that the bones weren't anything to do with their watch, so they suggested calling somebody in from the junior college. An expert needs to come in and figure out exactly what the find entails. Is it a burial ground? A village site? Is it Native American at all?" said Charley. "Sometimes it turns out that what farmers or construction workers turn up are animal bones and no big deal, but even if that's the case, the bones have been reported, someone is going to have to take a second look, complete the paperwork, and sign off on it."

"You would be that pair of eyes?" asked Oh.

"I've got the whole month before school starts. August is usually when we try to go away somewhere, but we didn't make any plans. Nellie said something about an old log cabin on Fuzzy's farm, and I was thinking maybe we could set up a camp there for a few days — it'd be fun. I could teach Nick some more stuff, and Jane, you could go poke around in Kankakee basements with Tim," said Charley, hope raising the pitch of his voice slightly, sounding just like Nick when he *really* wanted to do something.

"Or I could dig with you guys," said Jane.

Charley and Nick looked at her with such surprise, she laughed out loud.

"Come on, a treasure hunt's a treasure hunt. I could —" Jane began.

"Okay," said Tim, "I give you one day in the field before you call me on that cell phone of yours and beg me to find an estate for us to sell." Jane started to protest, but Tim continued. "Besides, I've got a huge deal cooking. Huge. A deal that will make you eat your little 'self-loathing' dig, dear. And you are seriously the person I need to make it happen."

Jane was a sucker for flattery and for being needed. Combine the two and you had her right where Tim knew he had just put her.

In fact she was so pleased that she didn't notice Tim give a subtle nod toward Claire Oh to indicate that the timing would never be more perfect.

"Please, Jane, while we've still got customers coming, how about I just clear out a bit of stuff for you?" Claire asked.

"Okay," Jane said. "Go ahead."

Claire raced toward the garage.

"I'll help," Tim offered. "We'll just thin the herd, ma'am. We won't sell off any of the good breeding stock."

Jane sniffed the air. *Eau de she'd-been-*

played was wafting toward her.

"There better be some big deal," Jane called after Tim. "Huge. And don't you dare sell the ladders or cigar boxes."

Jane looked under the kitchen table. Good. The two boxes she had dragged inside from the garage last night were still there. Did Tim and Claire really think she was going to part with her sets of Alice and Jerry readers? She reached into the box that held the old grade-school textbooks and pulled out *Runaway Home*. This book held as much sway over her as *Charlotte's Web* and *The Catcher in the Rye* put together. It was a sensational story of a family that traveled across the country in an Airstream trailer. The father was an artist and painted landscapes and portraits along the way. The kids picked up odd jobs. Jane had begged Don to buy a house trailer so her family could follow the example. Don, however, had pointed out that the EZ Way Inn was anchored to the ground, and, for better or worse, Don and Nellie were anchored to the EZ Way Inn.

The other box Jane had snatched back from Claire's and Tim's clutches held old autograph books that Jane had been collecting from estate sales and flea markets for years. She caressed the small, velvet-covered book, the first one she had acquired that had belonged to Maud Gomel. Most of the entries in her little keepsake were dated 1900. Who would take care of that if Jane let it be sold out there in the cold, dusty garage?

With all of the self-control she could muster, Jane did not follow Claire and Tim to the garage. She had saved the important things, she told herself. If she didn't see the other stuff when it was carried away, maybe she wouldn't miss it. It was the idea of the stuff being sold, being carted out in old, brown grocery bags, wrapped in last week's newspapers. She had gathered all of these objects to save them from the rubbish bin or the rummage table; now their rescue was being transferred to someone else. Jane swallowed hard and fought the urge to run out to the garage and throw herself on top of the folding metal tables Claire had loaned her for today.

Instead she turned to Charley, Oh, and Nick, all sitting at the kitchen table. They were waiting to see which side won the tug of war. Jane placed the copy of *Runaway Home* on the table in front of her and resisted the impulse to begin paging through Maud Gomel's autograph book. Instead, she tucked the little treasure into her bag by the door. Three pairs of eyes watched her, followed her movements. Would it be the stuff or them?

Jane picked up *Runaway Home* and considered the illustration of the family in front of the Airstream trailer. Squinting just a bit, she made herself substitute Charley and Nick for Dad and son and slipped an image of her own self into Mom's apron. Yes, they should hit the road, take off on a working vacation.

Pulling up a chair, she sat down, took another cleansing breath as she heard the garage door go up, and said, "Let's talk bones."

Chapter 3

"I guess Fuzzy just wants somebody there who can explain what's going on, somebody on his side," said Charley, turning up the car's air conditioner, "an interpreter and an advocate."

"My mother explained it that way?" Jane asked, closing Maud's autograph book. It had become a habit, reading a page every time she opened her bag. The entries had become daily affirmations, and Jane thought she owed it to Maud to piece together some of her friendships, some part of her life, by reading the messages. After all, why else would the book have fallen into her hands? Jane shifted the vents away from her, directing some air toward Nick in the backseat.

"Not exactly. She said Fuzzy had dug up some rocks that somebody thought they could make a buck off of, so everybody wants a piece, and now they're trying to screw Fuzzy out of his own dirt," said Charley.

"What about the bones?" asked Nick.

"That's what we have to find out — whose bones, how old? If Fuzzy has been growing those tomatoes on a significant site . . ." Charley let his voice trail off.

Jane saw a faraway look in Charley's eyes. Desire, curiosity, and what was that deep glow? Lust? Oh my, Jane recognized this. It was her own look when she stood in the doorway at St. Anthony's rummage sale and saw a box of vintage flowerpots that everyone else had missed.

Nick was looking through some of the boxes Jane had stuffed into the backseat. "Are we going to need tent stakes, Mom? Are we really camping out?" he asked.

Jane had agreed that in lieu of the family vacation she had failed to plan, they would take a few days and camp on Fuzzy's land. Although her mother had claimed there was a cabin, Jane wasn't sure what they would find. Since she didn't have time to locate the perfect Airstream camper for them, she had packed tent, sleeping bags, stove, the works. They had put everything together in record time and now, at 3:00 p.m., just two hours after Claire Oh had made the last deal with a Willie Nelson look-alike — fifty dollars for everything that was left — closed the garage door, and rubbed her hands together over the till,

Jane, Charley, and Nick were on the road to Kankakee.

She had nodded in agreement with everyone when they admired the empty spaces in the garage, the clear path to the side door, and she had marveled at (a) how easy it was to find the camping gear now that all the other stuff in the garage was gone, and (b) how easy it was to pack when you could park the car in the garage. Jane didn't mention how the clean shelves and empty corners cried out to her to be filled. That could wait. *Want less,* she told herself, *want less.* The rest of this weekend, she was going to devote herself to Charley's profession, to his and her son Nick's passion. No sales, no auctions, no . . . The *William Tell Overture* interrupted her thoughts.

Nick laughed at Jane's puzzled look. He stretched his arm over the seat and lifted her cell phone out of her bag.

"I like this ring, Nick. Can we keep it for more than a day?" Jane asked, pressing the answer button without first checking to see what number was calling. She steeled herself for Nellie since Nellie always caught her in the car, always scolded her for having a cell phone, always castigated her for answering it. She never seemed to think

she had any part in the technological con-
spiracy to ruin the world by dialing the
number. It was Jane's responsibility not to
answer.

"Baby, have Charley drop you off at the
store. I got a job for you right away."

Tim had left Jane's home in Evanston
immediately after the sale and was already
back at his store in Kankakee.

It took Jane a moment to switch gears
from Nellie's bossiness to Tim's.

"I can't, Tim. We're setting up camp at
Fuzzy's. I told you —" Jane said, but was
interrupted.

"Honey, let Charley and Nick do it. I
didn't get a chance to let you in on the big
deal at your place. I need you. And, besides, you don't know a tent pole from a
ski pole."

It was true. Jane was a dreadful camper.
She could pack a vintage hamper with a
great lunch, fill it with Bakelite picnic
ware, and fill an old plaid picnic thermos
with homemade lemonade, but she
couldn't make heads or tails of the pop-up
tent. It never popped up for Jane, it turned
inside out as quickly as an umbrella on a
windy day. She could accessorize the
campsite with the best of them, make it
look all jolly and gingham and photogenic,

but the construction of it was not her forte.

"I promised Charley and Nick that I'd help them —" Jane began, but was cut off quickly, too quickly, by Charley and Nick.

"No, honey, we'll drop you at Tim's, no problem," Charley was saying at the same time Nick said, "Dad and I will take care of the campsite, Mom."

How desperate were they to keep her from standing proudly on uneven rocky ground and declaring it the best place for a tent?

Jane turned to look Nick in the eye.

"Please," he said, "Dad and I like to do it. Male bonding and all."

Nick was getting smarter every day. How would she ever keep up?

THE WORLD'S LARGEST GARAGE SALE

Hosted by
KANKAKEE, ILLINOIS
FORMERLY THE LEAST LIVABLE CITY IN NORTH AMERICA,
NOW THE HOME OF THE TWIN GAZEBOS

September 14–16 and 21–23
throughout the town of Kankakee
Discover the treasure next door!
Questions? Tim Lowry, T & T Sales

"Ta da," said Tim, holding the poster up as Jane came in the front door of his flower shop.

"What gazebos?" Jane asked.

"The ones Letterman gave the town," said Tim. "But that's not the important part of the poster, dear."

"David Letterman gave you gazebos?"

"Remember when Kankakee was named the least livable city?" Tim asked, not looking up from the poster he had placed on the counter and was admiring. "Letterman made it into a bit and talked to the mayor and presented the town with gazebos, which he guaranteed would make the town a better —"

"No," Jane said. "I didn't know."

"Well, it doesn't make any difference, I —"

"What was the criteria for this? Who decided?" Jane asked.

Tim sighed. Jane wasn't going to listen to the plan for turning the town around until she heard about the latest detour on the road to Kankakee's recovery in detail. He told her about the organization that rated cities on livability.

"They assign points based on unemployment rate, cost of living, cultural opportunities . . . I don't know, a bunch of quality-of-life questions," said Tim. "Seems like Kankakee came up a few points short."

"Did they go sit by the river and watch the sun on the water?" asked Jane.

"Uh-oh," said Tim, "ladies and gentlemen, the prodigal daughter is now working up a head of steam."

"Did they feed the ducks at Bird Park? Get a peanut buster parfait at Dairy Queen or a sauce bun at the Root Beer Stand?"

Jane paced the length of Tim's store.

"Did they go collect buckeyes at Cobb Park? Did they walk the vita-course and do chin-ups in full view of St. Martin's? Go to the gladiolus festival in Momence? Try to win a pie at the rhubarb festival at the Civic Auditorium?"

"Janie, dear, your outrage is endearing, but you know the sad state of affairs here. Business ain't so great, pal, and there's a lot of debate over what might improve the town. A lot of folks believed a new airport was the answer, but . . . ," Tim said.

"New airport? To solve the overcrowding at O'Hare?" asked Jane.

"So you do read a paper now and then?" said Tim. "Kankakee and Peotone were all over the place being floated as airport sites."

"How do you feel about that?" asked Jane.

"I'm on the fence," said Tim, shoving a carved walnut chair away from a display and toward Jane. "Sit down, for god's sake, you're making me dizzy." He poured coffee from a thermal carafe for Jane and himself and spoke deliberately and more seriously than Jane was used to.

"There is a part of me that wants to shake everyone in town by the shoulders and tell them to accept the gift of business and jobs and tax revenue and all the rest. Would there be a downside? Absolutely, but what's the upside to unemployment and boarded-up stores downtown? I hate that. Remember Saturdays when we were kids? You'd go downtown, and it was classy and busy and Kankakee people spent their money in Kankakee. Three movie theaters. A bookstore. Two candy stores. Remember the caramel apples at Carolyn's next to the Paramount? There was stuff to buy and places to go and a lot of pride," Tim said, sighing. "I know it's the same in all the midsized industrial towns — factories leave for cheaper labor and the slide down begins — I know the drill. But I can't help but think that if people had just held on, shopped local, tried harder to keep down-town alive . . . oh hell, I don't know . . ." Tim let himself drift off, then recovered.

"I'm sounding like you with your river watching and buckeye picking. Maybe we're nostalgic for stuff that was never really as wonderful as we think we remember. Anyway, maybe a dose of prosperity might bring something back."

"So why the fence? Why not an unequivocal yes to the airport? Or whatever else is offered?" asked Jane.

"I'm realistic enough to know that what I'm longing for is some kind of 1950s idea of what small-town life was, and getting the airport or any other big business to move in here would not enable us to time travel," said Tim. "We might as easily become some crappy Chicago suburb, dirtier and with a bunch of cheap-ass housing: sans charm, sans movie theaters, and sans candy stores. Sans everything, to paraphrase Shakespeare."

"Hell of a stretch to call that a paraphrase, Timmy boy," said Jane, "but I see what you mean."

"Hence, my plan," said Tim, once again waving his poster.

She read the poster again, trying not to fixate on the gazebo reference, and held up her hands.

"I give. What's the plan?"

Tim picked up a thick, paperback book

and held it out to her. "Herein," he said, "lies the key."

"You have got to stop trying to paraphrase W.S. You're knee-deep in hences and hereins now," said Jane, taking the book from him. "*The Guinness Book of World Records?*"

"Kankakee is going to make it in as the home of the largest garage sale. I'm going for 100 percent participation," he said.

Tim explained that he had almost every family within the city limits of Kankakee and plenty in the adjoining communities of Bradley and Bourbonnais on board. He had asked that all households put out at least one tableful of stuff, and people were really getting excited about it. Block parties were being planned, and local farmers were planning a giant market in the downtown area.

"If everyone is selling," Jane began, "who will . . ."

"Buy?" asked Tim. "We're advertising in every local paper from Chicago to here and south of us, too. Plus, you know how it is. People will watch each other's place and take turns checking out other blocks. Some neighborhoods are trying to specialize — one subdivision is calling itself the toy department and doing tons of kids' stuff, there's a book and vinyl record block, oh, and the public library is going to have a sale of books on one of the weekends. Some schools are even selling old desks and chairs . . ."

"St. Pat's?" Jane asked. "I would love to have an old teacher's desk and chair. Oh, and maybe some bookcases," Jane said, feeling the want creeping up from her toes, taking over her whole body. "Is the library selling anything besides books? I want an old wooden card catalogue from the Kankakee library so badly I . . ."

Jane stopped herself. She was trying to want less. Jane Wheel was a detective now, a partner of Bruce Oh, as well as a picker for dealers Tim Lowry, Claire Oh, and her old friend Miriam in Ohio. Jane Wheel was a professional. She didn't have business cards yet, but it was only a matter of re-membering to go down to the copy shop and have them made up. JANE WHEEL/ PPI/PICKER and PRIVATE INVESTI-GATOR. She was supposed to be coming to grips with her undisciplined style of not only buying everything she knew was valu-able, but also buying everything she knew was being neglected by all the other pickers. The chipped pottery, the cracked plates, the foxed books, the flea-bitten crystal, the boxes of mildewed photos were what Claire and Tim were trying to cull from her houseful of stuff. That was what the garage sale was supposed to do. And despite the fact that Claire and Tim declared it an unqualified $1,487 success before the day was over, Jane knew it had only been a drop in the vintage leather fire bucket. She hadn't the heart to tell Claire that there was still a whole storeroom full of boxes bursting at the seams in her basement that she had conveniently forgotten to mention.

Jane snapped out of her card catalogue–induced reverie. "What about parking? Won't the whole town turn into a parking lot?" she asked.

Tim handed her another brochure. This one had a Kankakee street map with a dozen or more red stars printed on street corners. "Those are the shuttle bus stops. The buses are already hired from an Indiana company. They'll run all weekend; people will buy an all-day pass. They'll pick up visitors at all the parking lots — churches, schools, motels on the outskirts of town — and do a continuous loop. Locals can just pick up a bus on a corner near where they live and visit every neighborhood in town," Tim said. You'll see, Janie, people will be talking to each other and getting to know each other and the whole town will be better for it."

Jane saw the glow in his eyes.

"I've never seen you so excited . . . this is bigger than the MacFlea for you, isn't it?" she asked, referring to the fund-raiser Tim had invented for their old high school Bishop MacNamara.

Da da da, da da da, da da da da da. The *William Tell Overture* played, and Jane was quick to recognize the sound this time. Nick hadn't had a chance to change her signal since the last time it rang. It was disappointing. She realized that it was a bit ordinary to actually know it was her own. This call had to be Nick and Charley telling her the tent was up, the cabin was swept, and it was safe for her to make an appearance. She pushed the talk button without even glancing at the screen.

"Charley," she said, at the same time she heard her other most frequent caller growl a *yeah?* into the phone.

"Hi, Mom," Jane said. Couldn't Nellie ever begin a conversation with hello or even an acknowledgment that she was the one calling? It would be up to Jane to determine what the call was about using a kind of give-and-take, no, make that a *take-and-take* dialogue that would drive most adults to hair pulling and gnashing of teeth.

"Yeah?" Nellie repeated.

"Your dime, Mom," said Jane.

"A damn cellular phone costs a hell of a lot more than a dime a call. I don't know how you can afford something like that," Nellie said.

"It's tough, especially when people phone during the day and use up a lot of minutes not getting to the point of the call," said Jane.

"Yeah?" said Nellie.

"Yeah," said Jane.

Jane could hear her mother breathing, and then she heard her dad ask in the background if Jane liked the cabin.

"Tell Dad I haven't seen it yet. The boys are setting up camp, and I'm at Tim's. He's driving me . . ."

"What the hell you want to be over there at that Tim's for?" asked Nellie. "You're going to be late for your own cookout, for god's sake."

"What cookout?"

"Fuzzy's roasting a pig and invited the whole town, people who drove out to see the junk he dug up. He said he's invited scientists and newspaper reporters. That means Charley and the kid who delivers the *Daily Journal.* Lot of work for a bunch of freeloaders if you ask me."

"Are you and Dad going?" Jane asked.

"I made potato salad, for god's sake."

"I'll take that as a yes."

"Lula's going to make too much damn Jell-O and all the damn politicians are going to show up and yap about the airport or a new factory or some damned idea to make money and I . . ."

Jane heard Don interrupt Nellie, telling her to save it for later, that cell phone calls cost money.

"Hell's bells, I know that," said Nellie. "That's what I'm always calling her about. I'm the one who tells her not to use the damn thing so much."

Jane held out the phone to Tim who did a flawless static sound, and Jane said haltingly into the phone over the sound effects that the connection was breaking up. "See you. . . ." Jane pushed the END button decisively.

"Teach me how to do that," Jane said.

"Got to be born with it," Tim said, shaking his head. "What was Nellie's gripe?"

Jane shrugged. What was Nellie's gripe most days?

For a man who had recently passed out cold, from stress or pressure or the heat or Nellie's scrutiny, Fuzzy was proving an able party giver, picnic master, and pig roaster extraordinaire.

Dressed in denim overalls and a plaid shirt, the required John Deere cap, and steel-toed work boots, Fuzzy presided over the sizzling pig like the farmer king. He used a long-handled brush both for basting and pointing out to the carloads of arriving friends and neighbors the various locations around the farm, shaking his head and laughing at the idiocy of somebody not even owning the dirt they dug in. Jane watched him, all friendly handshakes one minute, then, in a lull in the arrivals, she saw him stare out into the cornfields, stock-still, his weathered face all cracked into puzzle pieces. *Why me?* he seemed to be asking. *Why is this happening to me?*

Jane had not been out to the farm in years and had forgotten what a storybook spot the Neilson place really was. The white clapboard farmhouse was set back from the road, a long drive weaving between giant oaks leading to it, and a barn that Judy Garland and Mickey Rooney could have tap-danced in for two hours and indeed saved the school. Or the show. Or the college. Or whatever it was they saved in those old musicals when putting on a play in Dad's barn was all it took.

"How about we put on a show and save the town?" asked Jane, staring at the weathered wood, thinking about how the scenery would fly down from the hayloft.

"That is so twentieth century," said Tim, waving at a knot of people surrounding the fire pit back behind the house. "If Judy were alive and Mickey could still tap, they'd be having a city-wide garage sale."

Jane spotted the cabin about half a city block behind the barn. Nick and Charley had parked the car next to it, and they had set up the tent twenty feet from the porch. Jane walked toward them, marveling at how much Nick looked like Charley. They were both watching her approach, hands on their hips, tossing the hair out of their eyes. Just like that, Jane had switched movie fantasy genres and, instead of a musical playing in her head, she was watching one of those epic frontier movies. Gary Cooper or James Stewart, one man — and boy — taming the Midwest, one farm at a time.

The movie stopped when Jane saw the taped-off area on the other side of the cabin. A chill ran over her, a wave of ice when she saw the yellow tape. Crime scene. She hadn't found another body yet, had she? She'd just arrived. Surely she'd remember a murder.

"It's the site, honey," said Charley, coming over to her. "It's where they found the bones."

Jane nodded, but the warm relief that should have replaced the ice bath did not come. She wasn't sure she wanted to camp out next to this taped-off area that was a dead ringer for an open grave. She tried to console herself by reflecting positively on the fact that none of them were sleepwalkers.

"How's the cabin?" she asked.

"Great, Mom," said Nick, "you're going to love it. The furniture looks like it was built from the same logs as the cabin and there're a lot of cool hooks for the pots and pans and clothes even and built-in shelves. It's kind of like a camper or something, except, you know, it doesn't move."

Jane stepped over the threshold. The light was still decent because of the high windows that lined the perimeter; but with no electricity, Jane could already feel how dark it would be in a few hours when the sun had disappeared. The back door stood open and Jane saw the outhouse. Oops. Why hadn't the if and where of working

71

plumbing crossed her mind until now?

When Jane and Charley had taken Nick on a driving vacation to the South, they had stopped in Tupelo, Mississippi, to visit the birthplace of Elvis. Who could resist? The *Birthplace* was touted in every tourist brochure like the must-see spot of hallowed ground where you might find a splinter of the true cross, or at least a Bakelite guitar pick. The guide there explained that Elvis's home was called a shotgun cabin because you could fire through the open front door and the shot would fly right out the open back door. Jane followed that trajectory now as she walked through the one-room living space of the cabin and turned back to look at it from the back door.

A wood-burning stove defined a kitchen area on her right, and two large handmade beds with a low bookshelf between them designated sleeping. A large, square table sat just off center in the room, big log chairs pulled around it. A shelf had been cleverly built under the table, and a few old board games were stacked on it.

"Fuzzy said his great-grandkids stay out here when they visit from Montana. His granddaughter-in-law and grandson run for the nearest motel to get away by themselves, and the kids come out and have a ball, living in the cabin," said Nick, who had followed his mother inside and watched her take in the space with her picker's eye. He knew she had already sized up the cast-iron pans as collectible and was dying to see if the tins of spices over the stove were as old as they looked. Even the few dusty books by the bed looked like they had been placed by a propmaster on the set of *Little House on the Prairie*. Nick knew his mother was aching to open the trunks by the wall and examine the underside of the hooked rug in front of the washstand.

"Lula says we can use the bathroom in the house, too, Mom, but I told her Dad and I wouldn't need it," said Nick.

Jane raised an eyebrow.

"We've got some light out here if we want it," said Charley. He pointed out a large cord that was taped along the entrance to the cabin. It was an industrial-size extension cord that Fuzzy had run out from the house. There were two lamps plugged in, a small table model from the fifties by the bed and a forties floor lamp with a lush green shade standing in the corner. Jane hadn't even noticed the lamps as out of place. They fit in with the furnishings, and she hadn't thought twice about how they might be lit.

"We have a couple of lanterns and some battery-powered lamps with us, too, for the tent," said Charley.

"I'm not afraid of the dark, Charley," said Jane, about to launch into her litany of all the things she wasn't afraid of. Which was her roundabout way of avoiding thinking about all the things that did frighten her. The two-page color illustration of snakes in the *S* volume of the encyclopedia, Marilyn Manson, unlabeled canned goods, illness or injury befalling her family, ski lifts, and body piercing below the neck.

"You really going to sleep in this hole?"

Jane hadn't heard Nellie come up behind her — people never heard Nellie creep up behind them — and she jumped when her mother's voice barked in her ear.

Oh yeah. And Nellie. Jane was a little bit afraid of Nellie.

Jane backed out of the cabin, thinking about how best she might defend its rustic beauty to her mother, who was eyeing suspicious holes in the walls and pointing out mysterious small tracks left in a thin layer of corner dust — all details that Jane would have preferred not to notice. Nellie liked to explore every nook and cranny that might hold something dirty, germ laden, or disgusting. Anything Jane's mother could wipe away with a rag and a bottle of Pine-Sol was the treasure she wanted to find. Sure, Jane could look all she wanted for a wooden library card catalogue; and if Nellie were anywhere in the vicinity, she would creep up right behind her daughter, pulling out each drawer and going for the corners with a Q-tip and a bottle of disinfectant.

Her dad, Don, was a little easier on dirt and a whole lot easier on Jane. Jane could hear him just outside the cabin. Instead of coming in for inspection, he was looking at the hole in the ground with Nick.

"I don't get it," said Don. "What's stopping Fuzzy from selling his own dirt?"

"If there are bones here, Grandpa, something important. It might be a historical site that is protected, and Fuzzy can't do anything to the land."

"Protected by who?" asked Don.

"The Illinois Historic Preservation Agency," said Charley, coming over to shake Don's hand.

"When any property owner or developer turns up something unusual," Charley began. He was interrupted by Nick who offered, "Like bones."

He sounds so cheerful, Jane thought. *Is that because he takes after his father, who looks for ancient skeletons, or because he takes after his mother, who finds fresh corpses?*

"If human remains are found, the coroner has to be called and the police. If it turns out that it's not a crime scene, jurisdiction is under the Human Skeletal Remains Protection Act."

"Still doesn't sound much like a who," said Don.

"The *who* would be the director of the Illinois Historic Preservation Agency. He'd have to call the shots."

"It's Fuzzy's dirt, isn't it?" asked Nellie. She and Jane joined the rest of the family, all of them now looking into the hole in the ground. "He owns it. He paid for it. He farms it. He tracks it into Lula's kitchen and the EZ Way Inn every day. Who the hell has a right to tell him what he can and can't do with it?"

Jane pictured Nellie somewhere in the mountains of Colorado with a caveful of canned goods and a shotgun on her shoulder. Yes, her mother could easily be a survivalist. She didn't even have to close her eyes to conjure it. Clutching her bowl of potato salad and squinting up at Charley like he was the "guvmint" come to collect back taxes or bust up the still.

Charley, obviously not realizing how much damage she could do with a bowl of potato salad if she believed it was her only weapon and he was the enemy, ignored the fire in her eyes and looped his arm around her shoulders.

"Nellie, you wouldn't want somebody rearranging your bones or, worse, tossing them into the trash heap if you had been minding your own dead business, resting peacefully in your family cemetery, would you?" asked Charley.

"I'm going to be cremated," Nellie began. Jane had heard this speech a number of times, after every wake, after every funeral. "I don't want anybody looking at me and saying it's so sad and she had a hard life and look how old she looks and she really suffered and . . ."

"Maybe they won't say anything like that, Nell," said Tim, who had stopped off at the food table and was carrying a plate heaped with chips and dip and salad.

"Maybe they'll take one look at you, all decked out in your Sunday best, wearing rouge and a smudge of 'Cherries in the Snow' on your lips, a little iridescent green on your lids to bring out the green in your . . ."

Jane and Charley watched Tim look off into the distance, waxing poetic, and looked back at Nellie, who was now stoking the fire in her eyes.

"Listen to me, Tim Lowry, you call me 'Nell' one more time and they're going to be talking about how you looked laid out with barbecue sauce all over your face and coleslaw in your hair."

Jane gave her mother round one, but was relieved that Tim had gotten her off track in the great cremation speech she gave every chance she could. A half-second later Jane had to give Nellie round two as well when her mother started up again, undeterred.

"I want to be cremated, you hear me? Everybody here is my witness on this. Nobody looks at me and moans and groans over me when I can't look back at them. Hear me? I want to be cremated," Nellie said.

Don looked at his wife with the same even stare he had been giving her for forty-five years. "Should we wait until you're dead?"

"I don't even know you, but I believe you and will honor your wishes if I should be in the vicinity."

Jane, Charley, and Nick and Don, Nellie,

and Tim all turned away from the taped-off hole in the ground. The man who had spoken had a small, gray goatee, carefully parted hair, and wore a suit and tie, even though the evening was warm and most of Fuzzy and Lula's guests had arrived dressed *pig-roast casual.*

"I'm Dr. Jaekel," he said, a defiant edge in his voice. He looked directly at Tim, sensing the quickest mouth and the most ready smart-ass in the crowd. "J-a-e-k-e-l, and no, my assistant is not Mr. Hyde. I assure you, I have heard every permutation of the joke." Dr. Jaekel held his hand out to Charley. "I'm acting coroner for the county. Borrowed while Kankakee's own good doctor is on vacation this month."

Nellie circled him like a bantam-weight.

"Who died?" she asked.

"Many people, every second," he said. Jaekel looked toward the hole in the ground. "Not necessarily, however, where we're standing." He sighed and Jane couldn't tell whether he was relieved by his own pronouncement or disappointed that he was currently surrounded by living bodies. "Professor, may I have a word with you in private?"

Jane and company watched Dr. Jaekel

steer Charley to the other side of the taped-off area.

"There's a man who had to grow up to be coroner. That sad, droopy face," said Jane. "Did you see his hands?" Jane watched him clench and unclench his long, bony fingers as he talked to Charley. When he pointed at the table full of bones and rocks, he jabbed the air, hurting something invisible to everyone but him.

"Yeah. Looks at you like you're not quite interesting enough to him yet," said Tim, "predead and all."

The yard was full of people waving to one another and filling plates with food. All the men seemed to be wearing hats identical to Fuzzy's, and all the women carried large, disposable foil pans. Jane squinted a little and tried to make this into the kind of jolly, rural homecoming she liked to imagine.

"What do you think, Timmy? Is this more like the clambake from *Carousel* or the big dance in *Oklahoma?*"

Nellie and Don began to inch closer to the crowd, and Nick was crouching over one of the mounds of dirt next to the hole. Tim looked over the crowd of people, grim-faced men, shaking their heads over weather or unemployment or the Cubs or the White Sox, and the bustling women, hand-wringing over the children or the grim-faced men.

"The cemetery scene from *Our Town*," said Tim.

Jane saw two unlikely guests approaching Don and Nellie. She could usually pick out nonlocals because of the way Nellie eyeballed people she hadn't known for sixty years. But even without Nellie's suspicious posture, Jane would have picked the taller, older one of the pair as a visitor. The man had a city haircut and shiny, black shoes that screamed out-of-towner.

"Joe Dempsey," the taller man announced. "Don and Nellie, I've had the pleasure, but maybe you could introduce me to this beautiful daughter of yours," he said as Jane moved closer.

Sales. He has to be in sales, Jane thought. Just as Jaekel might be pegged as a coroner, Jane thought she could peg Dempsey. He was as angular as Jaekel, but he caressed the air with his hands, making graceful gestures that drew everyone around him into his circle. He was used to being thought charming. Jane watched Nellie toss her head when he smiled at her. Nellie never trusted moustaches. She had always told Jane that men grew facial hair to cover something up, no other reason. Even Dempsey's pencil-thin moustache would raise Nellie's suspicions. Jane wasn't suspicious of the moustache. Dempsey was in his midsixties with a beautiful full head of silver hair; he would want to cultivate as dapper a look as he could. Who could blame him? It was his manner of conversation that Jane noted. He didn't speak; he announced.

"My associate, Michael Hoover," Joe Dempsey said loudly, waving his arms and presenting the shorter man with a kind of formal flourish. Hoover, younger by twenty years, dressed more casually in khakis and a sport coat, looked hungry, thirsty, and anxious, in that order. He nodded, licking his lips.

Fuzzy yelled to them to come over and fill their plates, and Jane realized she was starving. The two men headed toward the food, but not before Dempsey took Jane's hand as if to kiss the back of it. He didn't complete the act, but smiled and told her she was a darling girl. Jane was about to follow them to the picnic tables and find out who they were and why they had ended up at Fuzzy's pig roast when she noticed Tim motioning to her from the door of the cabin.

"Timmy, you already have your food," she said. "I'm going to go and find Nick . . ."

Jane followed as Tim backed into the cabin and pointed to the small table under a crude, almost blacked-out mirror. He had set a small tray out with a bottle of Grey Goose; two glasses; a jar of tipsy olives; fat, juicy, vermouth-soaked bites; colorful plastic picks. Under the table was an ice chest. Tim fixed them both a drink and clinked his glass to hers.

"Here's to innocent bones and profitable gazebos."

"This is so sweet, Tim. You thought of everything," said Jane.

"Yeah, there's beer in the chest for Charley and soda for Nick."

Jane sipped her drink, feeling warm and loved and happy down to her toes. This is what mattered in life. Scrounging stuff and solving mysteries was all well and good, but this is what mattered . . . being with family and having a best friend like Tim.

"You're going to need the booze, honey. This place is a dump."

Charley poked his head in, nodded to Tim, who reached down to grab a beer for him.

"Janie, we have got to get people away

from the site. If we stay around here, everybody and his uncle will stroll over. Jaekel's ready to call in the police to clear the area. Why, I don't know, since he and I both know there's probably nothing . . . still, a site is a site. I don't know what Fuzzy was thinking, inviting all these people," Charley said.

"Fuzzy thinking," said Tim, "oxymoron or apt description. You be the judge."

Tim assured them he'd lead the way back to the food and tables Fuzzy and Lula had set up closer to the main house and down by the cornfield and went out. Charley stopped Jane at the door, stretching his arm across the opening.

"You okay? Staying out here and all?"

"Charley, I love the cabin. This is a great little vacation, and you can teach me about what you do at a site. Watching you and Nick will . . ." Jane stopped. Charley was looking at her with . . . what was that look? He was smiling and with every second his eyes were locked on hers, they seemed to probe deeper. Oh yeah, Jane remembered that look.

"Charley, are you feeling" — Jane began, then wondered what a noncorny, non-loaded word was for an old married couple like them — "amorous?"

"I am always feeling amorous," said Charley. "All men are."

"Yeah, right," said Jane.

"True. Women stop seeing it, that's all. You find other things to look at."

Maybe Charley was right. Jane had been looking around a lot lately. Right now, though, she couldn't take her eyes off his.

"I'm crazy about you, Jane."

"I'm crazy . . . ," Jane began, but was interrupted.

"Mom, Dad, I'm going to get food with Grandma. She says you guys better come on because the moochers are going to eat the pig down to the tail in a few minutes."

"Okay," Jane and Charley answered together.

"He's one of the other things I look at, right?" said Jane.

"Right and proper," said Charley, kissing her on top of her head. "I love watching you watch him."

"I think the great outdoors and a digging site brings out the Harrison Ford in you," said Jane. "Not that I require movie star mystique."

Charley cleared his throat and stood a bit straighter. He looked over at the site and saw that it was clear of onlookers. Everyone, captivated by the smells that were now almost overwhelmingly delicious, had headed back closer to the farmhouse. Charley took Jane's hand and led her outside to the taped-off area.

"What do you see, Jane?"

"Besides the obvious?"

"Obvious first. That's often the most important," said Charley.

"You sound like Oh," said Jane, and imitated the soft-voiced detective. "See what's there, Mrs. Wheel, see what's there. . . . Okay. A hole in the ground. About five by five, maybe five or six feet deep."

Charley, holding her hand, walked her over to a shed on the opposite side of the hole. A tarp had been tied from the shed roof, extending a shaded, covered area about three feet from the small building. Two picnic tables were next to the wall and on them, small bones were laid out, some stones, a few pieces of metal.

"Is this the *find?* It seems . . . ," Jane began.

"Paltry for the amount of commotion it caused?" asked Charley.

"Small, I was going to say small."

"Yeah. There are a few other things in the boxes, but not much more. Look at this, though. It took Nick a few minutes.

I'll give you five," said Charley. "Even without a bone map, you can do this."

"Bone map?" asked Jane.

"When bones are found, if we're the ones finding them, before removing them we sketch out exactly how they're situated in the ground. Gives us the clues to construction, to the events surrounding the death — you know, how the bones ended up there before they were bones, when they were animal."

"Charley, these aren't human bones. Look at the little leg. Legs. There are four of them," said Jane.

"Yup," said Charley.

Jane fingered a few of the stones on the table, then picked up one of the bits of rusted metal. "The metal's definitely old. Hard to fake rust this dark. You know when people try to make new ironwork look old, they always try to rust it up, but it's always too red. Look how dark this is," said Jane, rubbing at it. "There's a little hole, here," she said. "Oh."

"Are you calling for your detective partner or do you get it?" asked Charley, laughing.

"Wouldn't you think Fuzzy and Lula would remember what this is?"

"And it is?" he asked.

"Their dog. It's his little tag and his skeleton, right?"

"Cat. Tag's maybe ten or fifteen years old. Hard to see the date, but you can make out the name."

"LITTLE OTTO," read Jane. "Poor baby."

Charley told Jane that she shouldn't mention it to anyone at the picnic. He didn't want to embarrass Fuzzy, and besides, there were some other things that had been dug up he wanted to take a look at in the light of day.

"Jaekel knows of course. Told me he took one look at the bones and couldn't believe anyone had called him and asked him to drive thirty miles to look at a long dead family pet," said Charley. "He assured the police it wasn't a crime scene, but there are a few fossils and something that he thought might be a stone ax head. Probably what Fuzzy hit with his gardening equipment."

"Is it anything?" Jane asked.

Charley shook his head. "Not sure. Jaekel was stuck though. Even if the bones just belonged to Otto the cat, once someone calls something like this into the state, there's a mile of paperwork to get the land cleared."

"Who did it?"

"Offed the cat?"

"No, I mean, who called it into the state? Wouldn't someone realize they were causing a lot of trouble for Fuzzy for no reason if . . ." Jane stopped when she and Charley reached the food table and Nellie appeared at her elbow.

"Four," she said, almost spitting. "No, five."

Jane looked at Nellie. She knew she was supposed to know what her mother was talking about. Nellie's language was primitive, a kind of guttural, one-word shorthand that required the listener to make many strange and dangerous leaps through what Jane had long referred to as "Nellie's mindfield," as dangerous to one's psyche as an actual minefield would be to one's limbs.

Jane's defense against the mindfield was silence. If she waited patiently, Nellie's next burst of linguistic puzzlement might give her the clue, lead her across the bridge, so to speak, to an island where they, for a brief moment, would communicate.

"Orange with bananas, cherry with pineapple, raspberry with some whipped cream crap in it, and green with marshmallows and nuts. And that wasn't enough." Nellie seemed, even for Nellie, unnaturally upset about the Jell-O variety laid out on the table. "Blue Jell-O with . . . what the hell is that on top?"

"Cool Whip, Nell," said Tim, holding a plate with a scoop of each flavor. "Where but in Kankakee are you going to get a groaning board of Jell-O like this?"

"Red with oranges is good enough," said Nellie, sniffing. "Lula's got better things to do, and she ought to be doing them."

As swiftly and silently as she had appeared, Nellie was gone, probably to point out the appallingly egocentric Jell-O display to the rest of the crowd.

"What flavor's red?" asked Tim, sticking his tongue out to show Jane the proof of the rainbow of Jell-O he had already ingested.

"Every Sunday, Nellie made Jell-O for dessert. She combined raspberry and strawberry and cherry, whatever she had in the cupboard and put oranges in it. She thought the combined flavors tasted better. You know," said Jane, "redder."

"Sort of makes sense," said Tim.

"Then you've got to get out of town," said Jane, but she was thinking of how cold and delicious that Jell-O had tasted, she and her brother eating it on the couch and watching those Cartwright brothers ride through the burning Ponderosa map at the beginning of *Bonanza*.

Fuzzy and Lula's barbecue went the way of most large, outdoor gatherings. Lots of people all talking in tight little clusters, opening up to engulf a newcomer, then closing in around him or her like some kind of amoebalike digestive motion. Jane noted the grim faces of the men softened with every trip to the beer keg; and with every trip they watched their husbands make, the women's faces grew harder. As the mounds of food diminished and those foil pans were emptied and crumpled, the crowd began to thin. First a couple, then two or three, then all the cars starting, and Fuzzy and Lula, Jane, Charley, and Nick watched a caravan of cars travel down the highway.

The EZ Way customers who had been there had given Jane the obligatory once-over. They had known her since she was a baby and still felt the need to comment on her height, weight, and the length of her hair. Jane often felt like the only adult woman, all grown up with a child of her own, who went home to be surrounded by dozens of people who told her she was taller than the last time they saw her. Jane knew she had been five foot three for at least twenty-five years, but she knew enough to keep it to herself.

Jane hadn't wanted to interrupt Lula, who had kept one eye on Fuzzy and the other on the roasting pit most of the evening, so she hadn't yet had a chance to visit with her hostess. Jane realized that although she had heard about Lula most of her life, she had only met her a few times. Fuzzy was a daily EZ Way Inn customer who talked about his wife as though everyone knew her, and Jane was surprised to see that she was nothing like the heroine of Fuzzy's stories. She wasn't round and jolly and warm and playful. She looked overworked and hard-edged and had an expression of wary concern that reminded Jane so much of Nellie that if she didn't know better, she would think the two women were related.

Jane checked her watch and was surprised that it was only 9:15. It had been a long day — a lifetime or two since she had let Claire Oh and Tim thin the herd in her garage that morning. Jane stacked some of the large pans that had been filled with Jell-O and three-bean salad and started toward the kitchen.

"Can your husband help us out?" asked Lula, wiping her hands on her apron and reaching out for the pans. "With the state and all?"

"I'm sure he can," said Jane, looking out to the yard where Charley and Nick were stuffing giant garbage bags with the empty plates and cups scattered around the yard. Fuzzy was out by the barn, talking to some men. Rather he was being talked to by one of them. Joe Dempsey. Dempsey was waving his arms in the air, describing something wonderful by the dreamy look on his face, and Hoover was walking another man toward the cornfield. The third man seemed to be staggering a bit, and Jane thought Hoover might be trying to walk him around a bit, sober him up. Surely they weren't going to let that one get into a car. The big yard lights had gone on at dusk, and although they illuminated the areas immediately near the buildings, the rest of the grounds were swallowed up in the summer night. Once Hoover and the other man got to the cornfield, they disappeared.

"Lula, who are those men out there with Fuzzy? What do Dempsey and Hoover do?"

Lula squinted her eyes in the direction of

the barn. "The forty-dollar suits?" she asked.

Jane didn't have the heart to tell her that a forty-dollar suit hadn't existed for more than forty years.

"They're trying to start some business here. They showed up a while ago, wanting to take polls and ask questions and price land. Carpetbaggers, if you ask me," said Lula.

Jane couldn't imagine what motivated anyone to move to Kankakee to seek fame, glory, or profit. And wasn't that what carpetbaggers were supposed to be after?

"Ever since we got famous with that list and those porches that the talk show sent us," said Lula.

"The gazebos?" asked Jane.

"Yes, our mayor was on television, too. We were all the rage for a while. It's died down a little though."

Jane helped Lula dry the last of the big pans. It didn't seem worthwhile to mention that being known as the least livable city in North America was not exactly a magnet for business.

Jane wished Lula a good night, expecting her to remain in the kitchen, but Lula walked outside with her instead. "Just got to round up Fuzzy. He loses track of time when he's checking up on things."

"Lula, who reported the bones and the fossils on the property? Did you or Fuzzy make any calls about them?"

Lula's dark eyes almost disappeared as she narrowed them. "I'd like to know who made that call myself. There's a word for people who meddle in other folks' business."

Something in the way Lula spoke made Jane not want to ask any follow-up questions. She and Charley might be there by request to help do the paperwork to clear the land, but Jane had the feeling that that was all they were supposed to do. Despite all the Jell-O being passed around that night, Jane had a feeling the party was Fuzzy's idea. He appeared to be the partner who kept their social life active.

"Go ahead and use the electric if you need it. And don't worry about any noises. Fuzzy's not sleeping so good, and sometimes he goes roaming."

Jane wanted to reassure her, tell her that Fuzzy could rest easy. The only grave they had disturbed was that of an old family pet. He could keep right on growing his tomatoes and sell all the dirt he wanted. But when Jane looked back, ready to give her that comforting news, Lula had disappeared. Just as well. She should let Charley make sure that everything was okay and give the news. Looking back over her shoulder, Jane saw that the kitchen light was already out and only a greenish glow from the television set in the front parlor illuminated the house.

Hoover and the other man had not re-appeared, and Dempsey and Fuzzy were nowhere in sight. Jane thought she heard Lula call to Fuzzy out beyond the barn, but when she looked in that direction, she couldn't see anyone.

For no good reason, Jane felt a chill down to her toes and walked quickly over to where Charley and Nick were coming out of the tent. Jane, shivering despite the warm night, suggested they bundle up inside the cabin and investigate a board game by candlelight.

"Me and Dad are sleeping in the tent, Mom," said Nick. "You want to?"

Jane looked into her husband's brown eyes, which had sent her such loud and clear come-hither signals only a few hours ago. They were sending signals now, too — Jane was certain she could see the white flag of surrender waving in his pupils. She couldn't blame Charley.

When you had a son like Nick — who

didn't really ask for much, who, most of the time, treated Jane and Charley with reason and patience and a minimum of eye rolling — it was hard to say no when he really did show some interest. They both knew that soon enough there would be high school and a gaggle of new friends and more interests and weekends away at sports events and science fairs. Then there would be a driver's license, and a girl-friend, college visits, applications, and ac-ceptances. Then four years of college, grad school, hiking through Europe, job offers, an office across the continent, marriage, wife and family, and holiday visits few and far between. Then he'd be signing them into assisted living, and that would be that.

Of course Charley had to sleep in the tent with him. He'd be out of his mind to say no. Jane, however, knew that she should not say yes to this adventure. Her own tolerance for sleeping in a tent and the nighttime sounds of the outdoors had decreased in inverse proportion to her age. Strapping on a backpack and unrolling a sleeping bag had held some charm in her college days, but her older bones begged for a firm mattress, a decent pillow, and a reading light. In the cabin she might not get any of those, but she would be a whole lot closer than out in the pop-up tent next to Fuzzy's tomato patch.

Charley caressed her shoulder slightly, and she wavered for a moment. *If Nick weren't here,* she thought, *maybe I would explore the great outdoors one more time.* A sky full of moon and stars, barely visible in the city, might draw her for one last campout. In his element here, Charley reminded her of someone she'd known in another lifetime, someone who'd made her hover a few inches off the ground just thinking of him. Who was that man all those years ago? Oh yeah, it was Charley.

But Nick was here, waiting for his father to fetch some bottled water and a few flashlights.

"You okay here?" Charley asked.

"Of course," Jane said. "What could happen? The ghost of Otto could come in search of catnip or something, but I think I could fend him off. Go camping, my little Boy Scouts," said Jane. "I'll keep a light in the window."

Jane meant to keep a light in the window. She had already planned to plug in the rickety bedside lamp and conveniently fall asleep reading so that there would be some light on all night, in case Nick got scared and needed to find his way inside the cabin. Jane repeated that several times to herself as she got herself ready for bed. For Nick. A light in the window for Nick. But just as she was about to crawl under the covers, she looked out the window toward the farmhouse, and saw Fuzzy coming out the back door.

"You people," he yelled, and not waiting for an answer, he continued, "decided to turn off the generator for the night! Don't let the bedbugs bite."

The cabin went dark and, if possible, the outdoors became even inkier than it had been before. Clouds covered the moon. The stars were visible, but not as dazzling as a Wyoming sky or a Montana night might be. No, Kankakee might be the least livable city in North America because of its dearth of cultural opportunities, but it was close enough to Chicago, with enough cultural activities for any number of cities and enough candlepower to still have an impact on the night sky of its little neighbor to the south.

When Fuzzy cut the power, Jane was shocked at the sudden silence. She hadn't even been aware of the hum from the generator, but when it stopped she heard the stillness. It washed over her and filled in all the spaces, curled in around her like a body pillow, a down comforter. It might have been soothing except for a skittering noise and the occasional hum of a mosquito. And what was it Fuzzy said not to let bite?

Jane squeezed her eyes shut, thinking that if she closed them tightly enough, she could forget how dark it was in the cabin. Eyes closed, she would not know if there was a little hall light on or a little nightlight glowing in the bathroom. Damn, don't think about the bathroom because there isn't one except out the back door, where it's even darker than this dark. Charley had told Jane to wake him if she needed to go out, but she was too stubborn to do that. Too stubborn to admit that this place was the darkest rabbit hole into which she had ever been dropped and too stubborn to ever go to the bathroom again if that's what it took. Stop thinking about it, she commanded herself.

Instead, Jane decided to think about everything that was crazy about this campout/pig roast and what Charley had referred to as archaeological dig lite. Fuzzy had invited them to stay there on the land, invited them to use the cabin, and had, just the other morning, asked for their help in figuring out what exactly they were digging up on his land. And yet tonight, as he heaped Jane's plate with food and walked her around the garden, pointing out the eggplants and cucumbers and peppers and tomatoes, he wasn't himself. One minute he was talking about heirloom seeds and grafting pumpkin vines and the next he was staring off into the cornfields beyond his property, looking for all the world as if he expected visitors to come walking out. Had he seen *Field of Dreams* once too often? Were the ghosts of baseball players about to drift out from behind the stalks? Jane had even joked with him about it, asked him who he was looking for.

"Who?" Fuzzy had asked then, looking at Jane so helplessly that Jane saw him struggling not to finish with ". . . are you?"

No, Fuzzy was no Kevin Costner, and his small farm was no field of anyone's dreams. Right now, it was a farmette of extremely minor expectations.

When Jane had asked her dad about Fuzzy, wanting to know if he was all right, if they knew anything more about the fainting spell, Don had shaken his head. "Just getting older, honey, just like me and your mom."

Jane and Don had both looked over at

the food table then, acknowledging that Nellie might be passing through the years at the same rate as everyone else standing around munching roast pork and salads slathered in mayonnaise and too many different colors of Jell-O, but knowing that Nellie wasn't really getting older. She had probably been a crusty sixty-one, give or take a year, when she was born and had remained there. Now, pushing hard on seventy's door, she didn't look any older than sixty, with a trim figure, a weathered but unwrinkled face, and the bottled-up energy of a rattlesnake on speed.

Don had reintroduced Jane to Joe Dempsey while they were cutting into a giant chocolate layer cake. Joe Dempsey, one of the new movers and shakers in Kankakee, as Don had described him. Jane had guessed his age as the midsixties when she first met him; and by the way he gripped her hand and shook it, she told herself again he had been trained in sales. He described himself as an entrepreneur, and Jane couldn't help wondering what entrepreneurial venture he could possibly be pursuing in Kankakee.

"I see this town as the future, not the past," he had said, nodding vigorously. "Good land, good people, lots of opportunities," Joe had whispered, leaning forward, "if you've got the eyes to see it."

It wasn't all that different from Tim's assessment of Kankakee. He, too, felt that it had gotten a bad rap, a raw deal. And there was no reason why this pretty little river town couldn't make a comeback.

Jane had dozed off thinking about Tim and the world's largest garage sale. She was dreaming about a garage filled with what she thought were rubber balls; but when she got inside the garage, she picked one up and discovered it was a rock. A round, beach-smooth rock. She dropped it and the sound it made, rock on pavement, woke her up. Or did a sound wake her up and so direct her dreaming hand to open?

Interesting how darkness intensifies sound. Jane thought she heard a light scraping outside the window. Then a car out on the road. Was that thunder in the distance? Was there going to be a storm? How long had she been sleeping? She could call out to Charley and Nick in the tent, but she wasn't sure enough to wake them. Sure enough of what? That she was spooked by being alone in the dark not twenty feet away from them? Maybe she could use her small flashlight to find one of the battery-powered lanterns Charley had said he'd leave for her. So what if she ran down the battery — she was going into town to help Tim canvass people about the garage sale tomorrow — she could, and would, buy fifty batteries.

"Ow." For a bare-bones cabin furnished only with the essentials, a lot of things were coming out of the dark to bump into her. She crept over to the window and saw that the moon had come out from behind the clouds. The back lawn glowed and shimmered, the green of the grass transformed into a watery silver. Beyond the grass and vegetable gardens, the cornfield stood sentry. Row after row, a grid of green leaves and fat stalks crisscrossed the land for at least two acres.

Where lawn met cornfield, Jane could see something waving at her. Was it a man walking toward her, waving his arms? A breeze rattled the cabin; and in the moving air, Jane saw the arms go wilder, sleeves blowing in the wind. She let out a long breath, not aware of how long she had been holding it.

"A scarecrow," she said. Jane realized when she named what she saw aloud, her jaw muscles had been clenched so hard, her entire face ached at the release. She opened her mouth and closed it, trying to reclaim her features, and said aloud again, "It's just a scarecrow."

Normally by now everything would have relaxed, become unclenched, the adrenaline would have drained away, leaving her tired enough to fall asleep no matter how much scraping, squeaking, and scratching was going on in the dark corners of the cabin. And asleep she would undoubtedly be if she hadn't just seen the scarecrow get down from the pole and disappear into the cornfield.

Chapter 4

Jane Wheel might occasionally be a bit scattered, like a rookie picker faced with the decision in the middle of a church meeting hall of whether to first hit the costume jewelry or sewing notions station. Would the jewelry be fished out by the dealers who masqueraded as do-gooders and volunteered to set up? If so, she should hit sewing and maybe find a tin of vintage buttons left, tucked under a tangle of zippers. But what if? What if there was a Bakelite dangle pin in the bottom of a jewelry box, waiting there in the dark whispering Jane's name?

But perched by the window in the dark of Fuzzy Neilson's cabin, Jane realized she had become quite the decisive detective. She felt around with her toes for her canvas slides and slipped them on, all the time training her eyes on the spot where she had seen the animated scarecrow. Animated was just how she thought of him, since the scene resembled something she had seen in *Fantasia*. True, it had been a lot of years, but didn't something that was supposed to be inanimate come to life? Maybe it was Mickey Mouse's broom? Yes, that was it, a broom or a mop — not unlike the crossed poles that make up a scarecrow's limbs, Jane thought. Aha!

She felt around on the table for her flashlight. She was going to have to stop thinking, *aha,* every time she remembered some stray bit of flotsam from that tidepool of popular culture that passed for her mind. *Aha's* were for clues and leads and discoveries, not for conjuring up the sight of Mickey Mouse dancing around as the sorcerer's apprentice in a way-too-scary-for-children cartoon.

Flashlight and shoes and a decision to make. Wake up Charley? Jane Wheel had watched plenty of movies and read plenty of books, and she knew damn well that the heroine always gets herself into trouble when she goes up to the attic or down into the basement alone. She doesn't want to bother her boyfriend or husband; she doesn't tell her roommate where she's going; she wanders alone and stupidly right into danger.

Jane was not going to be the silly schoolgirl heroine of some bad mystery movie. She had a solid role model. What would Nancy do? She clicked on the flashlight, but pointed it away from the entrance to the tent.

"Charley," she whispered. She might not want to be the ingénue in a detective story, but she didn't want to be the hysterical housewife in one either. Nick did not have to be awakened for this . . . whatever this was. Apparition?

"Charley," she whispered again, bringing her light into the tent and slowly moving it up the sleeping bags until she could figure out which one held her husband. When the light caught Nick's hair, flopped over one closed eye, she quickly moved it to the other sleeping bag. Charley, her light-sleeping, always prepared as a Boy Scout spouse, would jump up as soon as the light hit his face; and Jane was ready to motion him to follow, one foot already outside the tent in a ready-set-go position.

When the light hit the pillow where Charley's sleep-creased face should be, Jane saw only pillow. She moved the light up and down, and chanced waking Nick by quickly flashing it up and down and over him and across to the other side of the tent. Then she circled the light around the perimeter. No Charley.

Jane stepped outside the tent and flicked off the flashlight for a moment. The moon was almost full and its brightness, once her eyes adjusted, enabled her to see the *lawnscape,* if not the entire landscape. She got her bearings and looked down to where the cornfield began. She thought she saw something . . . maybe there was something standing there. Maybe what she had seen so clearly, a scarecrow jumping down and running away, was merely a nighttime breeze picking up the patchy, ragged shirt and blowing it off into the fields, leaving crossed poles standing guard.

"Charley?" she whispered.

Jane figured the only path Charley would take that led away from the tent and his sleeping son would be one that led to his sleeping wife in the cabin, and she had not seen him. The outhouse? Must be, although that puzzled her. Wasn't the only real difference between men and women the fact that men reveled in peeing outdoors? When Charley and Nick had returned from South Dakota after Nick's first official dig, he'd spent twenty minutes telling her about the duck-bill dinosaur bones they had found, and the next thirty describing in glorious detail the wonders of outdoor peeing.

Jane walked slowly toward the cornfield, and since the outhouse was on the way, she expected to meet Charley any second. As she got closer to the field, she could see the stalks bending and waving. She was going to have to go online and Google Walt Disney and find out whether or not he was a farm boy. It hardly took any imagination at all to picture an inventive cartoon of the fields coming to life, trees lifting up their firmly planted roots, which would bend like knees stomping in time to an old-timey fiddle at a hoedown. Mickey and Goofy could grab rakes and hoes and whirl away into the cornfield as the scarecrows hopped down and formed two corners of a square; and that fat, old, waxing moon, almost a harvest moon, could call the do-si-dos and allemande lefts. Had Jane ever seen a cartoon like that or was she inventing it on the spot?

"Charley?" she whispered near the little wooden building.

"Huh?" A flashlight blinked on from inside and a deep voice whispered, *"Ocupado."*

Jane smiled. Charley must have picked that up from his South American trip.

"It's me, Charley. I'm going out to look in the cornfield; I thought I saw . . . ," Jane hesitated, "something." That ought to provoke his curiosity.

Jane approached the pole still standing, although it was no longer costumed as Ray Bolger, ready to sing and dance for little Dorothy and Toto. As a matter of fact, as she got closer, Jane realized it wasn't actually a pole or any type of construction. It was a long-handled spade stuck into the ground, an unlikely frame for a straw-filled pair of jeans and a flannel shirt. Still, it was a sight that might warn off some creatures from the cornfield.

The moon was high and bright enough, and Jane and her flashlight were close enough to illuminate the tableau. A large mound of dirt was piled up at least three feet, so the shovel standing up in it extended into the air at least six feet. Sitting, all loose-limbed and relaxed, his back against the garden spade, was a man Jane had seen at the pig roast, shaking hands and shoveling barbecue into his mouth while talking a mile a minute. He wore the green blazer of a real estate company. His mouth was still open, perhaps surprised at where he now found himself, sitting alone, no plate in his lap. Instead, a not-so-artfully arranged animal skeleton had been dropped across his knees, the animal's skull seeming to look right at the man's chest, right at the jagged hole torn through his blazer, his shirt, and, Jane could only assume by the amount of blood, his heart.

"Jane?" Charley whispered.

"Charley," Jane answered, as he came up from behind her.

"Nick?" she asked, turning around, fearful that her son might have come up behind her too, not wanting him to see this picture. Charley put a hand on her shoulder. He shook his head and gestured with his head toward the tent.

Charley's eyes were fixed on the dead man, and Jane, who had turned to her husband, was looking back over his shoulder in the direction of the outhouse, the tent, the cabin, and the main farmhouse.

"Otto?" Charley said to the dead man's lap.

"Fuzzy?" Jane whispered, watching the man tiptoe into his house through the kitchen door.

Chapter 5

When Detective Munson got out of his car, the sky was barely beginning to lighten. His face was still imprinted with the map of his bedsheets, and he had a faraway look in his eyes. Jane realized she was truly glad to see him. In fact she was almost giddy with delight. He was an old friend, a colleague. They were on the same side, and he would be happy to have her "work the case" with him.

"Mrs. Wheel," he nodded, hiding the delight he must have felt at seeing her back in Kankakee, literally camped out not a hundred feet from where an agent for Kankakee "K3" Realty, if the man's blazer was to be believed, had been shot through the heart.

Jane walked the still-sleeping Nick into Lula's kitchen, straight through the dining room, maneuvering him around a huge, half-round table made of walnut and into the front parlor, where she folded him onto a maroon camelback sofa and covered him with two of the six crocheted afghans that

Lula had piled on the hassock in the corner. Her hope, as always, was that Nick could sleep through the unpleasantness that was now going to permeate the air at Fuzzy's farm, the unpleasantness that might interrupt the dig he and Charley had planned to supervise, the unpleasantness that a murder investigation would bring to their campout. Oh yes, and the unpleasantness of the murder itself.

Jane watched sleep smooth Nick's face into that of a three year old. *If we could just snap our fingers and put them under a protective spell,* she thought, *let them dream through the hard parts.* She knew it was impossible, not even always desirable. After all, Tim had asked her many times, "Choose, Janie," he'd say. "You want a happy life or an interesting life?"

"Both," she always answered. Jane, when faced with the great dessert decisions of childhood — Chocolate or vanilla? Apple or blueberry? Red or redder? — had always asked for a bit of both. Nellie had always scolded her not to be so greedy. When Jane and Charley were at dinner, on a second or third date, and Jane was torn between Key Lime and tiramisu, Charley told Jane he didn't think it reflected greed; he thought it showed hope.

She looked down at Nick, anticipating his confusion when he woke up on the parlor couch, a prisoner of tightly tucked crochet instead of bundled up in his sleeping bag in the tent. She was wondering how she could prevent that — a note on the coffee table? While she stared at her son, a small miracle occurred. He smiled in his sleep and said, "Whatever." Clear as a bell. He could have been dreaming about any number of events, scenes, the realistic or the surreal. But wherever he was, his happy answer to his dreamy questioner had been, "Whatever." Jane decided to listen to that small glimpse into his unconsciousness. His intelligent face told her everything she needed to know. As long as he had the even-handed intelligence of his father and the . . . what was it Jane could gift him with? — touching his forehead with her imaginary fairy godmother wand as he slept . . . "interestingness" of his mother's life — maybe Nick would be okay. Perhaps, translated for the waking adult, the sleepy "Whatever" meant that his life could be happy and interesting. A bit of both. Whatever.

When Jane went back outside, she saw seven squad cars lined up in the long driveway that led to the house. An ambulance was parked on the gravel patch near the barn. Munson and a few others in plainclothes were directing uniformed officers not to trample the grounds, to tape off a perimeter that appeared to include the cabin and the tent. Jane was glad that her first instinct had been to get Nick out of the tent without asking permission or calling attention to it. There would be time later. Charley was crouched a respectable distance from the body, looking at the bones piled up in the victim's lap. He seemed to lean in, turn his head, lean back. Jane realized with a start that Charley had a camera, must have been in his jacket pocket, and he was photographing the bones. And although Jane had no idea what a law against that might be called, she had a feeling, if he happened to look over at Charley, Munson wasn't going to like seeing him playing photographer.

Lights had been set up, and the scene was being combed by three police officers that Jane could see. More could have been in the cornfields behind the first row.

Jane felt someone come up behind her before she heard the crunch of gravel, but before she could pry her eyes away from what, just a few hours ago, she had thought was a dancing scarecrow, a voice was in her ear.

"Sooner rather than later," said Dr. Jaekel, the acting coroner.

"Pardon?" Jane said, doing a little sideways jump so she was facing the man. She noted that his long face looked even longer, but his hair was neatly combed, his shirt pressed, his tie tied.

"We are meeting again, sooner rather than later," he said, and kept walking toward the cornfield. Charley had stood and pocketed the camera by the time Jaekel passed him, and Jane was relieved. She had the feeling he would have no problem holding out his hand and requesting the film, just as a stern teacher might stand before you, interrupting his lecture to demand that you surrender your gum.

Murder stirred up action, that was for sure. Jane had walked away from the porch, but she turned and saw that the chairs and table nearest the back door had been appropriated as a makeshift desk and there were two police officers writing furiously on lined tablets. Everyone had either a cell phone or a walkie-talkie. Munson was walking from uniform to uniform, asking questions, giving directions. Yellow tape was streaming out, being wrapped around little stakes pounded into the ground. And Jane knew that within a few minutes she would be questioned for the first time; and for the next five hours, the same questions would be asked again and again and again. She took a deep breath and walked toward Charley. Before she answered anyone else's questions, she wanted to ask her own.

"You okay?" Charley asked, turning to her and holding out his arms before she reached him. She found she was happy to fold herself in. Even though the temperature would climb and climb, this early sunrise air was chilly.

"Charley, before we get split up to answer questions, tell me, did you hear anything when you were in the outhouse?"

"Mrs. Wheel?" Munson had walked over. Munson and Charley shook hands and the police detective made some remark about Mrs. Wheel being, once again, in the middle of the mess.

"Well, at least we can agree this time on how we define the mess," said Jane. Unlike some of the other moments when Jane's detecting life had intersected with that of Detective Munson's and she had to convince him that it was murder or, at best, an aided and abetted natural cause, here on the edge of Fuzzy Neilson's cornfield there was no debate. Green-blazered Roger T . . . something — Jane could read the first name printed on Munson's notebook upside down, but the last name was under Munson's thumb — was definitely not a living scarecrow escaping from the farm as Jane had feared, but a Realtor who was now unquestionably a murder victim.

"Define away, Mrs. Wheel," said Munson, flipping through the pages, either looking for some elusive fact or trying to convince Jane he didn't really care about what she was going to say.

"Murder," said Jane. "I don't know much about guns, but I've been studying, and I believe the victim was shot and the bullet hit something major because of the amount of blood. And I . . ." Jane stopped. Did she want to say that she might have seen Roger T. fall, collapse onto the ground? Of course she wanted to tell the police investigator everything she knew, but before she did, maybe she could find out what woke Charley up so that he wasn't in the tent when she went to find him and why Fuzzy was hightailing it into the back door right after she and Charley found the body.

Munson nodded at someone behind

Jane's back and then looked directly into her eyes. "We do agree on murder, Mrs. Wheel," said Munson, "and I believe you knew the victim?"

Jane tried to remember the face of the man she had seen what? One hour ago? Two? It was light out now. How long had it taken for Munson and his people to comb the field, examine the body, set up camp, turn Fuzzy's farm into the beehive it had now become?

What was it about a body that made you remember everything and nothing? She could recall the position of his arms and legs, the company blazer he wore, the somewhat surprised look on his face. But did she associate the man with anyone living? No. She thought she had seen him at the barbecue, but she didn't know him, did she? Was it someone from Kankakee that she should recognize? The sad truth right now, as she racked up the numbers of dead bodies she had stumbled over, was that she practiced a kind of disassociation with the victim. After finding her neighbor Sandy murdered, she had experienced nightmares, periodic flashes of horror. Then came other victims. Since she now had a professional interest, she wondered if some kind of protective reflex had set in.

"I don't believe I —" Jane began.

"Roger T. Groveland?" Munson asked, again looking over Jane's shoulder.

Why is he avoiding my eyes? Jane thought, then realized he was not just looking past her but looking at someone.

She turned to look and saw a short, gray-haired man, still sleepy, but scrubbed and pink-cheeked.

"You are?" asked Munson, gesturing to the man.

"Oh no, I'm not him," he said. "No, no, I'm not Roger Groveland. I'm Henry Bennett. Hank," he said, extending his hand to Munson. When Munson narrowed his eyes at him and did not extend his own, Henry did a slight pivot and Jane found herself shaking hands with a man whom Munson seemed most displeased to meet.

"Hey, Bostick, you letting the world in here now? Not bad enough that we have a hundred and fifty sets of footprints from the damn pig roast? I told you, the Realtor to make the identification and that's it." Munson was waving his pad in front of the face of a frightened young man in a uniform — Bostick — who looked like the younger brother of someone Jane had gone to high school with. *Great,* she thought, *him I know, him I recognize. Sammy Bostick's little brother.*

"I'm the Realtor," said Henry Bennett, holding up the green blazer he was carrying over his arm. "I came here from the K3 office. I'm certainly not Roger Groveland."

"No, no, of course not," said Munson. He looked over at Jane accusingly, as if to say that none of this would be confusing if it weren't for Jane Wheel standing in the middle of this backyard-farmette-crime scene. This was a woman who complicated things. "I was simply telling Mrs. Wheel the name of the man out there. Roger T. Groveland."

What was Munson talking about? Yes, she did know Roger Groveland. He had lived down the street from her when her family had lived in the subdivision out west of town. Don's Folly, she and her brother had called the house. He had wanted something brand-new in their lives, something he had built from the ground up. So when ground was broken for the development, Don was there at the meeting, looking at maps of lots and selecting blueprints. He had bought the land and put a down payment on the house and come home proud as any poor-kid-makes-good, bootstrap-yanking, hard-working-provider-of-the-year kind of guy and been crushed when his children wept over leaving their neighborhood, which was within walking distance to Cobb Park and bicycling distance to school. Out in the subdivision, they would have to ride a bus for half an hour to go to a school with farm kids.

Don held firm. He had, after all, signed the contract. And they had moved to Western Hills Drive, into a three-bedroom ranch house with a cornfield just beyond their backyard. *Like right here at Fuzzy's,* Jane thought. And on moving day Jane prepared to hate it all, but was caught totally off guard when Roger Groveland had ridden up on his blue Schwinn and asked what grade she was in. They had been best friends in fifth grade, but due to the immutable laws of middle school, were unable to speak full sentences to each other during the next three years. They had gone to different high schools, but occasionally ran into each other. Adult Roger had stopped in the EZ Way Inn every month or so for a bowl of Nellie's chicken noodle and an update on what Janie was doing in the big city. Roger, Jane now remembered, had worked for a local real estate office and, according to reports from Don after chatting over lunch, done well for himself.

Hank Bennett fidgeted with his own name tag, lifting it slightly from his blazer that he now put on. *Carrying it over his arm had been a mistake,* thought Jane. *It was what had made Munson so angry at Bostick.* Without that ugly green jacket, Henry "Hank" Bennett had no business on the property. Bennett lifted his lapels and straightened his jacket, again fingering the name tag as if to make it clear that he was a Realtor, if not the Realtor that Munson had expected, and he was there to help sort out whatever needed sorting out.

"I'm sorry if it wasn't clear who I was," said Bennett, as much to Jane as to Munson, whose face he seemed to want to avoid. "I had an early appointment at the office, so I answered the phone when the policeman called." He straightened his shoulders.

"That wasn't Roger Groveland," said Jane.

Munson looked annoyed. "Oh no, Mrs. Wheel?"

"No," Bennett chimed in. "Rog is dead."

Munson's annoyance went from a simmer to a medium flame.

"I mean, Rog died about, let's see, six, almost seven weeks ago," said Bennett.

"Heart attack. Sudden."

"No?" said Jane.

"Oh yes, very sad," Hank said, shaking his head. "His wife had left him a few years ago, moved away. Niece came to town and took care of everything, had a house sale for the contents — Irene hadn't left him with much — then she listed the house with me. Still available. Nice potential there, if you're looking," he offered.

"Bostick!" Munson shouted and turned away from Jane Wheel, and Jane saw what she might have thought of as impossible, a man cowering away from and running toward someone at the same time. Poor Bostick. Jane could hear Munson lambasting him about the identity of the victim. Bostick, however, frightened as he might be, had had no reason to doubt the name tag, as it was affixed to the blazer, which seemed to fit the gentleman. No wallet, no other identification, which didn't seem unusual to Bostick. If the man was being robbed, of course his wallet would have been taken. Munson, in a quiet but deadly voice, suggested to Bostick that most muggings did not take place in a cornfield and perhaps the victim's identification should have been backed up with more than a plastic ID tag before he turned in the name to Munson.

Munson turned on Hank Bennett.

"If that isn't Groveland, who the hell is it?"

"I have no idea, Detective Munson," said Bennett. "I've never seen him before."

"I don't know why someone would wear a stupid green blazer unless he had to, that's for damn sure . . . ," said Munson. "Sorry," he looked at Bennett, who seemed to take the blazer slur somewhat personally. "It's been a confusing morning. I apologize, Mr. Bennett. I appreciate you coming over and I hate to ask you to take another look, but we need to make quite sure that this isn't an employee of K3 Realty who might have pulled the wrong jacket off the hanger at the office."

"Impossible," said Bennett. "We take our jackets home. There are no mix-ups at work."

Charley came over from the shed where he had gone to check out the rest of the findings from the dig. He placed an arm across Jane's shoulders and touched his forehead to hers.

"Sorry about your friend, Roger. When Bostick told me who it was, I recognized the name. I told Detective Munson that you knew Groveland."

"It's not Roger," said Jane.

"Nope," echoed Henry.

Charley look puzzled, then smiled faintly. "Well, I guess that's good news in one way, honey. About Roger."

"No." Jane, always aware of the inadequacy of language to communicate, felt like she was falling in a hole. "Roger's still dead. He's just not dead here." Jane pointed to the cornfield. "I mean there."

Munson told Bostick to take Bennett to the cornfield. Munson wrote something down and followed them, looking back and holding up a hand to Jane that seemed to mean he'd be back in one finger's time and that she wasn't to wander off.

"The man out there was wearing Roger's blazer," she whispered, "but Roger died a few months ago of a heart attack."

"And Bostick is catching hell for the bad ID?" asked Charley.

"I'm not sure that Henry 'Hank' would have been invited in just yet if they hadn't believed the murder victim was associated with the real estate company. Munson is pretty grouchy about the number of footprints he's dealing with here already. He doesn't want more than those his people have invited in to trample the evidence."

Charley was nodding as Jane talked, but

she noticed his attention drifting down toward the cornfield.

"What?" she asked.

"Otto," he said.

"Are you sure it's the same skeleton?" Jane asked.

"Yeah. I heard someone out at the shed. I thought I heard footsteps, so I got up to see if you were trying to make it to the outhouse by yourself. I saw a flickering light by the shed, you know, a flashlight or a lantern, and went over there, but I didn't have a chance to figure out what was missing."

"When did you go to the outhouse? After you had been to the shed?" Jane asked.

"No, I . . . ," said Charley.

"It was before?" Jane asked. "That timing doesn't . . ."

"I just saw you walking down the path and followed you. I didn't know what you were doing, thought you might be walking in your sleep."

"I wish I was," said Jane. "Anything else missing from the table over there?"

"It was a mishmash of stuff, Janie," said Charley. "There was the cat, and the old tag, and some interesting stones and pottery shards. There were two bottles. Things aren't arranged the same way on the table, but I'm going to have to go over the list with the professor from the junior college. If they let him in," Charley added, "or if they let us out."

Jane's gaze followed Charley's. The long drive up to the farmhouse was blocked at the road by two police cars. Jane was trying to decide whether or not Munson would take it as a personal affront if she went into the house to check on Nick before she was officially dismissed, when she heard a tinny-sounding bell. She was ready to dash back to the cabin, thinking it was her cell phone, newly tuned to some obscure melody by Nick, who would claim he just wanted to keep things fresh for her.

It wasn't her cell phone, though, or anyone else's. It was a pre–cell phone alert, a bronze triangle hanging from the willow outside Fuzzy and Lula's back door. Lula had carried out a huge basket of something and was using a metal stick to ring the triangle and shouting for everyone to come and get it. If there hadn't been a dead man who wasn't Roger Groveland laid out in the cornfield, Jane might have found it somewhat amusing and maybe even ironic that dozens of police officers were looking back and forth from Munson to Lula, who was luring them with the most deadly of threats to their well-being and profession-alism.

"Doughnuts, boys! Fresh hot dough-nuts," Lula sang out. "Come and get 'em."

Apparently Munson decided he wouldn't risk mutiny by denying his men a doughnut break, but he didn't indulge himself. Jane wandered over to the large tray and helped herself to the shaker of powdered sugar Lula had thoughtfully set out next to the still warm rolls. Jane didn't want the extra sugar, but she lifted the shaker above her head and read the mark on the bottom, UPICO, the signature of Universal Potteries. It was in Eleanor Blue with the circus decal. It wasn't particularly rare, but Jane admired the utility of it, the heft of its rounded shape in her hand, the warm, safe feeling it gave her to see it being used, the knowledge that it had probably been in constant use since Lula's mother had ordered it seventy-five years ago from the Sears catalog. Instead of gathering dust in an antique mall or dis-played in some retro kitchen, all kitsch and irony, here it was, doing what it was meant to do. Continuity? Was that what Jane ad-mired? Was it what she thought might rub off if she acquired enough stuff with the mojo of home and hearth? Would it protect them all? And what was it she thought she needed protection from?

"Quit Bogarting the sugar, baby, some of us want what's inside of that quasicollectible," said a familiar voice.

"Tim?" Jane turned to see Lowry balancing a cup of coffee and a plate with three doughnuts. "How?"

He took the shaker from her and liberally sprinkled his breakfast, smiling. "I've got my ways."

Tim explained between bites that he had been at K3 Realty when the call had come in. The real estate company was one of the sponsors of the Twin Gazebo Garage Sale, and Tim had been there using the street directories and making copies.

"At six a.m. on a Sunday morning?" Jane asked.

"I haven't got much time to put this thing together. There weren't any good sales this morning," he said, taking a large bite of doughnut. "You know me — my inner clock is permanently set at four a.m. on weekend mornings to get me first place in line at the sales. But Sunday mornings aren't as good as they used to be. So I told Hank I'd like to work there as early as he was opening the office, and he said he had a crack of dawn meeting."

Tim told Jane that Bennett had gotten flustered at the call and said that he could drive himself out to Fuzzy's, then realized that his wife had dropped him off and he didn't have a car.

"I thought you might need me, Nancy Drew," said Tim. He had driven Bennett, but he had laid low in the house, talking to Lula and Fuzzy about what they might offer for sale if they decided to come into town and take a table.

"Munson, you may remember, isn't my biggest fan, so I decided not to . . ."

"Get in his face," Jane finished, a cloud of powdered sugar now between them.

"Something like that," said Tim. "How would you price this shaker?"

"Twenty dollars," said Jane.

"You'd better be a damn good detective because you'll starve as a picker," said Tim. "No one would pay that."

Jane started to say something but stopped.

"Right, I know," said Tim, "you would. You'd pay twenty."

"I look at it this way, Tim. I just bought a stainless steel sugar shaker at a fancy kitchen store, and it cost over twenty dollars. Don't make that face, I did," Jane said, knowing Tim didn't believe she would ever wander alone into a housewares department anywhere and buy any item retail. He had seen her hyperventilate in a Target more than once.

"Lula's little ceramic one here has character and stories and is as cute as can be. Why wouldn't I pay the same price for it? More even?"

"Number one, it's in the blue, which is a common color. If it had the same decal and was in red, maybe you could go ten, but that'd still be high. You wouldn't buy it for twenty, honey, because you're in the business. You don't pay retail, especially not high-end retail. You can find another one. And it will be cheaper. So you move on quickly to find it," said Tim, his mouth full of fried dough. "And number two, why were you buying a shaker for powdered sugar. You open a can now and then, but you never bake."

"I cook," said Jane. She took the last two doughnuts on the platter to bring in to Nick. "The shaker was for Nick. He makes pancakes and the powdered sugar gets all over, so I bought the shaker. It made the kitchen seem more organized."

"Yeah, honey. That'll do it," Tim said, and laughed. He brushed his hands into the air and wiped his face with a yellow-and-green paper napkin from the crocheted holder Lula had set out. He waved as he stepped off the porch. "I'm going to see Charley and take my chances with Munson. Let's try to get out of here to do garage-sale canvassing ASAP, okay?"

"Eleanor," said Jane.

"Who?" asked Tim.

"The color is called Eleanor Blue. I know it's the most common color," said Jane. "But it's the prettiest," she added softly, since Tim was already out of earshot.

When Jane dropped off the plate for Nick, he was half awake on the couch. Lula had tucked in even more crocheted covers over him, and he looked like a caterpillar wrapped in a brightly colored acrylic cocoon.

"Anybody fill you in yet, Nicky?" Jane asked.

Nick shook his head no, blinked, and stretched. "But I'm thinking that all those police cars in the driveway mean something happened out there. Is Dad okay?"

Jane nodded, considering her son. He had those big, brown, anxious eyes that seemed so familiar. Where had she seen them? Oh, yeah. Mirror. Okay, but there were so many things about her son that she didn't recognize. He was calm, efficient, graceful, although he wouldn't like that word. He had Charley's stance and Charley's scientific reasoning. *Charley's hair,* she thought, brushing it out of his eyes. She only got to make those motherly gestures when he was still in the throes of sleep. As he became more and more alert, he stood taller and taller, out of her reach.

"Mom, did you find a, you know . . . another body?" Nick asked, trying to scoot up into a sitting position, but straitjacketed by granny-square crochet.

"Dad was right behind me," Jane said. "We practically found it together."

Nick nodded, an odd expression on his face. Jane tried to do a quick calculation of how much of his college fund they would have to use on therapy and the most cost-efficient use of the money. Would it make more sense to let the money keep earning interest so it would be available for adult psychiatry or should they chip away at the savings and the neurosis they had bestowed upon their boy by signing him up for weekly sessions now?

"So you and Dad are in this one together, huh?" Nick asked, grabbing a doughnut, blowing some of the sugar into the air between them.

Jane nodded. She guessed they were.

She promised to find Nick some milk while he unwound himself from the blankets. She warned him that Munson would want to ask him if he had heard anything, what time he had gone to sleep, all the usual questions. Nick waved her away. "I watch *Law & Order*, Mom," he said. "I know the drill."

Jane had often felt like she was being watched. Not paranoia exactly. No one stalking her or keeping any kind of Hitchcockian tabs on her behavior, but a feeling of being watched onstage. What was the movie about the guy whose life, it turned out, was a soap opera? A television show? She hadn't thought much of the movie as a movie, but she had certainly gotten the premise. Jane had thought it might have been because she had worked in advertising, producing commercials, that she was obsessed with seeing her life unfold as if it were on camera. But since leaving the business, she realized it was not a hazard of her profession, it was an epidemic that would overtake the twenty-first century. It had certainly gotten a head start in the good old twentieth.

Warhol's fifteen minutes of fame? Sort of. But it was more than that. People felt that their most private moments were now the fodder of the public. Oprah might have backed out a bit, but she was in on it at the beginning, that's for sure. To her credit, she seemed to have caught on and had the guilt-ridden decency to cut it out. But Jerry Springer and the string of no-names who had offered the masses a public forum for airing their worst selves? What would be next? Shows in which people manufactured falling in love, fought over money, strapped on lie detectors, let bugs crawl over their faces. Well, yeah. Jane had feared she was on "reality television" long before the term had been invented and now lived with the fear that somehow her thoughts about it had been revealed in the program of her own life.

Could she be responsible for creating reality television? More important, could she borrow some money from Nick's college fund and get the psychiatric help *she* needed?

Bottom line here: Did she *want* Nick to know the drill?

"Janie, we've got ourselves some excitement, don't we?" asked Fuzzy, who was sitting at the kitchen table when Jane came in after explaining what she knew to Nick. Fuzzy had poured nearly half of his coffee into a saucer to cool. For a moment Jane's eyes misted over. These days, everyone drank from coffee mugs. One seldom saw actual cups and saucers in use. She remembered, as a child, watching her dad pour the coffee out of his cup into its matching saucer, explaining to her that he did it to cool it off. Then he'd pour it back into the cup and drink it down. Why in the world did this scene make her so nostalgic, so emotional? Would a professional be able to explain it to her? Would he or she say that she channeled fears and anxieties into a kind of therapeutic nostalgia? Maybe Nick didn't need to go to college. He was pretty savvy, might get a scholarship anyway. And she needed the money right now to get a psychiatrist on retainer.

"Fuzzy, have you talked to the police yet?" Jane asked.

"Nope. Can't get anybody to talk to me or tell me who shot Johnny," said Fuzzy, carefully lifting the saucer and pouring the liquid back into the cup.

"Eggs, Jane? I scrambled up a mess of them?" asked Lula, still standing at the stove, spatula raised.

"Johnny who? You know that man out there?"

"Since he was a boy. John Sullivan. Grew

138

up on the next farm over. Went off to college, didn't he, Lula? Works for a newspaper now up in Chicago."

"He's a newspaper reporter?" asked Jane. "Does he work for Kankakee Realty, too?"

"No," said Lula, "he doesn't."

Jane noted that Lula used present tense and stabbed at her eyes with a tissue when she answered.

"Why was he wearing an agent's blazer, I wonder. With Roger Groveland's name tag," said Jane.

"Don't know," said Fuzzy. "Maybe he was doing an undercover investigator job like on the news? Like the people who get jobs in restaurants so they can show the filthy kitchens and such."

"Don't be so foolish, Fuzz," said Lula.

"What was he doing here?" Jane asked, more to herself than to Fuzzy and Lula. If Munson hadn't been in here yet to question the Neilsons, how furious was he going to be that Jane was hearing it all first?

"Don't know for sure, but I saw him at the roast last night and figured he was visiting his folks and came on by," said Fuzzy, handing his plate to Lula for seconds.

Fuzzy spent the next few minutes carefully buttering a piece of toast. He balanced a pat of butter on a knife, carefully spreading it from corner to corner, framing the bread in butter. Then, like an oil painter working on a canvas, he filled in his square with more butter, building it up on the toast so it looked like some dairy farming display, a topographical map carved out of butter. Lula glanced over from the stove and laughed.

"Stop playing with your food, Fuzz." She exchanged his buttered toast with a perfectly balanced slice from a plate near the sink. "You sure as heck don't need to put your cholesterol through the roof again."

Fuzzy stared at the toast for a few seconds. He shook his head at Lula and she stared right back at him. He turned the bread upside down, then back around and smiled and took a bite. Lula watched him like a hawk. Jane thought she might grab the butter away, so afraid did she seem that he was going to start doctoring *this* slice. Fuzzy shook his head again, then retrieved his thoughts about John Sullivan. He told Jane that John was a real go-getter, always on the job. He had been asking everybody there last night if they still wanted an airport and if not what the heck did they want to do with the town.

"Did he want the airport?" asked Jane.

"Don't know why he'd care. Lived up near Chicago somewhere. Farmed a little on weekends with his dad, but never cared for it too much," said Fuzzy. "I don't believe he did, do you, Lula?"

"Can't say as I can tell what anybody else cares for," said Lula. "They do one thing, but it's so they can do something else anyway. He probably farmed so his dad would leave the land to him instead of his brother; then once he got the land, he'd up and sell it right away. Folks do that all the time: throw some dirt up in the air and make it all cloudy so you can't see the sharp edges of what they really want. Us, we want to grow our vegetables and a few flowers and cook them and eat them and sell the extras." Lula wiped her hands on her apron. "And maybe sell a little dirt now and then to get some extra money to buy a big-boy bed for our new great-grandson. So he'd know it come from us. And look what happens to us and our farm — just 'cause we know what we want and we do what we want and don't bother anybody else."

Jane saw that Lula was about to cry, but she put the brakes on by putting dishes away and wrapping extra food. She slid the last piece of toast over to her husband.

"Here. Don't say I never gave you nothing," she said, and began running a fresh sink full of hot, soapy water.

Jane had never heard such a long speech from Lula. Like her mother, Lula was a doer not a talker. When Jane was in her twenties, she had gone a few times to a womens' discussion group that a colleague at work had begun. "What the hell you talk about with all them women?" Nellie had asked. Jane had told her that they talked about everything . . . their feelings, their hopes and dreams . . . and that it was great to have people who listened. Nellie had sniffed and remained silent, and when Jane couldn't stand the quiet anymore and begged her mother to tell her what she thought about it, Nellie had laughed. "I don't think anything at all of it. I don't think anybody goes to that thing because they want to listen, though. You all just want to hear yourselves talk."

Nellie had gone on to tell Jane that if they just cleaned a closet or wiped down their kitchen counters or made a pot of soup they were just as likely to feel good about all their hopes. Plus they'd have a meal on the table and nobody else would know all their business.

When Nellie or Lula gave up any conversation longer than a recipe or a grocery list or a harangue on the way their children dressed, kept house, or raised their children, it was an event. It sure as hell wasn't because they wanted to hear themselves talk. They weren't women who wanted that at all.

Jane considered what Lula said about Johnny Sullivan's weekend farming. Was he trying to butter up his father in order to inherit the land so he could turn around and sell it? Perhaps Sullivan was asking questions about the airport as an interested heir apparent to a desirable runway location? It sounded like John Sullivan might have been playing reporter or gentleman farmer on weekends in Kankakee, but the real question now was why, last night, was he dressed to play Roger Groveland, Realtor? And was that the role that had finished him, that ended with him playing dead?

When Jane went back outside, Tim and Charley were engrossed in a serious discussion with Munson. Jane could see the corners of Tim's mouth twitching, but she wasn't sure whether he was amused or angry. There was no doubt about Charley's expression. He was angry. He was using his right hand to count the fingers on his left. It was his tell. When she had first noticed it, Jane thought that it was his way of counting to ten to stay in control of his temper. Charley had denied this, explaining that as he counted, he gave himself reasons for whatever argument he was mounting in a conversation. As Jane walked over to the three men, she saw him start all over at the thumb and realized Charley must have a lot of reasons for the way he felt.

"You can't touch those bones anyway. Not your jurisdiction," said Charley.

"And whose jurisdiction is it, Professor? Yours?" asked Munson.

"I believe this site falls under the Human Skeletal Remains Protection Act, and if I'm correct, everything in the vicinity of this site has to remain untouched until we determine . . ."

"What do you mean by untouched?" Munson asked, his cell phone in hand.

"The act forbids anyone from disturbing what might be human remains in unregistered graves —" began Charley.

"Look, as far as I can see —" cut in Munson.

"And if I remember the wording of the act correctly, 'disturbing' includes excavating, removing, exposing, defacing, mutilating, destroying, molesting, or desecrating any skeletal remains, unregistered graves, and grave markers," said Charley.

Munson stopped, considering Charley's recitation.

"The way I see it, you have your work to do and I have mine. I am not forbidding you to continue, just hold up for a while. I am also informing you that my people will have to go over this area." Munson held his hand up to stop Charley from interrupting. "A murder has been committed here, and my duty is to the . . ." Munson stopped. "Your duty might be protecting the long-dead remains, Professor, but I have to work with what happened last night."

"The new body trumps the old bones, Charley," said Tim, looking back and forth at the two men. "Never thought I'd say this, Detective Munson, but I do believe I agree with you."

Jane was only a few feet away from the three men, but only Tim had noticed her; and after he spoke, he looked at her, expecting approval. His look said, see, I can be a good boy and behave even when I want to drive Munson, the homophobic son-of-a-bitch, crazy.

"Mr. Lowry," said Munson, his voice a

low growl, "how the hell did you get here?"

"Isn't it possible that Charley can continue to examine the site while your people comb the field and the yard?" asked Jane, trying to placate and distract at the same time. "If he limits his work to the immediate area?"

"This scene is already a mess. There were a hundred people here last night, tramping through the property, dropping plastic forks and napkins. We'll be lucky to turn up anything of use," said Munson. "Of course," he added, "the bones are kind of interesting."

Charley looked at Jane. They had been married fifteen years, and if you could average the number of looks, real eyeball-to-eyeball encounters that a married couple has per day — say, conservatively, ten, because meaningful, forget-everything-you've-ever-known-and-felt-and-thought-and-lose-yourself-in-my-eyes looks aren't as common as one might think — that would mean that Jane and Charley had exchanged 53,750 direct looks, and Jane could tell that out of all of them, this one was the one she was meant to recognize.

Charley's look was an iron hand clamped over her mouth.

No one said anything.

"Don't know what to make of someone who shoots somebody dead, then piles up a bunch of bones in their lap," said Munson.

Even Tim understood that it was no time to burst into a rousing chorus of "Dem Bones."

"Mrs. Wheel, we'll start our interviews with you up on the porch if you don't mind." Munson took her elbow, wanting to guide her away before she could consult with Charley, but she stopped him.

"Our son is in the house, Detective Munson, and he is naturally upset," said Jane. "I need to have a word with my husband. I'll join you in a moment."

No need for Munson to know that Nick was calmly munching doughnuts and watching cartoons inside. Jane waited until he was halfway to the house before turning back to Charley and Tim. "What?"

"Otto."

"Who?" asked Tim.

"The family cat. Some of his bones are missing." Charley talked low and fast. "I don't know anything about the gunshots and time of death or anything, but I'm guessing that whoever piled those bones into our Realtor's lap did it as an afterthought, carrying the bones over in his pockets or bare hands. I don't know. Maybe he either dropped them or maybe tried to set them up to make it look like it was something more . . . I don't know . . . ominous."

"Oh yeah," said Tim, "because someone getting shot down dead in a cornfield isn't really, you know, scary enough."

"Shush, Tim," said Jane. "Charley means that the bones make it seem like a cult crime or something. You know, some kind of sacrifice or something."

"Not just that, Janie. Remember, I was up last night. Out of the tent. Over to check on the site. I heard something or someone over there. They're going to find my footprints leaving the tent, leading them to the table set up by the shed, then going to the path following you. I'd like to think about all this . . . and see if I can find any bones scattered around. Maybe someone left a trail if they dropped anything they had scooped up from the table," said Charley.

"But I think I heard the shot. I thought it was thunder or something. I dozed off, then woke up. I couldn't get back to sleep," Jane whispered. "And when I got up and saw you weren't in the tent, I started down to the cornfield, and I talked to you when you were in the outhouse, remember?"

"What did I say?" asked Charley.

"Mrs. Wheel?" said a polite young uniformed officer. "You're wanted now."

"*Ocupado*," said Jane.

"Why would you think I would say that?"

"Because that's what you said. I figured it was a habit from the dig you were on in South America."

Charley shook his head.

"What?" Jane asked.

"I was never in the outhouse," said Charley.

Jane had pulled out her cell phone on her way to talk to Munson. She considered it carefully. Would it be Nancy Drew's best friend now? Would she need George and Bess if she had her trusty link to civilization and police backup? Jane dialed Bruce Oh's number, wishing she had remembered to ask Nick to record it as a speed-dial number. She knew she could learn how to do it herself, she was sure she could, but the time, the energy, the rapidly decreasing brain cells all seemed better spent on other tasks. Right now, stalling her way up to the porch, though, she realized one number would be so much easier than trying to remember seven. Of course, since it was so early in the morning, Oh would be out taking his morning walk before the world woke up and needed him. Claire would already be up and out at a sale. Jane left her usual cogent message:

"Hi, hello, I'm in Kankakee, well, outside of the town really, about three miles west at Fuzzy's farm; and last night I thought I saw a scarecrow fall, but it turns out it's this man who was misidentified as an old friend, but it's not. He's dead and everything, the old friend, but he's not this dead guy, but . . . damn it. A murder. As usual. Call me." And as the time's-up beep sounded, Jane remembered to say, "It's Jane Wheel."

As if he wouldn't know.

Chapter 6

Jane so badly wanted to know if Munson watched police television programs. Did any of these uniformed people watch those shows, the people running around the farm, armed not only with guns, but also with cell phones, evidence collection kits, and flashlights, which were still being used to peer into and behind bushes, even though it was now a bright, sunlit morning, to investigate Fuzzy and Lula's tomato plants and cucumber vines? They all looked so unreal, so costumed and made up and rehearsed. Social critics always worried that violent programs desensitized watchers to real violence, but Jane worried more that it made day-to-day, ordinary life less real. Yes, she worried that people believed that the only real reality was now televised and everything else people did from morning to night was a rehearsal for when they would actually get a chance to strut their stuff, when it was scripted, edited, and produced. Is that what television and movies did to the world? Or was it just what television and movies and her previous career producing commercials had done to Jane?

Munson had asked her in at least three different ways to describe her night. She told him the truth. She woke up. She had been restless. She looked out the cabin window. She may have heard something like thunder. Far away. She saw what she thought was a scarecrow fall down in the cornfield. She went outside to investigate.

"Alone?"

"I was sleeping alone in the cabin. Charley and Nick were in the tent."

"And you didn't go wake your husband? Ask him to go with you?"

Jane was a product of Catholic education. She knew her Ten Commandments and her sins from venial to mortal. And, being a Catholic-educated girl, she knew that it would be easy to tell a lie, confess it, receive absolution, and still arrive, soul intact, at heaven's gate. On the other hand, as a woman who was as uncertain of her girlhood faith as she was of every other religion she had sampled through college and adulthood, she couldn't in all honesty trust herself to lie. What if the confession didn't work the way it was supposed to? What if all those little lies piled up and became a rocklike barricade against getting

152

into the final look-see? What if all those lies and cheats and snide remarks and envies and pouts were all added together and, totaled up, became your number for getting into the biggest house sale of all? Oh my god, what if God made you wait outside the pearly gates until your number was called; and you, with your sinfully high number, watched all the afterlife trappings walk out the gate with the people who had lower numbers — read fewer sins — than you? In life how painful was it to watch the dealers who had slept in their cars walk out of the estate with the Bakelite and the fifties lamps and the vintage tablecloths? How excruciating would purgatory be if it were the longest line to get the best harps and wings?

Get a grip, Jane told herself. She didn't believe in wings and harps. Although she had bought an excellent old marimba at auction once, and she did have a fondness for musical instruments. A harp would be elegant in the sunroom.

No, she was pretty sure that the Vatican had erased purgatory from the rule books.

What she had left from Catholicism was a conscience, scrupulous and guilty at the same time. When Munson asked a question, she had to answer it truthfully.

"Yes, I did go to the tent to wake Charley," Jane said.

A uniform came and whispered something to Munson. He nodded and rose.

"To be continued, Mrs. Wheel."

The one thing that the police were unable to do with crime-scene tape was block off the scene from view. It might be possible to discourage people from walking through what they hoped was a clue-strewn, answer-laden piece of property, but no one tented it or managed to curtain it off from onlookers. Jane had clear sightlines from which to watch the man and woman who were being escorted to the scarecrow area, as Jane had decided to call the crime scene. Both silver-haired. Both tall and thin. They might have been brother and sister, but Jane knew they were not. John Sullivan's parents.

Mr. Sullivan was wearing worn jeans and a plaid shirt. He held a Cub's baseball hat in one hand and wiped at the corners of his mouth with the other. His wife walked beside him, unbowed. Jane noted that she had remarkable posture, and when she looked down at the face that an officer uncovered on the ground, her shoulders sagged only slightly, then rose up to their former position. She turned away and began walking back toward the driveway. John Sullivan's father lingered a moment. He waved the cap a bit and said something to the officer, who shook his head. Jane watched as he stretched the cap out toward the body of his son and realized, in that moment, that it was his son's hat. When the police had shown up at the Sullivans' door after Fuzzy had finally told someone the name of the dead man in the field, after someone had finally listened to him, someone had fetched Mr. and Mrs. Sullivan and driven them directly to the scene, not waiting for a morgue and cool concrete floors and fluorescent lighting. And Mr. Sullivan had picked up his son's baseball cap, maybe from a hook by the back door. He had probably clutched it for dear life in the backseat of the police car, wanting to shout to the uniforms whispering in the front, "Can't be my boy. Not Johnny. I got his cap right here."

The human drama that was unfolding around them slowed the police officers who had been combing the fields and lawn. Everything slowed during the Sullivans' walk to the field and their return to the driveway. Jane watched Mrs. Sullivan shake her head when an officer brought her a glass, and noticed she did not even

acknowledge the folding chair that someone had placed behind her. Mr. Sullivan
placed his hand on the police car in the
driveway, but he did not lean on it. He
stood tall, supporting his own weight.

Jane watched them respond to Munson's
questions. She tried to imagine what they
might be. Do you know what might have
brought your son to the area? Was he
working on a story? Had he mentioned any
problems he was having at work? Trouble
in any relationships? Girlfriend? What did
he do outside of work? Did he gamble?
Does he have any friends who might be
able to tell us what he was doing here?

Jane's question? Why did a murder
victim, the one who was dead, always have
to be so accountable? Why did the first line
of questioning always seem so accusatory?
Why did Johnny Sullivan, weekday journalist and weekend farmer, go and get
himself killed?

Once, when Jane had overheard a police
officer comment that a victim had been at
the wrong place at the wrong time, she had
to restrain herself from pointing out the
fact that anyone who got him or herself
murdered was in the wrong place at the
wrong time, yes? The problem with a
cliché was that it developed from a kind of

truth, and people so quickly get cynical about truth since they can't do anything else about it.

Jane watched Johnny Sullivan's parents shake their heads and nod slowly, answering the barrage of questions that must have sounded like words in another language. Jane thought about what the rest of their day would be like. A conversation about when they could have their son's remains, a totally violating search of the room that Johnny stayed in on his weekend visits to their farm, the shattering realization of what an autopsy was going to do to kill their son all over again, the phone calls to relatives and friends, finally, funeral arrangements. Those are the parts of the family's day that the television programs don't show. Nick and all other television watchers might know the drill of what happens during the peaks of actions, but during those valleys, those lulls in confrontation, those quiet moments of dealing with the messiness of murder, there was nothing that made it on the air. Nothing prepared people; no instructional videos were available for those whose lives were turned upside down by violence. Because Jane knew all of this, because she felt sorrow and pain, she wanted to be the kind of person who could offer a prayer and a soft smile and the gift of silence to the Sullivans.

But Jane had questions, too.

Why was Johnny in the cornfield? Sure, she wanted to know that, but her most pressing question was why was he wearing Roger Groveland's real estate company's blazer?

Jane looked around and located everyone. Tim and Charley were still at the shed, and Nick was now on the back porch with Lula, who looked like she had more food on a tray. *Jeez, she's treating this like a barn raising or something,* Jane thought. How much can one woman cook in a day?

Jane decided to find someone whom no one else was questioning and practice her own detecting. Oh had been telling her to never waste time watching others work.

"Mrs. Wheel, there is always someone who knows something. Always someone who is holding a secret only because no one has asked him to tell," Oh had said. "Find that someone, and you will have an answer that no one else has."

Jane found her someone pulling weeds in the flower beds in the front lawn. Why hadn't anyone told Fuzzy that he shouldn't be touching anything on the grounds? Everyone was inspecting every square inch of earth between the house, the backyard, the vegetable garden, the shed and digging site, and the cornfield, but no one was stationed in front of the house on the far side of the front lawn. There was a perennial flower bed there, and Fuzzy was down on his hands and knees pulling up tiny weeds and putting them into a brown paper grocery bag.

"Fuzzy?" Jane said.

He put his head even closer to the ground and kept pace with the creeping charley that was probably invading the garden as fast as he could pull it out.

"Fuzzy, I don't think the police want you to be digging around until they —"

"If one more person — man, woman, or child — tells me what I can do or I can't do on my own goddamn dirt, I swear I'll . . ." Fuzzy turned around with his trowel raised over his head and his eyes blazing a kind of confused anger. Jane didn't feel threatened exactly, although she knew he wasn't kidding about being in charge of his own home, but she felt uncomfortable. She was seeing a part of this man that she had never known and shouldn't know. They had an intergenerational friendship. The elderly friend of your parents was someone you should be able to wave at and exchange a few innocent jokes with, maybe even ask for advice. But the raw emotion Fuzzy was displaying was disturbing. She wasn't remotely scared. He was close to eighty years old, and strong as he might be, Jane was pretty sure she could protect herself. Or outrun him. His behavior was just uncontrolled, and it left Jane feeling odd. Jane would feel the same if Lula, instead of exchanging recipes or advising her on Nick's care and feeding, came to her with questions about what kind of lingerie she should order from a Victoria's Secret catalog. There were just things that belonged to them and their friends. She was a generation removed, and she shouldn't be witnessing anything as intimate as Fuzzy's anger right now.

Fuzzy shook the trowel at her then turned back to the ground.

"Fuzzy, please . . . ," Jane began.

Jane stopped herself and saw that Fuzzy was not, as she had at first thought, using the brown bag for weed disposal. He was, instead, removing something from the bag and planting. Tulip bulbs? Not exactly the right timing for planting flower bulbs, and

160

the objects he was palming and burying were small.

"What are you planting?" Jane asked.

Fuzzy turned around, his face, a seeming mask of delight at finding her there behind him. "Janie, old girl, where'd you come from?"

Jane dropped down on her knees beside the old man.

"Fuzzy, what are you doing here?"

Fuzzy, with a big smile, allowed his watery green eyes to roam her face before coming back to meet her own. He shook his head as if she had asked an improper but amusing question and stood, unfolding one creaky knee and pushing up slowly. He clutched the paper bag in one hand and the trowel in the other.

"I'll betcha Lula's made sandwiches," he said, running his tongue over his lips. "Let's get us some."

Jane nodded and pushed herself up by putting one palm flat in the dirt. She followed Fuzzy to the house, hanging back just a few steps to examine what she had pulled out of the shallow grave Fuzzy had been digging.

Brushing off the dirt with her thumb, she could just read the date on one of them.

Nineteen thirty-nine. And the other looked like it might be 1940.

What was significant about the years 1939 and 1940? Maybe nothing. It was probably more important to find the answer to the bigger question. Why in the name of heaven was Fuzzy Neilson burying pennies in his flower garden in the first place?

Chapter 7

Jane saw her husband and son hunched over the specimen table at the site. Nick held something up for Charley's reaction, and Jane walked faster, afraid he might actually have been digging, which she was sure was against all of Munson's scene-of-the-crime rules. But as she got closer, she saw they were only cleaning up some of the items that had been boxed up and stored in the shed.

"Turns out Fuzzy has always been a pack rat," said Charley. "He's a collector of all sorts of things."

He held up a tiny skull in front of Nick, but addressed his remarks to Jane. "I think Fuzzy has saved every single object he's ever pulled out of the ground."

Jane fingered the pennies in her pocket, thinking hard about the boxes of bits and pieces Fuzzy had so carefully packed away.

"Squirrel, Dad?" asked Nick, turning over the small bony shape in his hand.

"Yep."

Jane leaned over the table and looked into the wooden crates whose contents

Charley and Nick were examining. Broken flowerpots, bottles, rocks, bones, pieces of ceramic tile. Fuzzy was a digger all right. Jane had heard bottle collectors refer to themselves as diggers, and although Fuzzy might not exactly display his finds like most collectors she knew, the amount of stuff he had gathered qualified him.

"What does it mean, all this stuff he saved?" asked Jane.

"You're the expert here," said Charley. "You're the one who claims to know people by what they own."

Jane held up a piece of ceramic tile that had some kind of raised writing on it. A manufacturer's date?

"I sure don't know Fuzzy. Not anymore. One minute he's his old sweet self, the next minute he's a fiery-eyed old tyrant. I have no idea what anyone's up to," said Jane, "except Lula. She's out to make sure that every one of us gains twenty pounds. Every time I turn around she's putting out more food. If I didn't know better, I'd think she was enjoying this. Her Aunt-Bea-come-and-get-it-boys role."

"People cope in all kinds of ways, don't you think? Somebody gets killed in her cornfield; she starts cooking to keep away scary thoughts," said Charley, fiddling with a latch on one of the cupboards.

"Munson said we could go over the stuff in the cabinet here. It had been locked up last night and the door hadn't been tampered with. It's as if," Charley stopped and smiled, "it's as if Fuzzy had his own little museum here, his own little curiosity shop."

"Charley, last night, you came over here, then saw me, and followed me out to the field?"

Charley nodded.

"Are you sure you didn't stop in the outhouse?"

"We pee outside, Mom," said Nick. "I've told you that's what we do on-site."

Jane nodded, considering her son's words. Every man she had ever known seemed to take advantage of the great outdoors in that manner. What was it about men and marking their territory? Jane suspected that all those manly men, the ones who chose an outdoor profession — forest ranger, construction worker, fisherman, farmer — they all just wanted unlimited opportunities to pee outside.

Tim came into the shed, wiping his hands on a *Nice 'n Clean* antibacterial wipe.

"My dear, Munson has given me permis-

165

sion to take you away from all of this for a while," he said, peering over Nick's shoulder at the tiny squirrel skull that Nick was carefully cleaning with what looked like a delicate paint brush.

"Shouldn't we be playing catch or tossing a football around or something?" Tim asked. He shook his head and assumed his deepest protective voice. "This doesn't look like a healthy hobby for my godson," said Tim.

"Let him teach you about bone preparation for a second, Timmy." Jane took Charley's hand and led him outside. They stood on the flat, concrete slab that served as a kind of porch area for the shed. The tables with some of Fuzzy's more recent dug up treasure, including the fossils that accounted for their presence at the farm in the first place, were in front of them. They looked the same as last night, except for the bare space where the bones of Otto the cat had been.

Jane pointed to the path from the cabin to the cornfield, marked midway by the old outhouse off to the side. If Charley had seen her walking out to the cornfield from here, cut over across the lawn, and followed her down the path, the outhouse would already be behind him. Whoever spoke to Jane from there could have run off toward the road while they were discovering Johnny Sullivan.

"If you were here and not in that outhouse, who talked to me?" asked Jane.

Jane knew the answer and wished she had not posed the question out loud. She was beginning to get comfortable in this skin. The Jane Wheel, girl detective, role was beginning to feel right. Then there was Charley's hand holding hers. The way he had looked at her last night, that was feeling right, too. All of her restlessness and boring middle-aged angst and wonder about the rest of her life, the whole chapter 2, the one door slamming, but the next door opening kind of crap was beginning to feel less clichéd and more real. If Charley became too protective, all flannel-shirt-and-chino, strong-man-husband-I-pee-outside guy, what would become of her sudden I-am-woman-hear-me-rummage-and-be-a-detective surge of well-being?

"The killer," said Charley, matter-of-factly. His grip did not tighten, did not pull her away from the scene, but remained steady. He kept hold of her hand while he pointed to the road. "If a car had been parked out there on the road, you know, if someone didn't bother with the driveway, no headlights would have shone into the house. The killer could have parked there, met up with Sullivan in the cornfield, shot him, and taken off for the road," said Charley.

"Ducking into the outhouse when he saw you by the shed or heard me come out of the cabin," said Jane.

They both stood there for a moment, considering how differently the night could have gone. Someone with a gun who had already killed a man had stood within a few feet of them and their son, a few feet farther away in the tent.

"If he had decided that we . . ." Jane didn't need to finish. She wasn't sure which made her feel instantly cold — the fact that she and Charley so easily could have been killed last night or the more frightening thought that Nick would have come running out of the tent and found them.

"I'll finish telling Munson about the someone in the outhouse," said Jane.

"Yeah. He'll be more interested in that than what I think I figured about the bones," said Charley.

Her husband explained that he pointed out a few of the tinier bones belonging to Otto on the ground near the body of

168

Johnny Sullivan. They appeared not to have been part of the setup on his lap, but it looked like they had fallen from his pocket when he fell. Charley pulled out a tiny fragment encased in plastic from his pocket.

"I'm giving this to Munson now. I picked it up before the police even got here. There was a little trail from the shed to the field to the body. I didn't find any on the cabin path or out in the lawn heading toward the road."

"Maybe Munson's men . . . ," Jane began.

"I knew what I was looking for, these little bones and fragments, so I admit it was easier for me. But the police didn't find anything like this where they were looking on and near that path because that isn't where the person carrying the bones walked.

"Somebody scooped up Otto from here and headed toward the cornfield," continued Charley. "And the thing is, Otto's skeleton wasn't very big, but there's no way somebody could pick up all those bones and carry them out there while carrying some kind of gun, put them all down, shoot Sullivan, then replace them on top of him," said Charley, "because you saw

Sullivan fall, then headed right out there. There wasn't time for such a deliberate maneuver."

"Were the bones placed correctly in his lap, Charley?"

"Not exactly. I didn't really get that good of a look, I . . ." Charley stopped himself, and Jane knew what he meant. Neither of them had wanted to study the sight. "But it's pretty obvious where to put the skull in relation to the ribs and the legs . . . ," Charley said, "you know, for the right effect."

"Maybe the killer didn't carry the cat," said Jane. "Maybe Johnny was over here, grabbed the bones, and was heading out to the cornfield to cut through and go home, back to his folk's house."

Charley nodded. "That's what I think, that Sullivan came to get the bones, or something out here, then headed off when he heard me coming from the tent. If he was cradling them just so," said Charley, demonstrating by hugging his arms to his chest, "then got shot and fell, the bones could spill into his lap in a recognizable pattern."

"Why would someone want those bones?" asked Jane aloud, then, listening to her internal *Oh*, counseling her to ask the deeper question, the question that the question demanded, as Detective Oh had phrased it, she amended her musing.

"Why would somebody kill somebody who wanted those bones?"

Tim drove fast and Jane knew from experience that if she mentioned it, he would drive faster. Fuzzy's farm was just about three miles due west of Kankakee, and zooming in on Route 17, Tim barely slowed, put on his turn signal, and jerked the Mustang into the parking lot of the EZ Way Inn.

"No," said Jane. She slouched down in the seat and covered her face. "I didn't get a lot of sleep; I don't have the strength."

"What do you think is going to happen if Nellie reads all about this in the *Journal* and her own daughter, an eyewitness, didn't even bother to tell her?"

"That's funny. I am an eyewitness, but I don't even know what I saw," said Jane.

After telling her story over and over to Munson, Jane began to have some respect for the method. The more she described the same thing, the more she realized what was missing from what she saw. And the more she realized what was missing, the harder she tried to remember, to envision.

That must be the method. Eventually, a witness remembered something new. That effort paid off with the filling in of some gap, some hole in the memory.

So far Jane's memory had not been spackled with some magical recall compound, but it had gotten her to think about timing. She got up and went to the window, but when did she hear what she had thought was distant thunder. Could that have been the gunshot? Is that what a shot sounded like? She didn't think so, but Munson didn't seem that concerned.

The memory that grew more and more clear was seeing Fuzzy on the porch, heading into the house. During her last interview with Munson he had not gotten called away or interrupted by a phone call and they had almost gotten to the point where her memory was, quite literally, Fuzzy.

"Did you see anyone else or hear anyone else out there in the yard?"

"Someone answered me from the outhouse when I passed," said Jane. "I thought it was Charley, but —"

Lula had interrupted then with a tray of more sandwiches and foam paper cups of vegetable soup. She was a one-woman, full-service restaurant. With a steady customer. Every time Fuzzy walked though the house or yard, he was chewing and holding something wrapped in a napkin.

"Anyone else?" asked Munson.

"After Charley and I found Sullivan, I looked back toward the house and saw Fuzzy going in the back door," Jane said. She tried to make it sound casual, neutral. She wasn't sure why she wanted Munson to be unimpressed with the information, but she did. Until Jane uncovered what Fuzzy was doing out there on the prowl, she didn't want Munson digging too deeply. And since Jane had reservations about Munson's inquiries, she hardly knew how to describe her fear of Nellie's heavy excavation equipment.

"Just tell your mother what happened out there, then we'll get on with the door-to-door," said Tim, flinging open the door to the Mustang.

"Why so concerned that we keep Nellie in the loop?" asked Jane. "She probably knows everything already. And what's the door-to-door?"

Tim consulted a small leather-bound notebook. Looking up, his face was one part Tim Lowry of T & T Sales, all business and appraisals, and one part Timmy, her bemused best friend who could not understand why she never remembered what he had told her a million times.

"Sweetie, the city-wide garage sale is going to put this town on the map, but if we want to make it work, you know, hit the record book and all, we have to get everyone to cooperate. No holdouts. So I have a list of houses where the occupants have been a little reticent, and I thought if you and I, together . . ."

"What in the hell is going on out at Fuzzy's?" asked Nellie. She had come out on the back porch carrying a case of empty bottles. Jane knew that her mother probably had given up carrying cases of full bottles, or pushing the loaded dolly that could handle three cases at a time, but still, seeing her hoist this box of empties was fairly amazing. Nellie had admitted that she was close to seventy for several years. Maybe it was time for Jane to pin her down to the truth that she still might be able to see seventy, but it was in the rearview mirror. In fact, maybe it was time for Jane to have the retirement talk again with both Don and Nellie.

"I've heard about a hundred sirens and seen all the cop cars in Kankakee racing out that way," she added, wiping her hands on an old checked apron that Jane had found, pristine condition, and given her mother as a collectible kitchen textile, one that could hang on the wall of the EZ Way kitchen and, as Jane had said at the time, *cozy up the place.*

"Fuzzy's farm isn't the only place located west of town, Mom," Jane said.

Nellie looked her daughter in the eye, and they stood locked for a moment, unblinking stare to unblinking stare. Nellie shrugged and raised her chin slightly. "Okay, you don't have to tell me."

Don opened the back door and reached out an arm toward his daughter. "Come on in, honey. Lula called this morning and told us you all had quite a night."

Nellie untied her vintage apron and used it as a bar rag, wiping off the top of the porch railing. "Yeah, I forgot. Lula called. You two want any coffee?"

Jane filled her parents in on what had happened. She didn't go into any details about the bones ending up on Johnny Sullivan's lap, about the voice from the outhouse, or about seeing Fuzzy outside after finding the body. Hell, Nellie probably knew all that anyway. Not only had Lula called, but Joe Dempsey and Mike Hoover were sitting at the bar. They had been over at K3 Realty when Henry Bennett returned from the farm. One of Munson's people had driven him back, and according to Hoover and Dempsey, Bennett was shaking like a leaf when he told them about the body in the cornfield. Next to the EZ Way Inn, the real estate office seemed like the happening place for gossip in this town. Why in this depressed, least livable city were two movers and shakers like Dempsey and Hoover hovering around the real estate office?

"Why were you two at K3 Realty?" asked Jane. "Looking for a house?"

"Maybe," Hoover said, at the same time Dempsey shook his head and said an emphatic, "No."

"Better get your stories straight," said Nellie, slamming down two cups of coffee, and pouring the shot of Jack Daniel's that Dempsey had asked for to "brighten" the coffee.

"Hardly a story," said Dempsey, glaring at Hoover while trying to smile at Nellie. The end result was a kind of frozen toothy stare. "Kankakee isn't down for the count yet. It's got a lot going for it. Great little town. Heart of the Midwest. River's pretty. Great old buildings."

"Great old *empty* buildings," said Don,

looking out the front window at the shell of the old stove factory that used to be one of many beating hearts of the town.

"Don't have to be," said Hoover. Dempsey tried to freeze him again with that look, but when he couldn't get Hoover to pay any attention to him, he gave up and joined in.

"Mike's right, Don. Maybe you all should consider bringing some life back into this all-American town."

"Errbert," Nellie said, without opening her mouth.

Jane and Tim both looked at her.

"Errrberttt," she said, more emphatically.

Don nodded.

"Nellie's right, and I'm not sure I'm for it, fellas. Haven't made up my mind."

"Do you have any idea what anyone here is talking about?" asked Jane.

"I'm enjoying it," said Tim, unwrapping a Slim Jim and taking a bite.

"Those aren't free," said Nellie, holding out her hand.

"It's not what you think, Don. We have other plans. We just can't unveil them yet," said Joe Dempsey, holding up his shot glass to signal for another.

"Okay, boys, whatever you say," said

Don, turning and nodding at Nellie. "But I'm betting with Nellie on this one."

Jane shook her head. Her mother was a mutterer, a riddler, had been all of Jane's life. She could, however, usually count on her father for clarification. If he was going to start agreeing with Nellie rather than interpreting for her, Jane could be in serious trouble.

Nellie had moved on from "errbert" to muttering about Tim and the rack of Slim Jims he was twirling. Tim coveted all the snack display racks and bins that rested on the wooden shelves between the barroom and the eight Formica-topped tables that made up the dining room. Each time he was in the EZ Way Inn, running his fingers over the lettering on the heavy plastic tray of Beer Nuts and the stepped tin rack for the cans of anchovies and packages of crackers, Nellie put herself between Tim and what he told her were "advertising collectibles."

"Stay away from those things, Lowry," said Nellie. "I need those."

"Nellie, you could get the more up-to-date displays from the delivery men. Why don't you update?" asked Tim.

"These work fine." Nellie, still holding the balled-up apron, wiped off each metal rung and clip that held the beef jerky snacks. "If it ain't broke . . ."

"Who's errbert?" asked Jane.

"Don't know, honey," said Don, shaking his head. "You know any Herbert, Nellie?"

"Who is he?" asked Nellie.

"Somebody Jane knows," said Don, moving over to the wash tanks to finish the glasses.

"No," Jane said. "What Mom was saying, 'errbert'?" Jane lowered her voice and tried to gesture toward Dempsey and Hoover.

"Airport, sweetie."

Jane stared at her father. He'd explain if she waited him out.

"These fellows think we're all too dumb to know, but they're trying to buy up land that they think will become valuable if an airport's built here."

"Fuzzy's farm?" Jane asked. This private detective business was a snap. She had this case figured out and could finish the day working with Tim on the Kankakee garage sale. Fuzzy's farm was probably designated as runway number three or something, and Johnny Sullivan was going to break the story before these two bought up all the parcels they wanted. Last night they went out and shot him. All Jane had to do was call Munson and tell him what she had discovered while sitting on a bar stool at the EZ Way Inn. These murderers would be arrested, and she could add another notch to her crime-solving belt.

Jane looked at the two whispering to each other over their coffee and whisky. Not exactly the embodiment of pure evil. Hoover had opened a package of Hostess cupcakes from the bread rack and was offering one to Dempsey, who smiled and shook his head. Not evil, but definitely shifty. Well, maybe not shifty, but clearly rascals. Maybe not rascals, but shrewd businessmen for sure. Hoover sneezed, grabbing the napkin from under his coffee cup just in time to cover his face. Dempsey put a fatherly hand on his shoulder and dug out a clean handkerchief and handed it to the younger man. Well, they were wearing suits that were more stylish than usually seen in the EZ Way Inn, so they were probably in business; but for some reason, Jane wasn't so sure how shrewd they were. And before she even began to dig for her cell phone in her bag, she had decided that while these two could not be counted out, she had no real proof of anything and a phone call to Munson might be premature.

Another phone call to Bruce Oh, however, might be timely. *Talk to Oh* was usually the first thing on Jane's to-do list whenever she found a body. Of course, she wasn't usually surrounded by her family and hometown police force when these events took place. It had been Jane's experience that meeting up with corpses was almost always private. Last night, having Charley walk up behind her wasn't only important for reassuring Nick that it wasn't just something peculiar about Mom that led her into the complicated lives of the newly dead, it was also a comfort to her that her new profession was shaping up as a kind of family business. At the very least, it was work she could bring home with her.

"Oh," said Oh.

"Oh," said Jane, too late to stop herself. He really had to learn a different way of answering the phone. "It's . . ."

"Yes," said Oh, "Mrs. Wheel."

Jane told the story to Oh that she had been repeating to Munson for most of the morning. She found that the time since leaving the farm and arriving at her parents' tavern had not helped her remember anything new. Oh's question, though, so different from Munson's, tilted her head and made her see the scene from a slightly different slant.

"When you saw what you thought was the scarecrow, did it make you laugh or shiver?" asked Oh.

"I think I was relieved to come up with an explanation," said Jane. "So I think I probably felt like laughing."

Oh did not comment.

"That's an odd question."

"Is it?"

"Okay, I give up. Why is it important? My reaction?" asked Jane, ignoring Tim who, having no luck in persuading Nellie to sell him any of the tavern display items, was now pointing at his vintage Patek Phillip and giving her the head jerk toward the door.

"Sometimes we laugh when we are sad. Occasionally we know something in our hearts, but we obey our head instead," said Oh. "But usually, our emotions, our feelings, how we act without thinking or knowing, tells us something."

"And in this case?" asked Jane.

"You don't remember being more frightened, you remember being relieved at an explanation. Which means you didn't see anyone threatening, menacing, to interfere with that relief; and I think it means you didn't hear anything resembling a gunshot because that sound playing with that picture of a fall would not have provided relief. It would have struck fear."

Oh's question had required Jane to replay the scene in her mind just as she had when Munson had talked to her earlier. More than once, Munson had asked if she remembered seeing anyone else, if a shadow had fallen across the moonlit scene, if she could recall anything unusual while watching the scarecrow, but she hadn't been able to come up with anything new.

"I remember why I felt relieved, why I smiled," said Jane.

"Yes," said Oh.

"The scarecrow turned and waved at me before it slid down," said Jane. "I mean it seemed like it waved at me. I had the feeling I was seeing something sort of dancing in a different direction, but it turned and seemed to be looking at me. That's when I thought I was seeing a scarecrow, and I smiled. In fact . . ."

"Yes?"

"If I only had a brain. I was humming that when I went to get Charley. The song's been in my head all morning."

Jane felt like she was seeing the scene

again for the first time. She had been watching out her window, watching something, someone out there, and that someone had been in profile, as if she were watching someone act with another onstage. Although the scarecrow's costar was slightly offstage, in the cornfield wings. When she realized, or thought she realized, she was watching the breeze blow around some old clothes, it was when the scarecrow turned and faced her way and seemed to wave.

"Mrs. Wheel?"

"What I saw . . . Johnny Sullivan . . . turned my way and seemed to wave. Although the cabin was pitch-black. He couldn't have seen me in the window."

"There were other objects, people in your direction?"

"Everything. The path to the cabin. The outhouse just off the path. The tent next to the cabin. The shed and digging site just off to the side of that, and behind all of that, the house itself," said Jane.

"And you said that Charley had gone to the shed because he thought someone was there?"

"When will you be coming down here? Charley and I can reenact the entire scene and . . ."

"Mrs. Wheel, why would I be coming to Kankakee?" asked Oh.

"I'm flattered that you think I can handle this case alone, Detective Oh," said Jane, wondering at what point in their relationship she would be able to call him Bruce, "but I think I'm not totally ready to . . ."

"What case?"

"Johnny Sullivan's murder."

"Police business, yes?"

"But . . ."

"In television programs and books, Mrs. Wheel, detectives always come in and do what the police cannot. The cab driver or the waitress or the lawyer . . . they all become detectives and solve the crime. This is fine, because — excuse me, Claire is talking to me, yes, that's right — Claire says, 'or the antique dealer and the picker'; they all solve crimes. But these amateurs all have something in common," said Oh.

"They're not realistic?" said Jane.

"They work for a client," said Oh. "Someone asks them to solve the case. Or they have to prove themselves innocent. Has anyone asked for your help?"

"Fuzzy asked for Charley's help in assessing the bones and fragments at the site," said Jane.

"So you have one case," said Oh. "See where that leads and be available when someone asks for your help."

Jane said she would and hung up.

What the hell was that?

First, Oh inspires her to think about what she saw, about what happened in a different way, then he takes it all away. Dismisses her involvement. What was this feeling? Dissatisfaction? Jane couldn't walk away from what she'd witnessed. She shook her head, trying to clear it, and looked at her father and mother bickering with Dempsey and Hoover. Tim was consulting his book and pushing buttons on something that looked like a cross between a cell phone, a camera, and a coaster. Jane looked at her own dinosaur of a cell phone, at least nine months old, and began to redial Oh's number.

No. Not necessary. What had Oh said? She had one case? He was right. If she and Charley could figure out why a bunch of bones unrelated to any peoples or creatures that would cause them to be protected had been reported to the government . . . if they could figure out why Fuzzy's farm was involved in any kind of dispute, they would, in all likelihood, find out why Johnny Sullivan was killed on that property. And if all this information did not lead to the big answer to the big question, she would find out anyway. She took a deep breath and dropped the phone into her bag. She had decided to get those cards printed, the ones that identified her as a picker and a private investigator — a PPI, as Tim had called her — and, by god, she was going to solve this case — client or no client.

Jane looked over at Dempsey and Hoover. They looked out of place sitting in the EZ Way Inn, but Jane wasn't sure that made them murder suspects.

"Why do you think Johnny Sullivan was out at Fuzzy's last night anyway?" Jane asked. She had picked up the glass carafe of overcooked coffee and topped off both Dempsey's and Hoover's green glass mugs. "You think he was interested in the *errbert?*"

"Could be. Nosy man," said Dempsey. "I've been here for about six weeks now on this . . . business deal . . . and every time that young man saw me, he'd start in asking inappropriate questions."

Nellie cleared her throat and nodded, stuck out her arms, and made a buzzing airplane noise. Jane laughed and had to give her mother some credit. When Nellie was on duty behind the bar, she could be pretty entertaining.

"Nellie," Dempsey said, leaning forward over his coffee mug, "if I tell you why I'm here, which by the way has nothing to do with a goddamn airport, will you stop telling everybody that I'm an airport guy? Nobody'll talk to me anymore because of that, and it's not true."

It was Hoover's turn to shoot a look at his partner.

"I thought we agreed to . . ."

"Shoot, Mike," said Dempsey. "There's a dead man in the cornfield out there. Probably one of these crazy farmers thought he was an airport guy and decided to take care of business. You want everybody thinking we're in the same club as Sullivan?"

Mike Hoover shook his head and dug the heels of his hands into his eyes. He asked Don if he had any tomato juice behind the bar.

Jane filed away that question, *the same club as Sullivan,* because it promised another direction she wanted to take in asking questions. For the moment, though, she was happy to hear whatever Joe Dempsey had decided to say.

Dempsey reached into his jacket pocket

and took out three pale green business
cards. He handed one to Jane, one to
Nellie, and one to Don, who held it at
arm's length, and invited Tim to read with
him.

HOMETOWN, USA
Joseph Dempsey

1-555-1DEJAVU

remember?@pcu.com

"Satisfied?" Dempsey asked, holding up
his shot glass for a refill.

Don, Nellie, Jane, and Tim all studied
and passed the cards back and forth. Nellie
turned hers over a few times before
throwing it back on the bar.

"What the hell does that mean?"

"What is the most universally loved fea-
ture of the major theme parks?" asked
Dempsey.

"Where do families gather and meet,
where do the ideas of wholesome fun get
planted in the brain?" asked Hoover,
taking a large gulp of tomato juice and
throwing back two aspirin.

Don, Nellie, Jane, and Tim stared at the two men.

"Disneyland," Dempsey practically shouted. "Haven't you ever heard of Disneyland?"

The four listeners nodded.

"What do you picture when you think of it?"

"Mickey Mouse?" said Don.

"Those spinning teacups?" asked Jane.

"Matterhorn," said Tim.

"Goofy," said Nellie, walking away, making it clear she was commenting on the conversation, not referring to a beloved animated character.

"No!" shouted Dempsey. "Main Street. You think of Main Street. White-washed buildings and picket fences. Sunshine and blue skies. No litter. Small-town values and Moms and Dads holding hands with kids in pigtails and baseball caps."

"Why do I have the feeling he's going to jump on the table and start singing, " 'trouble with a capital T and that rhymes with P and that stands for . . .'?" Tim whispered to Jane.

"Phooey," said Nellie. "Are you trying to tell us that there's going to be a Disneyland here? In Kankakee, Illinois? You're out of your minds."

"All fertilizer and no soybeans," said Don, tapping a finger to his head and nodding toward the two men.

"Wait," said Jane. "Who do you work for?"

Dempsey and Hoover looked at each other, and the older man gestured for Hoover to begin the story.

"We're partners," he said, looking at Dempsey, who had raised his eyebrows at the description. "We represent a group of people who have money to invest. Our idea is to develop a theme park based on a small town. I mean there'd be rides and stuff, but it'd be more like a county fair that's always going on. After all, Kankakee is located right next to a major population center with its own access to transportation —" said Hoover.

He was cut off by Dempsey who began to wave his arms as he spoke. "The layout, the look of the place, would be a cross between the movie *State Fair* and ice cream social in *The Music Man* . . ."

" 'Oh, we got trouble . . . ,' " Tim sang softly.

"The entertainment would be the real draw," said Dempsey, leading an imaginary orchestra. "We'd have concert halls, dance ballrooms, old-fashioned entertainment every weekend. There'd be family resorts based on old-time summer hotels on the river. We'd have a fishing pier and maybe a riverboat. A small town through the twentieth century, from the early 1900s through each decade — you know, arts-and-crafts bungalows through fifties ranches, with displays and entertainment."

"And a working farm with animals, a permanent county fair set up with not only the rides and midway, but display halls with quilting and needlework and stuff," said Hoover. "Everything people re-member from their small-town childhoods that was good."

"But most people remember the things that were bad," said Jane. She looked at Nellie, who was giving her an icicle stare, and added, "Don't they? I mean people my age? Dying downtowns, factories that move away, old houses being torn down for ugly, square apartment buildings. And when we were kids? Nothing to do on the weekends. Boredom, teenage drinking, drugs . . ."

"Was it that bad?" asked Don.

"No, not for me, Dad," Jane said quickly. "But you know, the majority and all . . ."

Tim shook his head. "Not for me either, Don. Don't know where she gets these ideas."

"I'll tell you," said Dempsey. "It's from the newspapers and magazines who print all those stories about the least livable towns. Didn't it make your blood boil when you read that stuff? Then Letterman comes along and gives Kankakee those gazebos. That's what started it."

When no one asked the right prompting question, Dempsey rolled on.

"That gazebo triggered it. Band concerts in the town square, sweet summer nights, and kids running around catching lightning bugs and putting them in peanut butter jars . . ."

"Okay," said Tim. "Let's cut to the chase here. You think you can use Kankakee as the location and basis for a theme park based on small-town America. A concept, I might add, that never really existed the way it's been portrayed, even during the time it was allegedly happening. I mean, you're going to gloss over the elitism, racism, and homogeneity that these nostalgic concepts really represent and just create some money-making venture in a declining town that you think is desperate enough to grasp at any straws you hold out?"

Dempsey and Hoover nodded.

"You want to cross a Disney Main Street

with Branson with a state fair?"

The men nodded again.

"Right here in River City?" said Jane.

"Have you actually bought anything? Any land?" asked Don.

"We've got feelers out for several vacant factories and warehouses. See, it would be the whole town, and we'd have a transportation system, busses, trolleys, carriages to go from one attraction to the next. Can you picture Roper Stove as a concert hall?"

Jane and Tim remained quiet when they left to make the garage-sale visits Tim had planned for them. Dempsey and Hoover had gotten Don's full attention when they planted the idea of a building across the street, the former Roper, becoming the new venue for big bands and polka nights and square-dance competitions. Not to mention wooing the national ballroom-dancing championships to use the facility. Jane had watched her father's face light up and grow brighter with each mention of an entertainment he had thought was gone forever. Nellie had hung back, quiet. Jane knew that when Nellie didn't have anything bad to say, Nellie didn't have anything to say. Did her silence mean she liked the idea?

"Tim?"

"It's not as if I don't come up with ideas to help Kankakee, too . . . ," he said. "But the city-wide, garage-sale business seems pretty . . . I don't know. Tame? Unambitious?"

"Hey! Wake up. Is this mind control? The people, Tim? What about the residents of Kankakee. Does a pair of jeans and a T-shirt and a John Deere cap suddenly become your costume? Are you a blue-collar man? Do people come and stare at you if you live in a ranch house and refer to you as midcentury modern man? This idea of theirs suggests that the town be vacated, vacuumed, and sanitized then reborn as a stage set. Everybody who lives here now, who owns businesses, has kids in school here, works, goes to church here . . . they all would become actors?"

"We do it anyway, don't we?" said Tim. "Some of us do — you know the whole gay-man-in-a-flower-shop business. I've told you that everybody who comes into the shop these days wants a queer makeover . . ."

Jane looked at Tim and saw the glazed look on his face. She had her work cut out for her. Keep her parents from investing their life savings with two animated nutcases dressed as businessmen, keep

Tim from abandoning the garage sale of his dreams, and donning an ascot for his role as the town's Noel Coward eccentric, and what was the other thing?

Oh yeah, "dem bones, dem bones." Solve Johnny Sullivan's murder.

All this before Kankakee becomes the next colonial frigging Williamsburg.

Chapter 8

"I make your life interesting, yes?" asked Tim, opening her car door with a flourish. It was uncharacteristic politeness, and Jane was immediately suspicious.

"Yes," Jane answered, "you make my life interesting, all right. You and everyone else I meet lately. What are we doing here?"

They stood in front of a brick bungalow in the middle of a block of bungalows. In the front yard, a family of stone geese were dressed in yellow pinafores and bonnets. There was also a bird feeder and a birdbath, three colorful, twirling wind catchers dangling from an oak tree, and a set of wind chimes hanging on the porch.

"This is the home of Mrs. Olivia Schaefer, retired schoolteacher. She said that she and her neighbors would not be participating unless some of her questions could be answered," said Tim. "And she is either the busiest woman in the world and never home, or she is not picking up my phone calls."

"So this is a pop in? A surprise visit?"

asked Jane. "I can't do this."

"Your shyness was an attractive quality for about five minutes when you were fifteen. Time to move on."

Tim ran up the steps and rang the bell, smiling back at Jane, then, turning to the door, prepared his sunniest face for Mrs. Schaefer.

Jane hadn't time to prepare herself for what Mrs. Schaefer would look like, but she had not expected the stylish young woman who stood at the door.

Suzanne Blum introduced herself as Mrs. Schaefer's niece. She was packing her aunt's things up for a move to an assisted-living apartment complex. Although she would be delighted to participate in the garage sale, neither she nor her aunt could be there personally for the weekends of the sale.

"Aunt Liv told me about it. She was in charge of the holdouts on the block and proud of it. She told me that if she agreed, they would all agree; but I can't be here for those sale dates and . . ."

"We have volunteers from the high school. A whole service club that has made the sale their project. Good kids who will either assist or run the tables for people who can't or don't want to do it. I can send someone by to meet you and your aunt," said Tim.

They all shook hands and Suzanne Blum assured them that she'd leave a note for the neighbors and that this block would be on board.

Back in the car, Tim was writing himself a long note, jotting down the addresses on the block.

"Did you see those lamps with the green shades? Hope those make it into the garage," said Jane. "That was easy, Timmy, what's next?"

"Got to get back to the store and take care of something," said Tim.

Jane smiled and said it with him. "Got to go sign up that crew of high school volunteers."

Before Tim dropped her back at Fuzzy's, Jane had run into the Jewel to pick up a few items for their cabin, although she was sure Lula had prepared some kind of a feast. In addition to food she picked up a few newspapers and as many kinds of batteries as they had lights to use them. If Fuzzy and Lula cut the generator tonight, she wanted light. Munson had suggested they stay elsewhere but said he wouldn't insist. Jane and Charley had already discussed the fact that they would all stay in the cabin and that there was a dead bolt on their door. The police would still be on-site as well.

Jane had been somewhat flattered when Munson said he thought there would be no harm in them staying on the land. For a moment she had fantasized that he wanted her there in case something else happened, as a kind of adjunct to his own people. She had felt that way until she heard him say to one of his uniformed people, "At least if she's here, we won't be finding any bodies anywhere else."

It took the shine off the compliment.

As Jane had predicted, Lula had, Charley told her, come over and said she expected them to have dinner at the house. As much as Jane did not want to have a farmhouse feast with Lula's wide world of Jell-O assortment laid before her tonight, she did welcome the opportunity to talk to Lula and Fuzzy under what might pass for more normal circumstances. She hadn't been able to ask any questions without interruptions or an audience since they had arrived. First, there was the picnic/pig roast with half of Kankakee there; and then, well today, they had had the crime scene unfold before them. Jane needed to talk to Fuzzy about what he had found in his topsoil and when and how this all connected up. The more Jane had thought about Otto's bones, the more she wondered who would have thought they had to call in the state to inspect. She was sure that animal bones . . . cats and dogs and squirrels and raccoons and so forth, were turned up all the time. Who would have called the state about a pet cat's skeleton?

"Damn good question, Janie, damn good," said Fuzzy, helping himself to more of the pot roast Lula had set before them.

Charley sat back in his chair, his hands in his lap. Jane watched him watch Fuzzy cut his meat and vegetables, everything all at once rather than one bite at a time, and Charley waited until Fuzzy had eaten a bite before adding another damn good question.

"Have you found things before, Fuzzy? Bones and such things?"

Fuzzy chewed more slowly and appeared thoughtful as he shook his head. The head shaking, however, didn't exactly match his verbal answer.

"I've found stuff before. Lots of neat little . . . bottles and such." Fuzzy looked at Lula. "What else? What's some other stuff I found?"

"Rocks. He's found some pretty rocks out there," said Lula. She was on her way to the stove to refill the gravy pitcher, and she paused at the windowsill where an aloe plant rose out of a pale green flowerpot.

"See?" Lula pointed to the plant.

"McCoy?" asked Jane, smiling.

Lula picked something out of the plant and held it up. "You call this rock, what? McCoy?"

"No," said Jane. "The flowerpot is McCoy Pottery."

"Oh, this old stuff. I got a basement full of that. I told Tim Lowry he could have it to sell at that big wingding he's having in town."

Jane shivered a little. She wasn't sure if she felt excitement over what might be in Lula's basement or horror at the thought of Tim having such total and complete access to the attics and cellars of their hometown. She wanted to believe her friend was thinking of Kankakee's best interest, but, she supposed, Tim might think Kankakee's best interest was not incompatible with the best interest of Lowry's company, T & T Sales.

"I'll take a look at your stuff for you, Lula," said Jane. "I'm working with Tim on this project."

"Can I see that?" asked Charley, holding his hand out for the rock that Lula had taken out of the plant and rubbed clean on her apron.

Charley held the stone up. Minute, elongated blades of crystal fanned out from its pale, yellowish center.

"Pretty," said Jane. "What's it called?"

"Nick?" called Charley. After eating his dinner, Nick had asked if he could watch television before they headed out to the cabin. Lack of even basic cable though had driven him to the stack of record albums that had belonged to Bill Neilson and the old stereo system that was still well used in the living room. Jane could hear a familiar voice coming out of the speakers, but not well enough to place it. She heard Nick laughing and called in to him again.

"Nick, did you hear Dad?" Jane said. When he didn't come, and they could all hear him laughing, Jane stood up. "Apparently not. I'll go get him."

If Nick hadn't been wearing saggy jeans, new Jordan shoes, and a baseball playoff T-shirt dated from last summer, Jane might have believed she was seeing her son transported to a different time.

Sitting on the floor, holding the album cover of *The Button-Down Mind of Bob*

Newhart, he was listening intently to Newhart ask, "Is your mother home?"

"You ever heard of this guy? Newhart?" asked Nick.

Jane nodded and smiled. "Finish the record later, okay? Dad wants you."

The four adults, Charley, Jane, Fuzzy, and Lula, all seated at the table, watched Nick examine the stone that Lula had fished out of her plant.

"Where did this come from?" he asked, balancing the rock in his hand, turning it over and holding it up to the light over the kitchen table.

"From my aloe plant," said Lula.

"From the rose garden," said Fuzzy.

Nick shook his head, smiling at his hosts. *He looks so adult,* Jane thought. *Indulgent and kind, but firm in his disagreement with their answers.*

"No, I mean, where did it come from originally?"

"Well, I suppose when I turned up the dirt in the vegetable patch, I could have shifted it over near the roses," said Fuzzy.

"If I'm right," said Nick, looking at his dad for confirmation and noting that Charley gave him the slightest of nods, "this mineral isn't found in Illinois. I think it's called Austinite, right, Dad? Not very common. Maybe Mexico?"

"Yes," said Charley. "Crystals are orthorhombic, color's right for Austinite, although I've seen samples that are white or a bright green, too."

"Definitely not from Illinois," said Nick. "Can I go finish the record?"

Jane held out her hand for the mineral specimen. She turned it over in her hand, held it up, just the way she'd seen Nick do it.

"How did that rock get here from Mexico?" asked Fuzzy, his voice thick with suspicion.

Lula shook her head and stood, picking up plates to bring to the sink.

The crunch of tires on gravel made them all look toward the window in the living room. A truck drove slowly up the driveway that adjoined the house. Jane thought it might be another policeman, one of Munson's people coming to work for another. Shift change, that was all.

But after two car doors slammed, there was a soft knock at the back door. Jane knew there had been no barricade across the driveway when she had returned, but there had been a uniformed policeman standing guard. Who would he have let approach the house tonight?

Lula opened the door immediately, as if they had company after dinner every night and no one should hesitate just because someone had been murdered on the property the night before. Fuzzy stood up and said he'd get more coffee started to go with the pie that he had spied cooling on the counter.

Lula stepped away from the open door and allowed Mr. and Mrs. Sullivan to walk into the kitchen. No one said hello. No one embraced. They took seats at the table and accepted the cups and dessert plates that were set before them as calmly as if this were any other night when they might drop in for coffee and a piece of pie.

"We didn't know where else to go," said Mr. Sullivan, looking from Charley to Jane to Fuzzy and Lula. His wife nodded. And in an oddly formal ritual, they each accepted a piece of apple crumb, cut through the flaky crust into Lula's secret ingredient–laden spiced apples, and sat silently chewing.

Chapter 9

"We don't have any family," said Jack Sullivan.

"Just each other and Johnny," said his wife.

"My people were from Pennsylvania, and they're all gone now. And Elizabeth has a brother somewhere out West, but we stopped getting a Christmas card from him, oh about two years ago, right, Elizabeth?"

Elizabeth Sullivan nodded.

Jane thought about all the movies and books and television shows that romanticized the small-town farming life, big families with all the adults working together, raising a barn or building a fence, then everybody eating at noisy picnics under big old trees, the children playing on the tire swing and running in and out of the barn.

In the empty, grieving eyes of Elizabeth Sullivan, Jane saw rural life the way it was today — lonely and isolated. These people had a small farm that they could barely hold on to and make a living. Their children and the children of their neighbors ran as fast and as far as they could from the physical labor, the uncertainty of production, and the dependence on weather and the whims of the marketplace. The Sullivans had been hoping to work a few more years and maybe their son, Johnny, would have taken over the land. What would become of them now? Would they have enough money saved to buy a little place in Florida or . . . wait. Hadn't Lula said . . . ?

"Don't you have another son, Mrs. Sullivan? Lula mentioned earlier that . . ."

"Dead," said Jack. "Helicopter accident in basic training. Over twenty years ago. Phillip was nineteen when it happened."

Lula stopped wiping the dishes. She was as still as Jane had ever seen her.

"You never said . . . ," Lula started. "Elizabeth, why didn't you tell anybody?"

The Sullivans looked at each other.

"At first, it was just too hard to talk about. There wasn't a . . ." Elizabeth Sullivan stopped and took a long breath. "It was an accident over water. There wasn't a body. Jack was still planting; it was spring. Johnny was just out of high school and going off to start college early, some summer opportunity he had. He never really came home after he left that summer. Until . . . until now. Until he started working on that newspaper and coming home on weekends. It was like . . ." She stopped and inhaled again, but couldn't go on.

Jack Sullivan said quietly, "It was like getting another chance."

Everyone drank coffee. Lula stared at Elizabeth Sullivan as if she had spoken gibberish. She appeared to find the news about Phillip Sullivan's death even more upsetting than Johnny's murder. The only sound came from the distant voice of Bob Newhart on the record player. Nick hadn't come back into the kitchen. Jane was sure he didn't even know the Sullivans had come over.

"We brought these," said Elizabeth Sullivan, handing Jane a large, brown paper shopping bag filled with newspapers. "Maybe they'll help you."

Jane shook her head without asking the obvious question.

"We heard Franklin Munson tell one of his people you were a detective. So we thought maybe you'd find out what happened to Johnny."

"The police . . . ," Jane started.

"We want you," Elizabeth said. "Johnny was working on big stories and I told the policeman that, but he didn't even ask to see the newspapers."

"They think it was something about real estate. They kept asking about that jacket he was wearing, that Roger Groveland's jacket."

"Do you know why he was wearing it?" asked Jane.

They shook their heads.

"Doesn't matter," said Elizabeth. "He was a reporter, and he was probably going to write something bad about someone. We want you to find out. Jack and I want to know."

"We'll pay you," said Jack.

"Mr. and Mrs. Sullivan, it's not about money. I'm just not sure I can find anything that the police . . ."

Nick laughed out loud in the living room, drowning out Newhart's hesitant stutter.

"You've got a boy," said Elizabeth Sullivan. "You'll know how to find out."

The Sullivans stood up to leave. Jane hadn't known how to refuse them or even why she wanted to say no. Hadn't she, just a few hours ago, been upset with Bruce Oh for suggesting that she was supposed to wait for a client before plunging into an investigation? Why now, when she had a client, did she feel so uncomfortable?

Jane's previous cases — and even when talking to herself in the smallest of silent whispers, she italicized *cases* and blushed from the inside out — because who was she, after all, to call herself a detective and to reflect on former *cases* — had fallen into her path.

But accepting this one, Johnny Sullivan's murder, was accepting herself in this role. Bruce Oh had already put her name on the letterhead, and Tim referred to himself as Helen Corning, the lesser known pal of Nancy Drew; but Jane hadn't stepped outside of her own circle of family and friends to take on an investigation, to solve a crime, to *crack a case,* for god's sake, and she winced at her own inner dime-novel lingo.

"What do you think, Charley?" Jane asked, as they walked out to the cabin, after the kitchen was clean and Nick had put all the records away, arranged in the order he planned on listening to them.

"We've got a few more days, and I want to write up something on the site here that will free up Fuzzy's land. I'm not at all clear on what any of these random minerals and bones mean, but I know the site itself isn't significant to the government.

But I have to fill out the paperwork and snoop around a little. So why not see if you can help the Sullivans?" Charley asked, smoothing back his wife's short, brown hair. "Not like you to shy away from a challenge."

Jane nodded and agreed that she should call Oh in the morning. On the one hand, she thought she might be hesitant because she would have to take herself seriously as a detective, and it all seemed too silly, too unrealistic. On the other hand, her previous career had been in advertising. She had produced television commercials, for heaven's sake, so it wasn't exactly like she was leaving brain surgery to become a fashion model.

Okay, so when she peeled away all those onion skin layers of resistance, what was she left with? The fact that Jane Wheel, girl detective, was of course going to take the case, had already in her head taken on the case, and that the only reason she thought she might refuse was that her most likely and only suspect was her parents' old friend, Fuzzy Neilson, whom she had watched tiptoe back into his house last night, not ten minutes after Johnny Sullivan had been shot dead in the cornfield. She could hear Oh asking her, shouldn't you be willing to prove him innocent rather than fear that you'll find him guilty?

As soon as she was convinced that Nick was sleeping, Jane told Charley about the pennies she had seen Fuzzy burying.

"It's just one more strange thing," said Jane. "His behavior's so erratic, and I don't know what to make of him being outside last night. I told Munson, so he's probably asked him about it, but . . ." Jane trailed off and absentmindedly reached into her jeans to take out the pennies, also pulling out the Austinite sample she had pocketed when the Sullivans had surprised them in the kitchen.

She noticed a little speck of green on the corner of the rock and was about to point it out to Charley — she wanted to show him she paid attention to all of his geology facts, and he had mentioned green as a color of this mineral — but Charley shushed her and cocked his head, listening.

She thought she might have heard the soft closing of a door, too, and although she told herself it would be one of the police officers on duty, she joined Charley at the window that looked back toward the house. They stood side by side in the darkness of the cabin and watched Fuzzy

Neilson walk slowly and stealthily out of his house. He headed first toward the shed where his collections were housed, then turned abruptly toward the cabin. He seemed to be heading straight at them, then turned again down the path to the outhouse and cornfield. He was carrying a sack, and Jane thought it was probably the same one she had seen him pulling the pennies from. Jane and Charley had moved quietly to a window at the back of the cabin, following Fuzzy's route. It was the same window where Jane had stood watching last night's events unfold. A few feet away from the outhouse, Fuzzy stopped and put the bag down. He seemed to be fiddling with something in his pocket and Jane had an urge to push Charley down and hit the floor with him. Was Fuzzy taking out a gun?

"Oh," said Jane, realizing what she was watching and turning away.

Charley continued to watch. He bumped Jane's arm, and she turned back to the window. Fuzzy picked up the bag and retraced his steps back into the house. Jane noted that the policeman stationed out at the edge of the cornfield had not even seemed to notice Fuzzy. Jane wasn't sure any other officers were within sight, but none came running. Well, why would they? Fuzzy was entitled, she supposed, to walk outside in the dark and relieve himself in his backyard, which, as Jane and Charley could see, was the extent of this midnight's rambling.

Monday morning, Munson confirmed Fuzzy's nocturnal habits.

"You mentioned seeing Fuzzy on the porch, and when I asked him he shook his head and didn't seem to remember being outside at all. Lula came in with a tray of food and started laughing. She told me Fuzzy's been peeing outside every night since they had young babies in the house. One of the kids was a real light sleeper, and Fuzzy got tired of Lula yelling at him when he'd forget and flush, so he started going outside. She said he never even wakes up anymore. Said now that he's an old man, he's out two or three times a night at least and never even remembers anything about it in the morning."

"So Charley could have heard Fuzzy by the shed and gone over there and by the time he got there, Fuzzy was already in the outhouse, then he just went back in as usual, not noticing anything or anyone else out and about," said Jane.

"Possible," said Munson. "Your partner said that if that was the case, the shooter could have been out in the cornfield and gone straight to the road through the corn like we thought yesterday. Would mean Johnny had taken the bones out there himself like your husband thought, and after he went down, the bones either fell out of his arms onto his lap or the killer . . . somebody with the killer . . . set them up in his lap where he fell. Maybe they were trying to see what the bones were or maybe just trying to send a message or something," said Munson.

"Who?"

"Oh," said Munson, feeling for his cell phone, which gave out a low buzz.

Jane tried to look as if she wasn't listening as Munson discussed guns and bullets and as soon as he hung up, she asked, "What partner?"

"Oh," said Munson. "I told you."

Jane always got that strange down-the-rabbit-hole sensation when she played the name game that always accompanied an unexpected invocation of Det. Bruce Oh's name.

"He called yesterday afternoon and said you two were on the case and could we share information, you know," said Munson.

"I've got to admit, I didn't like it much before, but the guy has sort of grown on me."

Jane nodded. She knew how that was. Oh did have that effect. However, although he might grow on someone, how did he also manage to keep her so off-balance? He called Munson yesterday afternoon before or after he had told her that they were not on the case because they had no clients? Was this how partners always worked?

As soon as Munson went to the shed to talk to Charley about the bones, Jane pulled out her own cell.

"If I have to wait for a client, don't you also have to wait for a client? How exactly does this work? I mean, I feel it's sort of embarrassing to find out from Munson that we . . . and besides now we have clients because last night the Sullivans came over after dinner and asked me, you couldn't know if, just please call me back . . . it's Jane Wheel; oh, you know who it is, you know everything before it happens any . . ." The answering machine clicked off and Jane, as usual, wished she could have made her message a bit cleaner.

Jane spent the rest of the morning going through the newspapers that the Sullivans had delivered to her last night. Johnny was writing a continuing series, it seemed, on airport expansion, concentrating on the plan that would bring an airport to Kankakee. He had written extensively on what an airport might mean economically for the individual citizens of Kankakee. He had explored the various sites and layouts for the proposed field. He had conducted a series of interviews, a kind of door-to-door reporting of the pulse of the townspeople on whether they thought the airport a godsend or a curse. One article quoted three different real estate companies — they were all in favor — and the piece included quotes from both Roger Groveland and Henry Bennett of Kankakee "K3" Realty. A man-on-the-street kind of sidebar, Jane was interested to note, included a quote from Joseph Dempsey, identified as a local entrepreneur.

"A town like Kankakee, rife with potential, is the kind of place people like to call home. An airport will only increase the likelihood that others will be able to find the joy and peace that this haven in the heartland brings."

Jane, who could fall in love with her husband based on Charley's confident and casual use of a word like *eschew*, could also smell a contrived and phony use of language. Her education in advertising had not been for naught. *Rife,* she knew, would not be the kind of word that tripped off Joe Dempsey's tongue when he was randomly stopped on the street. And how oddly random that Dempsey, a newcomer to Kankakee, would be Sullivan's main man on the street. In fact, Jane was feeling that there were a lot of odd coincidences in these articles. Sullivan was wearing Groveland's blazer, which was identified by Henry Bennett, who, although he had been interviewed by Sullivan in what the article described as a roundtable conversation, didn't mention that he recognized the murder victim, just the blazer.

Munson had mentioned that he had someone reading Sullivan's articles — his entire body of work e-mailed to them from the newspaper — which was why the police had not wanted to accept Elizabeth Sullivan's paper bag full of her son's clippings. Jane decided since they were all working on the same thing, she really had no reason to run all this by Munson yet. It could wait until she had a chance to run it by Oh, unless she had scared him off altogether with her phone message.

Jane had started a notebook on the case. She had always kept books on commercial shoots and had transferred that kind of organization to shopping garage sales and flea markets. She made lists of items she was seeking for others and a current list of items she was looking for herself. She had pages of "misses," the pieces she hoped would give her a second chance. There was that desk with the built-in typewriter that she had walked away from, left in the basement of a Skokie bungalow even after the older ladies running the sale had offered it to her for fifty dollars, including the oak swivel desk chair that matched it. What had she been thinking? It now had a place on her permanent list — as if she would ever find such an item again. There was the Weller vase she had walked by twice in a church basement, and when it finally registered what it was, she had reached for it and a tall man with a longer arm had lifted it past her face with a mean chuckle. She hoped these items, these "misses," would teach her about thinking quickly, being decisive, worrying about transporting it all home later, after writing the check and seeing the sold sticker with her name on it firmly planted.

In her case notebook, what was the equivalent of a "miss"? It was the question she had either been unable to ask or the questions that hadn't found the right form.

They were the curios of the case. The pieces to the puzzle that were just out of reach or camouflaged by all the other pieces. The pennies, the Austinite specimen, were misses — answers to questions not yet asked. She also made a list of the people who made her curious, even if she wasn't sure exactly what questions she would ask them.

Dempsey and Hoover were still on her list. Even if they had had nothing to do with Johnny Sullivan, if Dempsey's name hadn't popped up in Sullivan's interview, they would remain on her list. There was something fishy about turning Kankakee into a theme park, and she needed to get to the bottom of that before her dad became an investor in the Roper Stove Four-Burner Fun Ride or the Kankakee River Rapids Log Roll or something. Henry Bennett still had some questions to answer, and pretty soon she would come up with them. And her old friend Roger Groveland. How did his jacket get mixed up in all of this?

Jane tossed her notebook onto the bed and walked outside. Nick and Charley were still over at the site, and Jane could see boxes stacked. Charley was lifting items one by one out of the box on top.

His actions were so deliberate, so careful, they made Jane smile. These rocks and bones were as interesting and beautiful to Charley as a set of Depression-Era juice glasses, Heisey or Hazel Atlas. Go figure. Maybe she and Charley were more alike than she had recently thought. They were both collectors, preservers, protectors — problem solvers.

There was a barn on the property that Jane hadn't paid much attention to because of its placement in relation to the house and cabin. It was off to the other side of the house, not in the path to the shed or the digging site, not in the line of vision from the cabin out to the cornfield. The police had gone in and searched it, of course, but hadn't found anything disturbed. They had reported that the layer of dust on the rototiller and small tractor had been undisturbed. The cobwebs that were laced over the old tools piled in the corner were intact. The large door stood slightly open, so Jane decided to take a look for herself.

The tools the police had talked about were vintage gardening spades and forks that Tim might want to take a look at if Fuzzy had abandoned them. The stalls in the barn were empty except for some wooden crates stacked against one wall. There was some straw matted on the floor and it occurred to Jane that it wouldn't be obvious if someone had walked into one of the stalls. No footprints in the dust would register if someone walked along the wall into the stall and simply stepped on the thatches of straw covering the dirt floor. Jane followed that path to get a closer look at the boxes. The bottom was labeled WWII, Property of Ronald Neilson. Jane knew Fuzzy had been in the service because she had seen pictures in the house. He and Lula's wedding picture featured a young and upright Fuzzy with the same bristly crew cut, as dark then as it was white now, dressed in his army uniform.

Jane was so used to opening boxes in strangers' basements, she almost pulled up a hay bale and went to work. She stopped herself, realizing that she would have to ask Fuzzy and Lula's permission to take a look at what Fuzzy had brought home from the war. Except, of course, for what hadn't been placed inside a box. Behind the stack of crates, between the boxes and the wall, was an old leather bag as large as a postal sack. Jane figured it might be okay to sneak a peak at that. She pulled it out from where it was placed in the crevice and thought it was probably more old tools, felt like it might hold a hoe or a weeder of some kind.

Odd. Despite the fact that everything around her was labeled for war and even though a man had been shot not fifty feet away from the barn, the gun that tumbled out of the bag when she tugged at it caught Jane completely and terribly by surprise.

Chapter 10

Jane was sure that every neighboring farm for miles had heard Munson yelling at his officers. There had been five who had searched the barn and every one of them swore that the bag with the gun had not been there when they had walked through the day before.

Looking at their miserable faces, Jane believed every one of them. She waited until Munson had finished with them, then went over and took his arm, leading him back into the barn.

"I saw the bag behind there," said Jane, "pulled it out, and only after the gun fell into the dirt did I notice the straw around the bottom box. Look."

It was bunched up into little ridges. The box had been pulled out, moving the straw, then pushed back after the bag with the gun had been put behind it against the wall.

"This was just done. There are mice running all over this barn and at least two cats who prowl around in here. Those perfect little hills of straw were recently made or else they wouldn't be so perfect. You can see the little tracks in the dirt from the box being pulled. Your people didn't miss it yesterday. It hadn't been done yet," said Jane.

Munson had already wrapped the gun and sent it into town.

"It was a twenty-two. Gun that shot Sullivan was likely a twenty-two."

Neither Jane nor Munson had heard Fuzzy come in.

"You need a gun?" asked Fuzzy.

Jane instinctively shook her head at Fuzzy, trying to warn him not to talk. But he was looking at Munson.

"You need to shoot something?"

Munson shook his head slowly.

"No, Fuzzy, we were just talking about your twenty-two we found in here, wondered how it got stuck behind those boxes."

"No, it ain't in those boxes," said Fuzzy. "That was just an extra I stuck there. Hadn't put it in its place yet. I keep all my guns right here." Fuzzy pointed to the blank wall behind him.

Jane and Munson both remained silent and Fuzzy laughed.

"Don't see them, do you? It's a trick.

Learned it on a farm in England when I was over there. We stayed in a bunch of barns when we was there, teaching some of them Englishmen to take care of themselves if they were invaded. Me and an Englishman named Lester came up with a way to hide things in his barn."

Fuzzy felt along the wall behind him, then smiled. There was a popping sound as a latch unhooked and Fuzzy lifted a window-size piece of wood away from a recessed cabinet in the wall.

"See there? This was the window between the stalls, and I just hung barn wood up over it and made me a hidden cabinet. The farmers over there in England had these hiding places for the rifles they had just in case. And they had these silencer things put on them, see, so they could pick them Germans off quiet if there was an invasion."

Jane wasn't sure if the whole story Fuzzy was telling was accurate, but he was right about the hidden compartment behind the wooden panel. No one would ever notice it if they weren't looking over the wall inch by inch. The hinges at the top were stained to match the wood, but more important, the same layer of dirt and dust covered them so the hardware was indistinguishable from the wood. And in the cabinet were five guns, all outfitted with some kind of attachment the size of a juice can.

"I made these silencers just like the Brits did. Why not? I told Lula if I kept the guns quiet, she couldn't get mad at me for shooting the squirrels and the possums and such, not if I wasn't making any noise, right?"

Fuzzy took down one of the guns and walked toward Munson and Jane, pointing the gun directly at them. Jane could feel Munson stiffen beside her and put his hand on the holster inside of his coat.

"Fuzzy, set the gun down on the floor and let me take a look at it, okay?" Jane asked.

"Why?" Fuzzy asked, waving the gun in the air. "I can show it to you up close."

The next few seconds passed in slow motion.

Fuzzy was about three feet away from them when they heard someone come in the barn door and call out Fuzzy's name. The person was standing in shadow and was blocked from view by one of the doors to an adjoining stall. A man's voice, firm but nonthreatening. "Mr. Neilson? Mr. Neilson?"

As Fuzzy turned toward the voice,

Munson grabbed the rifle and pulled it sharply backward, jerking Fuzzy off his feet. He landed in a pile of straw, but it was still a hard knock to his old bones. When Bruce Oh — master of the surprise appearance and nonthreatening voice — came over to them, he knelt down and very gently probed Fuzzy's shoulder and patted him back into a lying-down position as Fuzzy struggled to his feet.

"Mr. Neilson, sit here a minute and make sure you are okay, that no bones are broken," said Oh.

"Sorry, Fuzzy," said Munson, "but you were making me awfully nervous with that gun."

"Good thing," said Fuzzy, "because the next time I get my hands on it, I'm going to shoot your nose off."

Munson made some phone calls while Jane and Bruce Oh greeted each other.

What Jane wanted from the greeting:

"Mrs. Wheel, please forgive me for calling Detective Munson about the case without first talking to you and explaining my strategy. I was wrong — of course, we should be working on this — and as usual, you were right in anticipating our involvement. Thank you so much for seeing the whole picture and leading

me into the light on this matter."

What Jane got was, "Mrs. Wheel."

"Detective Oh."

Jane was not that good at glaring, but she was making a splendid effort when Charley came in, followed closely by Nick.

"There's not a body in here, is there?" asked Nick, hanging back by the door.

"Of course not," said Jane. "Fuzzy was showing us some of his guns and he took a fall, but everything is fine."

Jane shrugged at Charley's raised eyebrows. It was the best she could come up with since she wasn't quite sure just what had happened. She knew with all of her heart and soul and logic and instinct that Fuzzy Neilson would not hurt another human being; and yet when he was walking toward them with that gun, every fear sensor in her body had gone off, wailing at her to fight or flee. Was it the presence of the gun that made the human being holding it disappear?

Lula arrived at the door, dropping her tray of whatever pastries she had whipped up this morning when she saw Fuzzy sitting on the ground. She rushed over, knelt beside him, and spoke into his ear in a low, cooing voice. It was a side of Lula Jane had never seen. She had regarded Lula as cut

230

from the Nellie cloth — all tough, no love — in the caretaking department, but clearly Lula had softer edges. Munson spoke to her, explaining what had happened, and Lula stood, fire in her eyes.

"Do you mean to tell me that you had to knock down a harmless old man because he was walking toward you? Is that what I heard you say? He was walking toward you? You haven't changed a bit since you were in grade school with my boy. You always did hit somebody in the nose first and ask questions later," Lula said, finally stopping for a breath. "I am not going to put up with this, Franklin Munson. As soon as I get Fuzzy into the house, I am telling someone about this." Lula, with Bruce Oh's assistance, helped Fuzzy, who had gone as quiet as a frightened child, to his feet.

"I am calling your mother," said Lula.

Munson rubbed his eyes. He watched Lula walk Fuzzy toward the house and shook his head. "I really should have left town," he said. Looking at Oh and Jane, he shrugged. "When I graduated from college, I was offered jobs in two different states, for Christ's sake, but I said no. I like the people in Kankakee, I said."

Munson gave instructions to the two of

his officers to wrap up the guns still in the barn and take them into town.

"We think that Johnny Sullivan was shot with a twenty-two. We know that Mrs. Wheel might have heard some kind of noise but not necessarily a gunshot, and now we find — literally — a stable of weapons, with what appear to be working suppressors — right under our noses."

"Supressors?" Jane asked Oh.

"No such thing as a silencer exists really. The noise from the gun can be suppressed, but not totally silenced," said Oh.

Munson told one of his officers to go ask Lula for something, and Jane thought she heard something about shoes.

"What are you doing? What's happening to Fuzzy?" asked Jane.

"We can't ignore the fact that all these weapons are on the property. A man was shot here; and you yourself reported that, besides you and your husband, the only person you saw in the vicinity was Fuzzy," said Munson. "We're just going to check the clothes he was wearing, his shoes."

"His shoes? He's a farmer," said Jane. "And a gardener. His shoes are going to have all the dirt on them from everywhere on the property, including the cornfield. What can you possibly prove by analyzing the dirt on his shoes and his clothes . . ." Jane stopped.

Between the house and the cabin was a relic from bygone days that had made Jane smile every time she passed it. A clothesline. Strung from two metal poles sunk in concrete were three thick, taut lines. A floppy cloth bag hung from one of the lines, filled with wooden clothespins. On one of Jane's trips into the house, she had given in to her craving for the feel of wooden clothespins and plunged her hand into the worn, pink-and-blue cotton bag. Pulling out a handful, Jane reviewed the history of the clothespin from the examples in her hand. There were the narrow wooden ones that someone had carved by hand, the more uniform rounded plump ones, then back to narrower, straight-edged pins with squared-off heads and wire hinged bodies. But it wasn't just the clothesline and the clothespins that made Jane smile, it was the clothes hanging from the clothesline. The constant parade of blue jeans, overalls, white T-shirts, socks, and men's pajamas that rotated positions on the lines announced to the world that Lula was a woman who did laundry and was proud of it. In fact she did laundry every day. Munson would get the clothes he asked for — clean as tomorrow, smelling of a fresh breeze and slightly stiff with sunshine.

In the flurry of "not exactly a new crime, but a new glitch in the crime scene protocol" that ensued — Munson barking orders, Lula escorting Fuzzy to the house, slapping away the extended hands and offers of help from all except Nick, who walked on Fuzzy's other side, asking him about the leaf fossils he had found in a box in the shed — Jane was left facing Charley and Oh. They formed a quiet oasis outside the barn, where once again, six officers were stationed by the door, waiting for the crime scene van to arrive. Again.

"How did you know about the Sullivans?" asked Jane.

Oh shook his head.

"They asked me to find out about their son, they . . ." Jane hesitated. Why was it difficult to actually speak the words? "They hired me."

"Clients," said Oh.

"How did you know?"

"You just told me, Mrs. Wheel. I am here because my wife insisted that she was needed to help Mr. Lowry with his record-breaking garage sale. When I reminded her that she had told me she'd outgrown garage sales, she informed me that she was revising her policy. She feels the sale Mr. Lowry is planning might have . . . what was her word? Potential."

"You phoned Munson," said Jane. "He told me."

"Yes, I did," said Oh. "After Claire decided we needed to come down, I called your cell phone, which you did not answer. I then called the EZ Way Inn and left a message with your mother. I think."

"You think you left a message, or you think you were talking to Nellie?" Charley asked. Even though he was a part of the conversation, he was using a stick to dig into the mulch around a lilac bush, one of the row that lined the path to the barn. Jane filed away the scene. The next time Charley gave her the evil eye for turning over a vase and checking the mark when they were a guest in someone's home, she would remind him that he had never met a patch of dirt he didn't like to scratch around in.

"I spoke with your mother," said Oh. "I was not confident the message would be delivered. She told me you already had enough problems and hung up."

"Then you called Munson?" asked Jane, forgiving Oh immediately. He had walked through the firestorm that was a telephone call to Nellie, and that was penance enough for surprising her.

"Here's something interesting," said Charley. "I thought I saw a little sparkle down here."

Charley showed them a piece of polished rose quartz that had been covered by the tree bark and mushroom compost.

"Not a sample you'd expect to find here?" asked Oh.

"I wouldn't expect to find a tumbled and polished specimen of anything in the ground," said Charley. "The soil here on Fuzzy's farm, though, yields many surprises."

Charley reached into both pockets of his khaki work pants and spilled the contents onto a tree stump a few feet away.

Jane was reminded of a bowl of shiny mineral specimens that sat beside the cash register at a rock shop they had visited on a South Dakota vacation. You could buy the polished stones by the "scoop," which was an old sugar shovel that Jane had been interested in for its red Bakelite handle. The woman behind the counter had treated Jane as if she were certifiable when she asked to buy the scoop.

"No, honey," she had said slowly, "you

buy a scoop of the stones, see?" And she demonstrated by scooping up stones in the bowl, then letting them fall back in. "You buy what you can *scoop* up in the *scoop*. You don't buy the *scoop*," she finished, speaking deliberately and carefully. Then she had placed the vintage sugar shovel out of reach, as if Jane might hurt herself with it.

Jane picked up a few of the specimens.

"Isn't this coral?" she asked.

Charley nodded, smiling.

"We're landlocked, right?"

Charley nodded again.

"A stream from the Kankakee River that might have run through here years ago wouldn't be offering up any coral specimens, would it?"

Charley shook his head.

"At first when I saw the cat skeleton," Charley said, "I figured it was just an honest mistake by an overzealous citizen — you know, someone heard that bones were uncovered, doesn't see them at first, just decides this might be an old graveyard or a historically significant site — calls in an expert right away. In fact I figured that's why there weren't any other people from the local college here. Somebody came in right away, saw that a family pet had been exhumed, and left without fully explaining to Fuzzy and Lula that they could go ahead with their digging," said Charley. "In fact I imagined an all clear from the state would arrive any minute. Since I was planning on being here a few days, though, Nick and I started poking around and found all kinds of stuff. We've got arrowheads and pottery shards, fossils, and a few pieces of bone. We've got leaf fossils and insect fossils. I've found South American amber and old glass beads. And these are for you." Charley fished a tiny object out of his shirt pocket and handed it to Jane. "I know they're buttons, but . . ."

"An underwear button made of bone and a leather shoe button, probably from the 1890s or so," said Jane.

"You've come to some conclusion about these findings?" asked Oh.

"If it had just been some animal bones and arrowheads, I would think that someone might be trying to salt the site. Make it look like something it's not. Fool the experts. I mean, Native American artifacts, even if it turns out that they're not from any tribe that ever lived around here, will still hold up any activity for a while. There were Native Americans on Illinois land in this area, so it would make sense that something was found, but not something that belonged to an Arizona tribe. Until someone proved that it had been phonied up, though, Fuzzy wouldn't be able to do anything to his land. No construction, no selling of topsoil, no development of any kind.

"But this is ridiculous. There are ocean specimens, minerals that are from all over the world planted around here. So I would say whoever's salting the farm is either not very bright or has a ridiculous sense of overkill." Charley stopped and looked at Jane.

"Or he just likes to plant things," said Jane.

Jane told Oh about the pennies she had seen Fuzzy burying near his roses. She also told him about the Austinite Lula had fished out of her plant last night.

"So it would seem that Mr. Neilson himself is hiding little treasures on his property?" asked Oh.

"It might," said Jane, "if he weren't so mad about not being able to sell his topsoil. I think what's got Fuzzy so discombobulated is that he's being prevented from doing what he wants on his own farm. I hardly think he'd be working against himself like that. I mean, if he is, he's a great actor; and I don't think Fuzzy's ever been all that theatrically minded."

"Who called and reported the bones being found?" asked Oh.

"That's the question," said Jane. "It wasn't Fuzzy or Lula, that's for sure. Is there a name of a complainant or anything on any of the papers Fuzzy showed you?"

Charley shook his head. "I asked Fuzzy for any documents he had, and he brought out land surveys and old deeds and papers on water rights, and everything that had been shoved under his bed fifty years ago and under his father's bed for fifty years before that; but there was no official letter from any government office. This morning I phoned a few people I know to see if they could find out who made the initial call and what the nature of the stop is on this land, but I haven't heard back."

Jane appreciated Bruce Oh's patience, the odd curiosity that led him to such interesting questions, his almost complete lack of irony, the absence of cynicism. He was the counterpoint to her impatience, her naïveté that begged only the simplest questions, and her sense of irony that always made her distrust the obvious. She was sure that because of their give and

240

take, their dialectic, their yin and yang, whatever path they took to solve the murder of Johnny Sullivan and the puzzle of Fuzzy's farmland would be a sensible one — straight to the core of the problem — held in place by their complementary views of the world. Jane Wheel looked at her partner and mentor and waited for him to tell her what he thought their first step should be.

"Let's go talk to your mother," was not what she expected to hear.

Chapter 11

Nellie was in the kitchen of the EZ Way Inn, slicing onions. When Jane was five or six years old, a first grader waiting for her parents to finish up at work so they could all go home together, Jane loved to watch her mother chop vegetables for soup. It seemed so satisfying, so decisive. Making soup had a beginning, middle, and end; and the beginning part, the chopping, was so purposeful. Jane stopped enjoying the soup making, however, the first time she saw her mother cut herself.

Unlike contemporary chefs who might have a complete array of expensive, finely balanced knives, one appropriate for each task he or she might encounter in meal preparation, Nellie's collection of kitchen tools included two knives. A big one, approximately the size of a broadsword, and a small one, which was a cross between an ice pick and a straight razor. Every time she picked up either knife for any task, Nellie swiped the blade across a sharpening steel, so each was always deadly at the ready.

Nellie always wore at least one bandage on one hand. She'd nick a finger making barbecue or burn her thumb on the grill. She worked so fast and so efficiently, she usually never knew she had injured herself until a horrified Jane asked her why she was bleeding or blistering. Nellie would look down at the cut finger and swear out loud. Then she'd take the bottle of hydrogen peroxide she kept above the sink with the dishwashing detergent and bottle of ammonia, douse her finger with it, and slap on a Band-Aid.

Four times that Jane knew about, Don had to take her into the emergency room for stitches when she almost severed a digit in the name of onions for the cubed steak sandwiches. After one of these harrowing accidents, Don bought a fancy electric slicing machine, but when he saw Nellie using it without the plastic hand guard because she said it got in the way, he boxed it up and gave it away.

Jane's mother no longer fed the great crowds of factory workers who used to pour in the door when Roper was churning out stoves across the street, but every few weeks she made a pot of soup and hung up a sign outside the kitchen. SOUP TODAY, $1 A BOWL UNTIL IT'S GONE. It never lasted more than two hours.

"It sure as hell wasn't me called anybody on them," said Nellie, her fingers holding the onion on the board dangerously close to the blade as it came down. "Wouldn't have been my business what Fuzzy or Lula dug up on their own damn farm. Belongs to them."

Jane winced every time the blade met the board. She tried to watch her mother's face instead of focusing on her hands, scarred road maps of food-preparation disasters.

"No one thinks you did it, Mom," said Jane. "But maybe Fuzzy was in here talking about it, you know telling the story of digging up bones, and somebody heard and reported it."

"Does Mr. Neilson come in at a regular time? Are there others who are also here whom he talks to?" asked Oh.

Nellie stopped chopping and tried to scratch her nose with her shoulder. She was beginning to look red-eyed from the onions, and Jane enjoyed the vulnerable look it gave her mother. Even though the tears were artificially induced, Jane liked pretending that her mother's emotions were occasionally allowed to surface. Jane's pleasure was short-lived, since the scratching motion was making Nellie wave the knife around through the air, endangering all those in the kitchen. Jane and Oh stepped away from the counter.

"Fuzzy comes in around eleven most days. He usually talks to himself, but it's out loud. Anybody at the bar could hear him if he decided to tell a story and they decided to listen. Fuzzy's one of those guys likes to entertain the crowd."

"Do you remember him talking in here about digging on his land?" asked Jane.

"Ask your dad. I'm making soup here, Jane."

Don remembered. Not the date, but the morning.

"Fuzzy told the whole bar that he almost broke the blade on his rototiller, running over a bunch of bones," said Don. "Nobody pays any attention to Fuzz. He exaggerates everything."

"And the 'whole bar' translates to whom?" asked Jane.

"Francis the bread man, Gil, maybe Dempsey and his buddy, they come in just about every day around lunchtime, hoping your mother made soup. You know, I think Tim was in here, too. It was the morning he had his meeting with the real estate people and the owners of the Ford dealership. Yeah, because I made about four pots of coffee. Some kind of sponsors' meeting for this big sale," said Don. "I'm sure it was that morning because the bigger the audience he has, the more Fuzzy likes to tell stories. He was being real dramatic about how scary it was to uncover bones and not know whose they were, who he was waking up to haunt him. He was acting up a storm."

Jane dialed up Tim to ask him for a list of everyone who was at the meeting. He answered his cell phone on the second ring.

"Where are you? I'll drop it off at the tavern for you," Tim said.

"Not necessary, I'll pick it up," said Jane. "Where are you?"

"Claire and I got access to a most remarkable basement. You would love it down here, and the funny thing is, it was all Claire's charm and down-home manners that got us in."

Jane was almost sure Tim was teasing her. He knew she thought Claire a bit chilly and a little too tall and polished and poised. Jane was, perhaps, just a touch jealous of Claire's well-bred good looks, her majestic presence, and her incredible inventory of antiques. Claire Oh knew her collectible kitchenalia and her vintage neckties all right, but her real passion was for the real, the old, and the exquisite. She had traded up from Bakelite bracelets to vintage Cartier watches a long time ago, and next to her Jane felt rumpled and linty. It didn't help that Jane usually was rumpled and linty, while Claire dressed in elegant clothes with shoes and bags that matched. She even wore silk scarves tossed over her shoulder, looking like she was ready to pose for her fashion spread in *Vogue*. When Jane tried to achieve the same kind of panache with accessories, she ended up with a bandana knotted around her neck looking like the cover girl of *Modern Scoutmaster*.

Jane wasn't so keen on the cold calls that Tim was going to want her to make for this garage sale, so she could probably convince herself to appreciate the fact that Tim and Claire could do the door to door. When and if the time came that someone was needed to actually help someone sort through their stuff, though . . . well, that was Jane Wheel's forte. For the reluctant Kankakeans who thought nobody'd want that old junk in the basement, Jane was just the person to convince them that nearly everything had a value.

But Tim said that he and Claire were actually *in a basement,* and Jane didn't like the idea of Tim and Claire working a basement together. Claire was probably as clearheaded and directed while going through sealed-up cartons as she was when she planned Jane's briefly aborted garage sale. Jane admired efficiency, so why did it bother her so much that Claire could cut to the chase, label the items, price the goods, cull the keepers? Claire could probably do that sort of job in half the time Jane would take . . . yes, that was it . . . Claire could do the job in half the time.

Jane was slow and dreamy when she went through housefuls of goods. She unwrapped, dusted, read, admired, and speculated on each item that someone had thought enough of to put into a box instead of the garbage. Tim described this as Jane playing the tortoise to his hare. Jane herself described this method as *thorough.*

How dare he take Claire with him into a basement? Wasn't Jane his part-time, almost full-time, partner? The *stuff* of the sales was Jane's specialty. Tim might be the one who initially charmed the owners and eventually led the reluctant participants to the sellers' tables, helped them set up their cash boxes, told them how many singles and fives and quarters to put in their bank; but it was Jane, left alone with the good people of Kankakee who had been hoarding their childhoods wrapped in tissue, stored in attics, who would exclaim over every item, coax the owners into telling their stories, and convince them to either rewrap it, frame it, pass it on to other family members, or, as a last resort, sell it.

When Tim first heard Jane go through items with a family, he despaired because when he heard them weep over Grandma's china, he was sure they would decide to keep it. But it usually worked the other way. Jane listened to them and encouraged them to think about the object, remember the stories, wax poetic about the holiday tables that the Spode had once graced, and the cathartic action of remembering often was what allowed the owner to smile and let it go. The same person who had groused that all he had in the basement was old junk now saw that junk transformed into vessels of memory. It didn't seem like junk anymore. And Jane's eyes, shining at the thought of these memories being passed on into the world, convinced the owner that yes, if there wasn't room in their house, they could keep the story in their heart and let the objects go — for the right price. And Tim was right there, a handful of paper tags and a fine-point Sharpie pen, to mark that right price and seal the deal.

"Look, I'm at the tavern now with Oh, and I can come to you. I'll get the list of names and maybe take a look at that basement. I mean Claire might not be so familiar with what would be valuable here in Kankakee, so . . . Wait a minute." Jane stopped talking when she felt a tap on her shoulder.

Jane turned around, expecting Don or Nellie or Oh. She certainly did not expect Tim Lowry, holding his cell phone to his ear.

"Hi," said Tim, still speaking into his phone.

"Hi," said Jane speaking into hers.

"Nell, some of these glasses and pitchers are divine, but you're right about the finish on those trays. A shame, really," Claire said. Jane couldn't see her, but she imagined her towering over her mother who would, by now, be stirring all of the ingredients simmering in her enormous soup pot.

"This basement? She charmed her way into the EZ Way Inn basement? Here?"

"I swear I didn't even ask her. She

looked at my 'holdout' list for the sale and saw that Nellie was on it. The EZ Way Inn and the house. And she wanted to meet Nellie anyway, so I didn't think you'd mind if we just stopped by . . ."

Jane heard Nellie answer Claire in the kitchen, but couldn't make out the words; then she heard Claire laugh in response.

"Put your phone away, hon," said Tim. "I'll write down that list of names."

Tim sat down at the bar, waved to Oh, who was still talking to Don, and took out a small leather case with monogrammed 3 x 5 cards. Jane had wondered who the people were who used those fancy leather pocket briefcases, the ones she coveted from the catalogs. Tim, of course. He would be the one.

"How did this happen?" Jane asked. "You know I've been trying to get into that basement for years. Half of it is probably vintage tavern stuff I gave them, stuff that never made it out of the box."

"What can I say? Claire was just . . . I don't know . . . charming."

"Nellie doesn't speak charming," said Jane. "Furthermore . . ."

"Jane," said Claire, entering the barroom through the kitchen door, looking like she just stepped off the *Queen Mary*, wearing a peach silk suit, bone sling-back heels, and a pastel geometric print scarf. "I know what you're thinking. Please don't be angry about it . . ."

"I'm not angry . . ."

"She's in good hands, frankly she'll be better taken care of this way," said Claire.

Holy Toledo. Claire had charmed her way into the basement, and she had gotten Nellie to agree to psychiatric evaluation?

"You know, Sergeant Miles welcomes every opportunity to be with that dog of yours. And, you know, I don't have the way with animals that I . . ." Claire dropped her voice and inclined her head toward the kitchen, "that I do with people."

Jane sorted it out quickly. She had forgotten that Claire and Bruce Oh were supposed to be caring for Rita, the German shepherd she had taken in. It was Sergeant Miles, though, who had loved the dog at first sight and taught it some lifesaving tricks for which Jane was enormously grateful. Miles would be a better dogsitter, but that didn't make Claire a better Nellie charmer.

"How did you get my mother to allow you to go into the basement?"

"I gave her my card when I introduced myself, and she said she had some old stuff in the basement I might be interested in," said Claire. "I don't know why Tim had her on his holdouts list in the first place. She's a darling."

Claire moved off to say hello to her husband and, Jane assumed, charm Don, too, while she was at it. Hell, she'd probably be going through Francis's bread truck and the trunk of Gil's car before the day was over.

Tim was still writing down names, and Jane was happy to see, checking his PDA for the phone numbers and addresses of the people who attended his meeting, so he could give her a complete list. He was probably trying to make up for bringing Claire into the EZ Way Inn in the first place, and he probably liked writing on those cards, just the right weight of cardstock, printed with that grid and a bold T & T SALES across the top. Whatever the reason, Jane was glad Tim was just honoring the request and not smarting off about her being the girl detective on the case. *Ah,* Jane thought, *maybe he's jealous that I'm working with Oh right now instead of him, so he's trying to force me to choose.*

"Tim, I'll try to save some time to work on the sale with you, it's just that Fuzzy . . ."

"Hey, no problem. Whenever. Claire's said she's willing to sign on for the duration."

"Nellie. Darling," said Jane, standing in the doorway of the kitchen.

Nellie looked up to see if Jane had lost more of her mind.

"Mom, why'd you let . . . ," Jane began to ask, peering into the soup pot, closing in on her mother, who was getting out bowls, spoons, and packages of saltine crackers.

Nellie shushed her.

"See that woman?" asked Nellie. "The one who's all dressed up?"

"Claire Oh," said Jane.

"She's an antique dealer," said Nellie, "and she thinks some of the old tables and chairs and glasses and junk in the basement can bring some money."

"I've told you that for years, and you kept telling me there was nothing down there and I wasn't allowed. You told me you thought there were rats," Jane said, her quiet voice getting louder.

"Shh. I let her go down there because she's a professional," said Nellie.

"So am I," said Jane.

"Yeah? Look how she's dressed," said Nellie. "I got her card."

"We have different styles, Mother, but

I'm just as professional, and I should get to go in the basement and go through the stuff and . . ."

"Why?"

"What?"

"Why should you get to any more than anyone else?"

"I'm your daughter." Jane felt her voice rise, and Nellie didn't bother to shush her. She just made her own voice very quiet and calm.

"Jane Wheel, if I let you go into that filthy basement, I know what would happen. You'd get me down there and ask me about every spoon and ladle and box of napkins and old stove parts and even the old wash tanks that your dad never threw away," said Nellie. "Then you'd haul it all up here, and we'd have to clean it up and you wouldn't sell it. You'd say how it's vintage and part of the history of the place and all that nonsense, and then I'd haul it out to the alley, then you'd go into the alley and put it into your car, and take it home and put it in your garage.

"You listen to me, Jane. You have enough stuff. You have enough stuff for your whole family and a hundred more. At least if you go into other peoples' houses to get stuff, you might be able to let go of some of it someday; but if I really let you into my house and my work, you'll never close the goddamn door."

Nellie grabbed a large, stainless-steel ladle, sloshed it around in the soup, and dished up a bowl. She shoved it into her daughter's hands.

"Now, go eat some of this soup."

Nellie wiped her hands on her apron.

"You know what's wrong with you, Jane?" asked Nellie. "You don't know how to accept what I give you. You just know how to ask for what you think I have."

Chapter 12

Everyone ate soup. Bruce and Claire Oh, Tim, Don, every customer at the bar. Dempsey and Hoover came in and made a production out of sniffing the air and claiming to know when soup was being made. They did a lot of nudge-nudge-wink-wink, telling Nellie she ought to have the opportunity to serve her soup to the world, and if they ever found a way to put Kankakee on the map, they'd make sure she had her own restaurant.

"Yeah, that's what I'd like. More work and my own damn restaurant."

Jane looked over Tim's list of names. She knew Dempsey and Hoover had been in the EZ Way, but she hadn't realized they had been there for Tim's meeting.

"They volunteered to be on a committee. Said that anything that helped Kankakee was fine by them."

"Where are they living? Are they staying in a motel?"

"They rented a house over by Cobb Park. Furnished. Nice old house, I hear. I suppose it's their headquarters for Hometown USA," said Tim. "Hey, is that a secret?"

"Nope," said Don. "I've been talking it up to a few people, and a lot of folks around here already heard and are pretty excited about it."

Jane didn't want to argue with her dad so soon after tangling with her mother, so she kept her thoughts about Prof. Harold Hill and his sidekick to herself.

"Henry Bennett. And these three others, Laura Brown, Marisa Brown, and Kenny Pollett? All from Kankakee Realty?" Jane asked, checking Tim's list.

"Not the Brown sisters. Laura's a photographer from Chicago. She's doing a photo essay on the sale for a suburban newspaper chain. Maybe going to take one block and document everything — prep, setup, sale days, and aftermath. Or she might try to cover the whole thing; we haven't decided. And Marisa is writing the story to go with it. The text. They're real excited about the whole event. Be a big story for them."

"Did Mr. Sullivan ever want to write a story about the garage sale?" asked Oh.

"Never talked to me about it," said Tim. "He was all airport all the time."

"Hey, how'd you do with the high school volunteers you promised Suzanne Blum you'd find for her aunt's block?" asked Jane.

"Service project for the National Honor Society at Bishop McNamara. Going over to speak at the high school later," said Tim, standing to take his bowl back to Nellie in the kitchen for seconds.

"Kenny Pollett?"

"He's a Realtor. Young guy who seems to have neglected the real estate tenet about location and moved here from Chicago."

Jane looked at the list and tried to focus on the names. She looked up and into the kitchen where Tim had plunged into an old argument with Nellie. Both of them clearly enjoyed their roles. They knew what to expect from each other, navigated through the give-and-take of a conversation, and ended up satisfied at the end of it. How did people learn to do that? If Nellie was right, if Jane kept refusing what her mother had to give, asking her for what she thought Nellie had . . . whatever that meant . . . Jane had better figure out how to stop it. She wanted that easy rapport Tim had with her mother. She wanted to be respected or at least taken seriously by

Nellie. Didn't she? Or was Nellie just deep down right? Did Jane just want to be taken into the basement?

Oh parked in what was almost the last space in the lot that adjoined the real estate company. A large sign was lettered on the brick wall of the building:

Kankakee "K3" Realty
Let us take you home!

Jane wondered if the lot was nearly full because business was good or because it was poor. If all the cars belonged to the Realtors, it meant they were inside rather than showing property to potential buyers. If the cars were those of customers, Kankakee must be in the middle of a housing boom.

Bust. There were three people sitting in the large, open room, wearing those bright blazers that announced they were proud employees. Henry Bennett was on the phone, writing something on a notepad. A forty-something woman was paging through a thick computer printout of some kind of listing, carefully lining through certain points with a pink highlighter. A third member of the K3 team was a young man who appeared to be cleaning out his wallet. He sat back in his chair and was emptying each pocket and fold of receipts, ticket stubs, business cards, and small bits of paper with scrawled names and numbers.

Jane and Oh walked into the office and the Realtors looked up with such obvious hunger that Jane wasn't sure whether they were going to try and sell her a house or throw her into a stewpot. Henry Bennett remained on the phone but kept his eyes on the two of them, waved, and made a gesture to indicate he'd only be another minute. As the older Realtor, the one with the bigger desk, he clearly wanted them to believe he was the man in charge, the one worth waiting for. The woman actually licked her lips before smiling and standing. She choked out a hoarse greeting that made her sound like she might not have spoken aloud for several hours. The young man looked up, his eyes eager, but his manner restrained. You could almost hear his inner voice advising him to remain cool.

The desperation made Jane want to buy something. If there had been a display of gum or pens at a counter, Jane would have stocked up. Unfortunately, the impulse to want to buy something when business is slow, to help out the folks in the store, had to be squelched when you were in a store that sold houses and lots and office buildings. Even though there were bargains galore, Jane knew she shouldn't be snapping up the downtown restaurant that was being sold at a tremendous loss or any of the magnificent old homes on the river that would have sold for millions on Chicago's North Shore but here in Kankakee were practically being given away. Real estate at rock bottom still demanded more commitment than pocket change.

Bruce Oh looked at Jane with one of his almost raised eyebrows that signaled that she should take the lead. She was getting used to his lack of expression, or at least she thought she was. She decided she would interpret what passed for expressions as best she could, and until he called her wrong on it, she would assume she could read the man.

Jane liked her chances of learning something interesting with the salesman who wanted to remain cool. After her years in advertising, dealing with actors and models, she felt she could penetrate the invisible shield behind which a young man who didn't want to showcase his need — his *got to get this commercial, got to be hired for this shoot, must get this voiceover* — tried to protect himself. This one Realtor had *I've got to sell four walls and some windows right now* written all over him, and Jane hoped that meant he would talk about anything to get her to sit down and look at some listings.

"Mr. Pollett?" Jane said, reading his name tag.

"Yes, how can I help you?" he asked, pulling two chairs over to his desk. Jane could see Henry Bennett out of the corner of her eye, anxiously trying to end his phone call.

Jane introduced herself and Bruce Oh, but did not immediately ask him about any of the recent happenings on Fuzzy's land. Instead she mentioned that she had been a friend of Roger Groveland's and had always meant to come in and visit him at his office when she was in town.

"I didn't know him very well," said Pollett. "I started a month or so before he died."

Pollett offered them coffee, swept his wallet debris into his top drawer, and pulled out a yellow legal pad. "Were you planning on contacting him about the sale or purchase of property here in the greater Kankakee area?" he asked formally.

"My parents live here. They run the EZ Way Inn," said Jane. Pollett nodded and Jane went on, hoping Oh would be ready to help bail her out if she began asking too much too soon. "With all this gossip going on about the airport, I was just thinking it might be a good time to find out about land prices, possibilities here for investment. My folks were saying that maybe there are some bargains that my husband and I might find, and then if the airport is built here . . ."

"Dead," Pollett said, shaking his head.

"Pardon?" said Oh.

"I want to sell you property," said Pollett, "don't get me wrong, but I'm pretty sure that the airport thing is dead. I can't try to sell you anything on false pretenses. Besides, all that farmland that people thought would be so valuable for the airport, that's not for sale. Now if you want a nice house on the river, I've got them, but land for development around here is so tied up because of —"

"Is there anything I can help you with, Mrs. Wheel? Henry Bennett. We met out at the Neilsons' farm?"

"I am Bruce Oh, an associate of Mrs. Wheel's," said Oh, standing to extend his hand.

"The Neilson farm?" Pollett rolled his eyes. "If you're thinking about finding someplace like that around here, forget it. The rumors have tied up everything west of town. Besides, most of the people around there are so dead set against development that they'd just as soon shoot us as talk to us about selling."

"Kenny," said Bennett. "You and Kay head over to Villa Europa now . . . some condos out by the high school," he said to Jane and Oh. "Make sure everything's ready for the opening and that you've got examples in all of the different floor plans ready to show."

Kay looked at Bennett, surprised. She shrugged, as if to say anything beats sitting here, and picked up her purse.

Pollett looked like he might protest, but instead decided on a parting shot. "If you're a friend of the Neilsons, you ask them who's made them promises so they won't sell to anyone or even talk to us about it."

"I apologize for Kenny," said Bennett. "I don't think he even knows about the young man who was shot out there. No newspaper story out yet. I didn't think I should talk about it . . . so if he seems insensitive . . ."

"Mr. Bennett, you were the man who identified the body?" asked Oh.

"No, I couldn't say who it was; I just said who it wasn't. Not Roger Groveland, not anyone who worked here."

"But you had met the man before; you did know the victim?" Jane asked.

Henry "Hank" Bennett shook his head.

"He was a newspaper reporter whose parents lived on the neighboring farm. He had been doing a lot of stories on Kankakee. You were quoted in one of Johnny Sullivan's stories," said Jane. "Don't you remember being interviewed by him?"

Bennett sat down. His eyes were focused somewhere behind Jane and Oh when he spoke. "I didn't realize that was him. I looked away quickly when I realized it wasn't . . . when it wasn't anyone I knew from the office. They had told me about the blazer and . . ." Bennett stopped. "I didn't know it was that reporter." He brought his eyes back to them. "Really." Bennett's hands were shaking.

Jane turned around, thinking she heard another car turn into the parking lot, and

266

she noticed behind them on the wall was a large map of Kankakee County. A table in front of it held a coffeemaker and a plate of cookies that looked like it had been there awhile.

"Do you need a cup of coffee, Mr. Bennett?" asked Jane, walking over to the table.

"Please call me Hank. Yes, that'd be good. I only met Sullivan once, but he seemed like a good boy. I . . ." Bennett stopped again. "It's funny, I could put the image out of my mind when I didn't know who it was. I just walked away from it and it didn't stay with me at all, but now I can see it so clearly. His poor parents."

"Do you know them personally?" asked Oh.

"Yes, but not well. Kenny and I have been working with landowners west of town. We had a Chicago developer interested in building housing out there; we were talking to a retail mall developer, too. See, if the airport . . ." Bennett stopped. "We thought that some of the more entrenched farmers, the ones who were holding on to their land so tightly, might be persuaded to sell some of their adjoining acreage. Then no one farmer would have to give up everything, but there'd still be enough to offer a developer to make it worth his while to consider an investment.

"The Neilsons and the Sullivans, for example. They own a lot of land, but they're getting older, leasing out most of it anyway, and we thought they'd consider selling some big parcels as long as we could structure it so they kept ten, twenty, even thirty acres, with their houses and buildings, enough to farm for their own satisfaction. None of them are making a lot of money right now. This way, they could sell before they were forced to and keep a place to live," said Bennett.

"On the morning of Tim's meeting about the garage-sale promotion at the EZ Way Inn, did you hear Fuzzy talking about the bones he's found on his property?" asked Jane.

Bennett nodded.

"Did you call anyone to report it?"

"Are you joking? Do you know what happens when your land gets tied up in that kind of red tape?" asked Bennett. He straightened and seemed to realize that he was talking to two people whose role in all of this he didn't quite understand. "I mean, of course I would have made the call if I felt it was truly an important historical find. I would always follow procedure on that. But Fuzzy was always finding things," said Bennett. "He often talked about valuable minerals and treasures he was turning up when he was gardening. We all laughed it off. He played jokes on us like that all the time."

"Like what?" asked Jane.

"When Kenny and I first approached him about selling some of his land, he agreed to come into the office for a meeting. He brought in a piece of gold and told us he'd found it on his land, so he thought we should raise the price considerably," said Bennett.

"I was taken aback because it did look like a piece of gold ore, and he was so serious about it all. I started asking him questions about it, and he burst out laughing, told us we were a bunch of dopes. Asked why he should expect us to make a good deal for him when there were smarter people in the world. He said he wanted to sell his land to somebody who had vision."

"So the deal was off?" said Oh, writing something down in a small pocket notebook.

"No. He'd play some trick and call us names, then he'd call and say he was sorry and want to know if we were still inter-ested," said Bennett. "Kenny had had it. He said Fuzzy was a crazy old man and he wasn't ever going to sell his land. He told me it was a waste of time to deal with these farmers. They'd never make a deal."

Jane asked about the Sullivans, if they seemed willing to part with a parcel of their farmland.

"They did until their son started writing about the airport all the time and coming home to work on the weekend," said Bennett. "They said maybe he should be making the decisions about the farm."

Bennett stopped talking abruptly and looked at the two of them, then, almost as an afterthought, looked at the clock on the wall. He stood and said he was going to have to go to a meeting that was sched-uled, couldn't be canceled. He picked up his phone, pushed a button on its base, and asked someone to work the front. The door to the back office opened and a young woman came out. She was carrying several file folders with her, and Bennett indicated she should sit at his desk.

"You cover the phones, Letty, and direct people to my cell phone if it's a client with a specific question. Pollett and Kay will be back in an hour or so. So sorry, but I'm late. I hadn't realized . . ."

Bennett was out the door before Jane could even think of how to phrase what she was thinking . . . that Johnny Sullivan's death would mean that his parents might sell the land Bennett needed to make his deal. Jane wasn't quite ready to accuse Bennett or anyone else. After all, less than twenty-four hours ago, she had been pretty certain that Dempsey and Hoover were guilty, that they had silenced Johnny Sullivan because he was going to expose all their plans for turning Kankakee into an amusement park.

Jane and Oh got up to leave the office, but they stopped at the giant map on the wall. Oh traced his finger in the air over the county map, and Jane watched him outline the large green shape marked Sullivan and the equally large blue piece marked Neilson. The land butted right up toward the edge of the town of Kankakee, its western border defined by a large structure, the former Roper Stove Factory, and a tiny structure south of it, the EZ Way Inn. Each building was labeled with its own tiny red flag.

"How long has Mr. Bennett owned K3 Realty?" Jane asked the woman at the desk as she and Oh paused at the front door.

"He wishes," Letty said, turning away from them to answer the phone at another desk.

Jane and Oh sat in the car in the parking lot while Oh studied his notebook. He closed it and put it away.

"Did you believe Mr. Bennett when he said he did not recognize John Sullivan in the cornfield, Mrs. Wheel?"

"I think so. He was there for a moment, just making sure it wasn't anyone from his office. There was so much confusion. What I don't believe," said Jane, "was that he had a previously scheduled meeting just now. He just realized that Johnny Sullivan's death could be good for him and his deal."

"And Mr. Bennett realized that we now know this, that John Sullivan's death benefited Henry Bennett. And . . ."

Jane's cell phone rang. No *William Tell Overture*, no "Happy Birthday," no "Take Me Out to the Ballgame," no funny little song or weird little pattern, just a regular ring. A telephone ring. Jane thought it must mean that her son had gotten tired of his game of changing the tone on her phone so often that she never recognized the ring as hers. Perhaps this ordinary ring was supposed to be the most confusing of all? Or maybe Nick changed it back to the recognizable tone that she preferred because he was growing up.

When she answered the phone, though, Jane Wheel thought her little boy didn't sound grown up at all. He sounded like he was upset, hysterical. Was he crying? Jane listened to her son, then directed Oh to drive as quickly as possible back out to the Neilsons' farm. She kept redialing Charley's cell, but got no answer. Either Nick had clicked the phone off altogether, the battery had died, or Nick had rushed back to wherever the action was taking place at that moment, dropping the phone in the cabin, the tent, or the farmhouse, whatever he had run to for privacy to make the call. The last thing he had yelled into the phone sounded like a loud and static-riddled *"Hurry!"*

According to what Jane thought she heard Nick say, someone had just tried to shoot Charley.

Chapter 13

If it were the case, if someone had indeed been trying to shoot Charley, he seemed pretty calm about the whole thing, lounging against Fuzzy's small tractor parked outside the barn.

Oh had barely pulled into the driveway next to the farmhouse when Jane had her seat belt unlatched and the front door unlocked. She ignored Bruce Oh's request that he be allowed to stop the car altogether before she opened the door and jumped out, feeling, she had to admit once she saw that Charley was unhurt and unperturbed, a little thrilled at keeping her balance while exiting a moving car. True, it wasn't moving very fast and she did stumble a little, but, she thought, she could add a picture of herself bolting from a moving vehicle to her inner reel. No one was going to ask her to audition for *Charlie's Angels*, but for a Kankakee-made detective flick, she was holding her own.

"Where's the fire, hon?" Charley asked.

Okay, even for a Kankakee movie, that

dialogue had seen better days. Was she going to have to direct, produce, star, *and* do the rewrite?

"Where's Nick? He called and said you were . . . that someone had shot at you," said Jane, a little more breathless from her dash out of the car than Cameron Diaz might have been.

"Misunderstanding," said Charley. "He overheard me talking to Fuzzy and Lula. I was presenting a hypothetical situation, and he jumped the gun, so to speak."

Jane had been with Charley for over twenty years minus a few months here and there for some marital questions and answers. She acknowledged that she had a prickly, sensitive side and that she often worked through her own self-doubt by overreacting to any little thing her husband said, willfully misunderstanding the well-intentioned remark, defending herself against an innocent Charley who, most of the time, had no idea what she was so upset about. But Jane had been working on that. She recalled their early years when they could read each other's moods and body language fluently. And this outwardly calm, almost lethargic Charley was sending her a message.

Neither had ever needed the sitcom gimmick of a secret word or a funny gesture to signal to the other that one wanted to leave a party. Charley knew that when Jane ran her hand through her hair that she was pulling on the roots to stifle a yawn, and he also knew that when she bit her bottom lip she was really listening to what someone was telling her. Jane knew that when Charley softened his voice and spoke with a slight shaking of his head, he wanted that conversation to end. And she knew that when Charley called her "hon" and held himself very still, she should pay attention because something was terribly wrong.

"May we know the hypothetical situation?" asked Oh.

"Let's suppose someone walked along that cornfield, at the spot where the path from the cabin ends, where Sullivan was found, directly south," said Charley, inclining his head in a southerly direction, but not pointing — as if he didn't want anyone who might be watching to know what he was talking about — then he continued, "and they kept walking, you know where they would end up?"

Jane looked south. One could barely make out some buildings, but she knew the closest neighboring farm belonged to the

Sullivans. Charley nodded when she said their name.

"Well, if one found something that might be incriminating or illegal, but one didn't know if it had anything to do with what had happened the other night, what would one . . ."

"Charley, drop the hypothetical *one* nonsense right now," said Jane.

"Look, Munson's going to call me in to talk in a second. I think he's pretty suspicious of Fuzzy — him being out there when Sullivan got shot and not being himself lately and all. Nick heard me talking to Lula about what I saw when I went walking . . . damn it . . . Munson's waving me in."

Charley waved and nodded. "Nick misheard me when I was talking to Lula and I think he panicked a little, maybe it finally hit him that someone was killed right outside the tent. I know it's hitting me. . . ."

"Professor?" called Munson, giving another wave.

"I'll finish all this later," said Charley. "Nick's fine. I haven't had a chance to explain everything to him either — not that I know what any of it means — but keep him in sight, okay?"

Jane nodded and watched her husband

slowly walk over to where the police seemed to have started their investigation all over again.

"It's the discovery of those guns," answered Oh, before Jane had a chance to ask a question.

"During an investigation, the only surprise you want is a discovery that moves you forward. Finding those guns in the barn takes Munson back around to the beginning," Oh said.

"Where's Nick?" said Jane. "Charley said keep him in sight, but he didn't say where he was."

Oh gestured for her to check the farmhouse while he went in the direction of the cabin and shed.

Lula was checking something she was baking, her right hand on the oven door, the left hand rubbing against her apron, when Jane startled her by asking if she had seen Nick. Lula stepped back from the stove and looked at Jane as if she had interrupted some secret act. Perhaps to Lula, cooking was a kind of private ritual, but Jane didn't have time to pay homage to the kitchen gods right now.

"Nick," she repeated. "Have you seen him? He called me."

"I want you to remember something,

Jane. I did not ask you to come and help us here. It was those bones that Fuzzy made a big deal about. Your own mother and father called you. I told Fuzzy to stop talking about everything, stop telling everyone everything he knows." Lula stopped and took a breath, "Not that he knows his ass from his elbow."

Jane wanted to know why Lula was so upset and why she was giving Jane this caution, but first she wanted to see Nick. She walked past Lula and through the dining room to the parlor, where she had tucked those crocheted blankets around him . . . when? Yesterday. Had Johnny Sullivan waved to her from the cornfield just two nights ago?

"Lula, where's Nick?"

"Fuzzy was out walking the field and the Munson boy wanted him, so Nick said he'd go get him," said Lula, pointing out to the field and waving her arm in the direction of the Sullivans'. Charley's walk. "The corn path," added Lula, "that's what we call it."

Jane ran out the door and headed down to the cornfield. A uniformed officer was still at the perimeter of a taped-off area at the end of the yard, but Jane turned and headed off at a right angle from the crime scene, walking along the edge of the corn-field toward the Sullivans' farm. Whatever Charley had seen, he had seen it walking this way.

Whatever Nick had heard his father say, whatever had stirred Nick enough to call Jane had its roots somewhere along this path. And this was where Lula said Fuzzy had gone and where Nick had followed. Something about shooting. Nick thought Charley thought . . . if someone had heard shooting and Nick was . . . Jane tried to stop thinking. Honestly, where had think-ing gotten her lately? She needed to look around and figure out what they all found out walking, where this path took them.

The cornfield was on her left, and on her right, the mown lawn and separate vege-table gardens that Fuzzy had nurtured had given way to less cared for property — scrubby trees and a rusty tractor, engine parts and tires. It was so obvious where Fuzzy's land ended. Or at least where the land he cared about ended. The farm equipment junkyard and chaotic tangle was land unloved. Not a farm, not a garden, just weeds and dirt.

Jane noticed the cornfield on her left; that grid of order and mazelike intensity had broken its geometry by a widening between rows. Was it a lane for a truck or a tractor to go into the field or was it a road to whatever Charley had found? She noticed a fencepost with a tiny wooden square nailed to the top. On it was painted a red circle. Within the circle was another, wider red circle. An agricultural symbol? A certain hybrid of corn planted there? Jane didn't recognize it but wasn't sure why she thought she might. Just because she had grown up surrounded by farmland, she wouldn't know her field corn from her bicolor extra sweet. At least not until an ear of it was on her plate, buttered and salted, with a vintage red Bakelite corn-holder sticking out of each end.

Jane turned left and walked down this wide row about twenty feet and saw another fencepost with another small red circle sign. There was another wide path to her right, so she turned and in the distance saw something that took her breath away, but she wasn't at all sure it would have affected Charley in the same way. Quilts. Dozens of them. It appeared to be a clothesline hung with stunning variations of appliquéd patterns in red on white. Quilted studies in solid color geometry, circles within circles, and squares within squares. So beautiful and unexpected, hung out here in the middle of nowhere, surrounded by cornstalks? Why would anyone go to the trouble of hiding them? Some kind of rural Illinois sweatshop labor deal? An undercover seamstress operation?

Were Fuzzy and Lula running some kind of killer quilting bee?

Somehow this made even less sense than everything else that Jane had seen and heard since arriving at Fuzzy's farm. Jane didn't see Nick yet but figured she ought to go closer and see if there was anything else here in the clearing, any place he might be. She did see off to the side a few prefabricated storage sheds, the kind one puts together from a mail-order kit. No activity around them. As she approached the stretch of red and white, hung against the green of the corn, she realized they were not what she had first thought them to be. The size was all off. They were small — crib quilts? Smaller. Doll quilts?

It was only when she got within about eight feet of them that she saw them for what they were. Not quilts at all. They were paper signs of some kind with red circles and squares. They were clipped onto old weathered boards that in turn were propped up by hay bales. Some of the paper squares were torn, their corners flapping in the light breeze. A few were riddled with holes.

Jane had never seen anything like this — a row of modern-art geometric shapes in the middle of a cornfield? Some new kind of scarecrow variation? She peeked around behind them and walked on the other side of the hay bales. No colorful shapes hung on that side, only the cornfield stretched out behind them.

Jane heard a voice then a pinging, popping sound. This had all the makings of an old childhood joke or a line from a tall tale. "Why I remember it was so hot, the corn started popping in the field" had a Paul Bunyan Pecos Bill ring to it. The muted popping sounds continued and she saw the hay bale on the end of the row move, as if it had been punched or hit or . . .

"Holy frigging mother of . . . Stop shooting!" Jane yelled, as loud as she could while throwing herself on the ground and trying to crawl around the corner. The fact that she was wearing a red T-shirt made her feel even more like a moving target. "Stop shooting!" she yelled again, as she maneuvered around the last hay bale. At least the two shooters were lined up in front of the target at the other end of the row. That was the good news. The bad news was the fact that Fuzzy was instructing Nick how to hold the rifle, and to Jane's knowledge, her son had never held a gun before in his life. If he pulled the trigger, he was as likely to move the barrel anywhere in the general vicinity of the targets, and she was certainly in that range.

With all the volume and breath she could muster while lying flat on the ground, she willed herself to be heard. What if she had been walled off behind soundproof glass, and she saw Nick walking out in front of a truck? That was the voice she called upon and let loose on the rural Illinois landscape.

"Nick. Don't shoot. It's Mom."

Nick froze and dropped the rifle, and Jane could see that she had unleashed a Freudian nightmare upon her son's psyche that an entire team from Vienna would have to be called upon to repair. Nick first looked up to the heavens, then down to his feet.

"Over here," said Jane, in the same giant voice, raising herself to her knees and waving her arms, hoping that the motion would convince the two of them she wasn't just another target in the cornfield. "Don't shoot!"

Fuzzy seemed to finally hear her and

turned slowly toward that end of the row. He still held the rifle, and Jane could only hope she was communicating with the Fuzzy she had known since she was Nick's age and not the aging stranger she had encountered over the past few days.

"What in the hell are you doing out there, Janie? You liked to scared the bejesus out of your boy."

Nick looked a little wobbly and sat down. Fuzzy told him to stay put and headed off to one of the sheds. He brought out two cold cans of Coca-Cola and handed them to mother and son who were still breathing hard and unable to look each other in the eye.

Jane kept telling herself that it was good news. She now had Nick in sight. She wouldn't have to tell Charley she had lost him. Of course she had found him out on a makeshift shooting range, holding a gun and taking instructions from an elderly man whose moods were known to shift rapidly and who seemed to have an endless supply of guns fitted with suppressors — not silencers — which she now knew firsthand did not mask the sound of a rifle entirely. Thank God.

Jane wanted to hug Nick and tell him how worried she had been, but she knew this was a tricky situation that demanded more clever and up-to-date parenting. Oh, damn it, what the hell did she care. She grabbed her son and pulled him close.

"I was so worried about you. You called me and I came, and then I couldn't . . ."

"Dad said he heard shooting, and I thought he meant someone was shooting at him and so I called and then . . ."

"Lula said you'd followed Fuzzy . . ."

"I found Fuzzy by the shed, and he asked me if I'd ever fired a gun . . ."

"Janie, this boy tells me he doesn't even own a BB gun. That true?" asked Fuzzy.

Jane was so thrilled to be hugging her son and so grateful that he was hugging her back, that she forgot her canned speech about guns. She couldn't remember anything except she was against them. Against owning them, buying them, selling them, trading them, admiring them, shooting them, hunting with them, cleaning them, oiling them, displaying them, loading and unloading them.

"Yes, that's true," she answered.

"Why?" asked Fuzzy.

"I don't think they're needed by many people who have them," said Jane. "And I think when something's not needed, no good can come of it."

286

"Ever shoot one?" asked Fuzzy.

Jane shook her head.

"How do you know you're so against it then, Mom?" asked Nick.

The situation seemed to be normalizing. Nick had let go of her and was sipping his Coke. Jane realized her teeth had stopped chattering.

"I don't know, Nick. Too many bad guys have them, that's all."

"Fuzzy isn't a bad guy," said Nick.

"I don't want you shooting out here. In fact I have a feeling that Detective Munson doesn't know about this, right, Fuzzy? And for God's sake, you have *more* guns?" Jane asked, realizing that Munson had nearly had a heart attack this morning when the guns in the barn had been discovered. She had a funny feeling there was going to be an explosion when these sheds were opened.

"What is this, Fuzzy?"

"It's a club. Me and my kids used to come out here and target shoot. Sometimes they'd bring their friends and I'd teach 'em. Sullivan and his boys used to come here. This is almost on the boundary line of our places. Six rows over's Sullivan's land," said Fuzzy. "Kids all grew up and moved away, and Sullivan helped me take the shooting range down. A few years back, though, I thought, why not put it up again, maybe make a few bucks? I invited a few folks to come out, and we collected some money and got the sheds . . . people pay at the house when they come out and use the range."

"You keep guns out here?" Jane asked. "Where kids could come out and get them?"

"Soda machine. No guns. Well, I had these two out here. But the rest was all in the barn and now the police got 'em. And no kids out here unless they come with their moms and dads. And they got to be at least twelve," Fuzzy said, looking at Nick. "That's Lula's rule."

"Who comes out here, Fuzzy?" asked Jane. "The people who were at the pig roast? Are they all members?"

"And guests. I make exceptions if I like folks or if they're new in town. Dempsey and Hoover, those fellas came out here one day with some real estate people who shoot. You wouldn't think they'd know what they were doing, but that Hoover's a pretty good shot. Turns out he was in the army."

"So all those guns in the barn, they had all been fired recently? And these two?"

"Sure. But most people bring their own. Summer's the busy season. Folks getting ready for hunting in the fall; dads teaching their boys. And girls, some people bringing wives and daughters now," Fuzzy said, nodding. "Janie, this is good money. I make more off this than I do selling tomatoes by the side of the road."

Fuzzy looked off in the distance, and spoke slowly and deliberately.

"I'm too old to farm so I lease a lot of the land to other people who farm it and give me part of the crop. I need to leave my kids something so I can't lose this place. Out on the other side of town, Rutland cut a corn maze through his field. Sells pumpkins in October and makes a haunted house, gives wagon rides and such. Wife goes out to the Jewel and buys apple juice, and they come home and pour it into old jars and sell it as fresh cider. Come November they let somebody from the city drive a truck in and set up a tree lot, and he has his wife buying wholesale cookies and wrapping them up on chipped plates and making 'em look homemade. They make a buck, but it's a lot of bullshit. I started charging people a fee to belong to my club out here, and all I got to do is make sure it don't get too muddy out there so people can go out and change their targets without sinking into the ground. And I charge my members something every time they come out here, too."

"Fuzzy, it's so dangerous. What if someone got hurt, if somebody had an accident out here?"

"Nobody has. Hell, kid fell off Rutland's hayride and broke her arm in three places. His insurance went sky-high. Everybody here watches out for everybody else. Nobody's a hotdog out here. We're all about safety."

"Don't people need a license or something to shoot a gun? Do you check on that stuff?" asked Jane.

" 'Sides, who's going to sue me? Somebody get hurt out here, I throw the hay bales into the grove back there for the deer, throw the targets in the fire, and park a few tractors out here. Then I accuse them of trespassing and using my land for their target practice."

"If they don't even have a license, and all this then gets traced to you . . . ," Jane began, but stopped herself. Who was this? Not Fuzzy Neilson. This man was a stranger.

"I made all them silencers like I learned about in England so we don't disturb anybody. Lula says she can't hear a thing from the house."

"Lula really approves of all this?"

"She's a helluva shot. Almost won the little ladies tournament we had last summer," said Fuzzy.

"You have contests?" asked Nick, standing up with his Coke can, looking for a place to put it. "Recycling bin?"

"Sure we do," said Fuzzy, taking the can. "We keep these. Some people still like to hear that sound of a can being hit."

"Does Sullivan know about this? That you rebuilt the shooting range?" asked Jane.

"This is a secret," Fuzzy whispered.

Jane saw the strange light flash in his eyes again when Fuzzy started whispering. She heard voices and could see flashes of clothes through the rows of corn. People were coming into the clearing.

"It's not going to be a secret anymore, Fuzzy," Jane whispered back.

"Holy shit. Go open up those sheds and see if he has any machine guns or cannons or grenade launchers in there," said Munson to two uniformed police officers who were following him and Charley.

"Hey, Dad," said Nick, "can I learn to shoot?"

"Not today," said Charley, putting his arm around Jane.

"Fuzzy, you son of a bitch, I'm arresting you right now," said Munson.

Fuzzy looked straight ahead, seeming not to hear.

"You don't really believe he shot Johnny Sullivan, do you?" asked Jane. She wasn't sure that she didn't believe it, but what she did or didn't believe wasn't going to affect where Fuzzy slept tonight. And he didn't seem capable of speaking up for himself right now.

"I'm arresting Fuzzy on a weapons charge. He's in violation of the Firearm Owner's Identification Card Act for every one of those guns in his arsenal, not to mention all the ammo. And on top of that, looks like he's been running an unsanctioned rifle range also in violation of the state law. That'll keep everybody busy long enough for all the tests to come back about the gun that shot Johnny Sullivan."

"But even if you find out he was shot with one of the guns from out here or the barn," said Jane, "how are you going to know who fired it? He has a whole club; people who come out here and shoot these guns."

"You want to know the best reason for

me to arrest Fuzzy Neilson right now?" asked Munson. "Because if I don't arrest him, I'll probably strangle him with my bare hands."

Jane looked at Fuzzy, who was staring hard into the cornfields. If he was listening to them discuss his future, he showed no sign.

"Can we do anything? Can he be released into our custody?" asked Jane.

"Let's start with the *custody* part before we get to the *released into* part. First, we get him into mine, then we'll see where we go next, okay?" Munson said. He called over a young woman officer and Bostick, who seemed to have survived the morning's harangue.

Charley was reassuring Nick that they were going to help Fuzzy, and the trouble he was now in had nothing to do with Nick being out on the shooting range.

"I don't think Fuzzy knew how much trouble he could get into with all this," said Charley.

"He was just trying to make ends meet; he wanted to keep the farm," said Jane, "for his children."

"If I hear one more sad-sack story about trying to hold on to the family farm, I'm going to explode," said Munson. He faced

Jane and spoke quickly and quietly, looking over his shoulder to make sure that his people were just out of earshot. "These farmers own more than half the county, and they keep crying about how they're going to lose it. My folks had to sell their house after my dad retired because my mom got sick and they couldn't make the payments. My brother lost his job when Roper closed and couldn't ever find anything that paid him enough to keep the place his family had, and he and his wife split up and you know why? Money. Lack of it. A lot of people have had hard times, and they haven't started target practice in their basements. Any ideas about what might have happened if a bunch of teenagers ever came out here with a case of beer one night?"

"Nobody can tell me what to do with my land. Nobody can make me sell it," said Fuzzy.

It was Fuzzy's voice, but behind his eyes the man was AWOL. He kept repeating that it was his land, and when Bostick took his arm, Fuzzy's tone became almost conversational.

"My land and you can't make me do anything I don't want to do. It's my land and nobody is telling me what I can do with it," he was saying, as they walked him back to the corn path.

"We have to talk to Lula," said Jane. "He's not right."

"How long have you known Fuzzy?" asked Munson, as they all walked back toward the house.

"He's been coming to the EZ Way Inn forever. I can't remember *not* knowing him."

"Fuzzy Neilson ever been right?"

Jane didn't answer Munson. She didn't want to debate Fuzzy's mental acumen with Munson or anyone else. She was actually trying to remember the first time she ever saw the man. Sitting at one of the tables at the EZ Way Inn had been such a constant of her childhood, she realized there were no "firsts" associated with the customers. Like parents or cousins or grandparents, they were always there, entwined with memories of songs that played, favorite teachers, books, and best friends.

Jane could trace her picker instincts back to the tavern and the people there. She spotted the Buffalo China that she remembered from Nellie's lunches at the rummage sales, snapped it up and set a table with it, picked the right colorful tablecloths, and mismatched the right Depression Glasses to make people smile, to make them feel that they were in familiar territory. Jane associated the restaurant pots and pans, the clunky glassware, the advertising clocks, the Bakelite perpetual desk calendars that the beer salesmen dropped by with the tavern and its people.

Fuzzy had not only shown up every day, flashing her a smile and tossing her a quarter for the jukebox, he always sat down and talked to her. He asked her what her favorite vegetables and flowers were; and if he had them growing at home, he remembered to bring them to her. When she had told him she liked pretty rocks — a long childhood before she met Charley and had shifted her collecting allegiances away from his — Fuzzy picked up rocks he found that he thought she might like. When he and Lula went on vacation, he always brought her back a rock. She set them on the windowsill in her bedroom, rose quartz from South Dakota and an agate from where? Arizona? A fossil from a stream in Wisconsin. He always remembered. What had he told her? He liked rocks, too, and shells, and foreign coins that looked prettier than plain old American nickels and dimes.

"Pick something up to remember a place by," he told her almost every time he saw her; "that's why God made pockets."

Back at the house, Lula paced back and forth. She had refused to call their son or their daughter. They both lived with spouses and children in California — William in Oakland and Mary Lee in San Diego.

"They've got jobs and kids. I can't be asking them to come here. I don't even know what to tell them," Lula said. She looked at Munson. "What do I tell them, Franklin? You played basketball with William; you were his good friend. You tell me what to tell him."

"Lula, I don't want any harm to come to Fuzzy or anyone else, but I've got to get to the bottom of this," said Munson. "We've already lost Johnny Sullivan, and we've got to piece together what happened." He asked Jane to call Don and Nellie. "Maybe they can help Lula figure out what to do here. Call a lawyer and all. I can't get anymore involved in this with her," he said to Jane in a low voice. "I've got to put on another hat now" — he sighed — "and keep it on."

Jane left Nick and Charley with Lula. Bostick was explaining to Fuzzy that he might want to bring some things for overnight in case he had to stay at the police station.

Fuzzy had that faraway look in his eyes, but he nodded.

"Lula?" he said. "Are there cinnamon rolls left? Can you pack me up some for my dinner?" He smiled his old smile. "And, I guess, for my breakfast?"

"Mrs. Wheel, does your father know a lawyer?" asked Oh. "Mrs. Neilson doesn't seem to know anyone."

Jane called her parents' home. Don answered, and although she could hear Nellie asking questions in the background, Don held the receiver firmly enough so that Jane was spared the inquisition — for the moment. Better Nellie should come and see it all for herself. After she hung up, Jane realized that she didn't know if Don knew about the shooting range. Soon enough. They were on their way.

Jane walked outside, and Oh fell into step beside her.

"Mrs. Wheel, I owe you an explanation."

Jane tried to think of a statement, any statement, that Oh could make that would surprise her more than that simple declaration. It might have been because she was worn out, but she couldn't think of a thing.

"I discouraged you from thinking of this as your case when you first phoned me about Mr. Johnny Sullivan. I was wrong."

Jane realized her mouth was slightly open, and she closed it.

"I was worried you would feel drawn in because it was Kankakee. I worried that it would turn out to be a domestic violence case, something uncomplicated that could be handled by Detective Munson, and that you would lose your . . ." Oh stopped and searched for a word. "Zest."

"My 'zest' is important?"

"Zest is vital. As is compassion. Everyone will tell you that compassion can blind you to the truth. It can also be the driving force behind finding the truth."

"The Fuzzy I know didn't kill anyone," said Jane. "But I saw him out there in the yard that night . . . and there is a Fuzzy that I don't know. He's . . ."

"Mrs. Neilson may not know if they have a lawyer," said Oh, "but ask her if they have a doctor."

When Don and Nellie arrived, they split up and circled the people there. Don went over to Lula, handed her the card of his lawyer, and told her that he had already called him, and he would be waiting at the police station to help get Fuzzy home as soon as possible. Nellie made a beeline for Fuzzy and looked him in the eye. "What have you done now?"

"Nothing much, Nellie," he said.

"You tell everybody the truth, you'll be okay. Understand?"

Fuzzy nodded. Bostick came over to tell him it was time to go, and Fuzzy got up with no protest, no fight.

Jane followed him to the door. She reached into her pocket and pulled out the pennies she had been carrying since she had picked them out of the rose garden. "Why do you bury stuff, Fuzzy?"

Fuzzy smiled and put a hand on her head. "So you'll find it and remember me," he said. "That's why God made pockets."

Chapter 14

Nellie went upstairs with Lula. Jane left Don, Charley, and Oh drinking a cup of tea at the dining room table and went into the kitchen. Although Nick knew his way around a stove, liked to cook, and even had a repertoire of breakfast specialties and sandwich combinations larger than Jane's own, she hadn't thought of him as a scrubber and cleaner, a Nellifier of the kitchen. But here he was, her son who lived the life of a middle-school jock except when he was spirited away to a digging site by Charley and his inner geology geek could secretly and safely emerge, washing dishes. His arms were in soapy water up to his elbows, and he was using steel wool in a brownie pan. Jane feared for the pan.

"It's my fault. I shouldn't have called you when I heard Dad talking. Should have left it alone and listened to the end of the story. Then I followed Fuzzy. If you hadn't seen me there with that gun, you wouldn't have let them take him away."

"Nick, no one could have stopped this.

Fuzzy has a shooting range. He keeps guns out there, he . . ."

"Just because you think there shouldn't be guns doesn't make them wrong for everybody. You say people should make up their own minds about stuff, but there's stuff you don't even listen to other opinions on. You decided guns were bad a long time ago, and instead of just letting Fuzzy have a different opinion, you're letting the police take him away."

Jane took a deep breath. For twelve years or so you can watch them and feed them and fool yourself that you're molding them into the shape you've chosen, then one day you look at your child and you don't recognize something. Maybe it's a new expression, or a dismissive gesture, or maybe, like now with Nick, it's the challenge in their eyes.

"I've never liked guns. It's true. I didn't grow up around them. Your grandfather never hunted or took Uncle Michael and me out to shoot at targets. I never went to a camp that had a rifle range. It's all foreign territory for me, Nick," said Jane, "but I swear that has nothing to do with what's going on with Fuzzy. Munson took him in because he was out there when Johnny Sullivan got shot. I saw him." Jane added, "And he hasn't been himself lately."

"He's out there all the time," said Nick. "He told me he can hardly sleep anymore, and he likes to garden in the moonlight. He told me that if he plants certain flowers at night, they grow taller because they learn to grow by the light of the moon as well as the sun."

Jane looked at her son who, at last, smiled at his mother's wide eyes.

"No, I know that's not true, but it's a great story. Fuzzy is a storyteller, Mom. You think if he shot that guy, if he thought he'd caught a trespasser or something, he would keep it a secret?" asked Nick. "Fuzzy talks all the time about everything. If he really did something or had some kind of adventure, you don't think he'd talk about it?"

Nellie had packed a suitcase for Lula and wrapped up food to take to the police station since Lula insisted that Fuzzy would be hungry. Even though Don and Detective Oh and Charley and Jane all assured the two women that Fuzzy would be ready to come home in a few hours — that they all should just go to the police station and be ready to take him home — Nellie insisted that Lula was coming home with her and that they would wait for the call there.

"If I leave her here, she'll be up all night cooking and roaming the house. She needs to sleep. We're closer to the police station," Nellie told Jane, "and I'm sending your dad there to make sure everything gets ironed out."

"Good," said Jane. "Fuzzy couldn't have killed anybody."

"That's the most ridiculous thing I ever heard," said Nellie.

"Right," said Jane.

"No," said Nellie. "It's ridiculous what you said. Of course he could kill somebody."

"What do . . ."

"Why the hell not? Who doesn't want to kill somebody half the time? Shoot, if I had a gun at that tavern, I'd probably kill somebody every day." Nellie dropped her voice to a rough whisper. "Now as soon as I get Lula out of here, you go check in her medicine cabinet. She's giving Fuzzy medicine for something. Made me pack it, but I left another bottle in there. Made me promise not to talk about it, but you can go in there and see it for yourself."

Jane surveyed the 110 pounds of contradictions and contrariness that was her mother. On the one hand she could kill somebody every day, and on the other, she was scrupulous about keeping a promise to a friend — and sneaky enough to find a way to tell without telling.

"And if those Sullivans call, don't tell them anything. They're strange birds," said Nellie.

If Nellie called you a "strange bird," was it the same as a double negative? Did it mean you were really a sensible human being?

As soon as Don and Nellie left with Lula, the telephone rang. Alan Bishop, the lawyer Don had asked to meet Fuzzy at the police station, had arrived and was having some trouble communicating to Fuzzy that he was there to help him, that he was on Fuzzy's side. Jane asked Charley and Oh to go down there right away.

"You can stop at Don and Nellie's and pick up Lula and one or both of my parents, but then get right over to the station. If Fuzzy gets disoriented, he acts fierce and I don't want Munson to start imagining any . . . you know. I'll stay here," said Jane, who didn't want to mention the medicine cabinet yet. She supposed that made her fairly scrupulous about secrets, too. She figured she might as well see what, if anything, was significant, before sounding an alarm. Besides, what if she found out that Fuzzy was on some kind of antipsychotic medicine? Wouldn't that make it more likely people would think Fuzzy had done the shooting? Start the lawyer strategizing about the deal he could make? An insanity defense might get Fuzzy off; but if Fuzzy didn't do it, it would only distract and delay them from finding the real killer.

"I don't like leaving you and Nick here alone," said Charley.

"I can see five police out the kitchen window. And there are probably more down at the cornfield and along the corn path. Munson's got them swarming the place. If another gun shows up, he'll shoot the one who brings it to him," said Jane. "We'll be fine."

Nick asked Jane if he could go out to the shed and keep going through Fuzzy's collection boxes, the ones shelved and sealed that Munson had said were okay to catalog. Jane walked over there with him and was assured by Bostick that someone would be at the shed door at all times. If Nick finished and wanted to return to the house, someone would walk him the thirty feet to the house.

"He won't be alone or out of sight for a minute," said Bostick.

"You're a better parent than I am," said Jane.

Returning to Fuzzy and Lula's house, escorted by a young woman police officer, Jane decided to work her way up to the bathroom. She walked through the kitchen and admired Lula's pantry, as neatly and efficiently organized as any Jane had ever seen. Lula's own canned tomatoes, green beans, pickles, jams, fruit butters, and chutneys. Jane had seen templates for making canning jar labels on her computer . . . retro, gingham trimmed, and folksy, but next to the real thing — masking tape and Lula's careful penmanship with a Sharpie marker, EARLY WONDER BEANS — those labels would be precious and out of place. So many people Jane's age and younger played at being farmwives, buying country antiques on a fall weekend and purposely mismatching dishes and silverplate at the dinner table. Jane would have to admit to a bit of Lulafying activity of her own — all those vintage linens, hand-smocked aprons, crocheted potholders, and Lu-Ray dinnerware on her shelves.

Lula would pronounce all the studied authenticity ridiculous. Farmers don't use chipped crockery and old cast iron because they think it looks cool and real, they use what they have because it's what they have, and there's nothing wrong with it — no excuse to replace it. And when they do replace it? It will be with something practical and sturdy and new. They will not look for something quaint and authentic at a rummage sale. Lula's name for "retro" would be *used*. And why the hell would she want something that someone else had already used up?

On the other hand, Lula didn't rid her kitchen of objects lightly. Even dishes that were sixty or more years old held their place in the cabinet as long as they were still viable.

Lula had some Hall Autumn Leaf kitchenware and Jane smiled to see it stacked and ready to use, instead of artfully arranged in a glass-front cabinet. Straight-sided ramekins and custard cups and an Aladdin teapot. Should she tell Lula that Tim could sell it for her at a good price? Jane didn't think she would care. She'd just have to buy new, and it wouldn't be as good.

Lula had a large Miss America Glass cake stand in the dining room. Jane had been tempted by one at an antique mall that she thought had been marked around two hundred. Lula used hers for breakfast pastries every day. Jane walked over and ran her hand around the edge. She couldn't feel one chip, not even a tiny flea-bite. A beautiful piece of Depression Glass. Jane had to make sure Tim didn't offer to come in here and tell Lula what to put out for the garage sale. He'd buy everything up for his own house or shop before it ever saw the light of sale.

Family photographs lined the stairway. Jane remembered Fuzzy and Lula's children, William and Mary Lee, but they had been just old enough to ignore her completely on the few occasions they had met. William, at least ten years older than Jane, was a grandfather already. Lula had hung a picture of her great grandson at the top of the stairs. He was dressed in a pumpkin costume for Halloween and was posed sitting amid pumpkins in Fuzzy's garden. Jane winced at the sight of the cornfields in the background. That fall, when baby boy here was toddling in the pumpkin patch, no one watching from the sidelines or standing behind the camera could have anticipated how this view of the farm would be forever transformed. The same vegetable patch sans pumpkin vines instead entangled with crime-scene tape.

In the bathroom Lula had shown her characteristic organization. As soon as they arrived, she had invited Charley and Nick and Jane to shower and use this bathroom during their stay. Jane noticed that although they had all hung towels over the shower door that morning, there were now three freshly laundered bath towels and washrags for the guests folded into squares on the counter.

On the other side of the vanity, everything was in its place. A wooden natural bristle hairbrush, a rat-tail comb, a large jar of generic cold cream, a bottle of Cornhuskers Lotion, and Vaseline. These items all pointed to an economical but efficient nightly beauty routine. Lula might not be up on Botox injections and niacin lip plumpers, but she knew the most important rule of skin care . . . moisturize, moisturize, moisturize.

Jane opened the medicine cabinet and felt that she had now invaded Fuzzy's territory. Metamucil, tiny curved scissors for trimming in small private places, several sizes of corn and callus pads, and toothbrushes. On the bottom shelf, a row of prescription bottles. Jane jotted down the names of the medication on the two bottles that belonged to Fuzzy — she recognized neither of them — and noted that Lula had a half empty bottle of Effexor. Wrong. These were antidepressants; this bottle was half *full*. Jane checked the date the medication had been prescribed. Lula had been taking an antidepressant for six months? That was odd. It wasn't impossible to believe that someone in Lula's position might need some help — she was aging and her children and grandchildren lived far away. Her husband, always a handful, was now behaving even more irrationally. And they had all this land that had to be worked, leased, managed, or, perhaps, sold. No, it was clear why Lula might *need* to visit a doctor and start a course of antidepressants, it was just highly unusual that Lula, a kindred spirit of Nellie, *would* seek help.

When she was in college, Jane had told her mother that she was feeling pretty low and had seen a school psychologist a few times. Nellie was shocked that Jane would share anything personal and private with a complete stranger, especially a doctor.

"They keep records of that stuff, you know," Nellie had told her.

"But, Mom, I was in such pain," said Jane.

"So?" Nellie asked. "Who told you you

weren't supposed to be in pain?"

So much for Jane's flirtation with existentialism as an alternative to Nellie — her mother suffered existential angst with the best of them, she just combined it with one-part paranoia and two-parts stoicism for a winning cocktail of neurosis.

Jane wrote down the names of the doctors who had prescribed the medications and stepped into the Neilsons' bedroom. Without removing the perfectly smooth white-and-blue chenille bedspread, Jane knew she would be able to bounce a quarter on the tautly pulled sheets. Neurotic maybe, but the Nellies and Lulas of the world were to be marveled at, too. They had energy and discipline in their housework and in their cooking, but what they did in and to their homes was more than cleaning and fixing meals.

They took such fierce pride in doing it all right. All the homemaking gurus and shelter magazines and television decorating programs in the world weren't going to make Jane's generation and the ones that followed hers any better at what these older women did as a matter of course. Nellie and Lula worked a solid sixteen hours every single day of their lives without ever once complaining about time for themselves, and they always got the damn beds made. Who was ever going to do it right when they were gone?

Jane walked over to the small oak desk in front of the bedroom window. Two 8 x 10 envelopes were lying open on top of the calendar blotter. Jane had felt authorized by her mother and her concern for what Fuzzy was going through to check out the medicine cabinet, but snooping in the bedroom was Jane's own spur-of-the moment decision. If the envelopes hadn't been right there, Jane told herself, she wouldn't have picked them up. She wouldn't have searched through drawers or pawed through files to find them but these envelopes, one with a familiar return address — K3 Realty — and the other with a name she also recognized in the upper left corner — Joseph Dempsey/Hometown USA — were too obvious to ignore.

Jane opened the letter from K3 Realty first and, by force of an old, work-related, memo-skimming habit, read it from the bottom up. It was signed by Henry Bennett. Glancing over the body of the text, Jane thought, at least from this cursory read through, that it was a standard form letter, offering to be of service if they decided it was time to "reassess their property needs."

The letter from Dempsey was more intriguing. It was some kind of a document . . . an option to buy a certain parcel of land. It didn't actually look like a sales contract or an invoice; it was an option to buy the land within the next five years or in the event of the owner's death. The language was confusing, but the gist of the agreement seemed to be that the owner would receive a small amount of money up front and give Hometown USA exclusive purchase rights that would expire in five years. It didn't seem binding exactly, since it stated that the seller was under no obligation to sell at all. Was this legal? Locking people into a price and a promise like this? Jane didn't know much about property prices in Kankakee County, but this seemed low. Nonetheless, both Fuzzy and Lula had signed on the bottom line.

Jane heard the kitchen door and felt as guilty as a teenager. Worse. She felt as guilty as a teenager's mom.

"Nick? I'm upstairs, just coming down."

What if Nick caught her snooping here and jumped to the conclusion that if she were nosing around in the Neilsons' bedroom, she would certainly be going through her son's room at home? Absolutely false. Jane prided herself on her respect for her son's privacy — she only read things that were left out face up and that didn't require touching. In other words, if a note from one of Nick's friends was folded in half and Jane would actually have to pick it up, unfold it, and smooth it out to read, she would not do it. If the same note were on his bed unfolded, peeking out from under something that she could legitimately pick up and put away — say his jacket or soccer shin guards — she allowed herself to read what was visible. She could contort herself into any position to read something thrown into a corner or slid under the bed, as long as she did not touch the paper, postcard, notebook itself. She was a curious and caring mother, sure, but she had her standards. Like Nick, she had watched *Law & Order*, and knew how far Briscoe and his partner were allowed to go when looking for evidence in a suspect's house. She knew the drill, too.

Jane replaced the envelopes on the desk, trying to make them look undisturbed. She kept equating Lula's household skills with Nellie's, but what about her eye for trespassers? Was it as sharp as Jane's mother's? Nellie could tell what Jane had worn to school by looking at her closet and seeing which items had been rehung crookedly.

She could skim the garbage can in the kitchen and name Jane's after-school snack. She knew if Jane had done her homework in front of the television by counting the wrinkles in the couch cushions. Mail in disarray on a desk — Nellie would have Jane cold — knowing that she peeked, of course, but would also be able to tell in what order she had read the letters. Jane squinted at the desk, trying to remember if the K3 Realty letter had been on top. Or was it the Hometown papers? She picked up that envelope and held it over the desk, trying again to picture it.

"I got one of those, too."

Jane jumped at the unexpected voice and made a sound between a scream and a stifled scream. As frightening as it was to see Jack Sullivan watching her from the doorway, she told herself that he was a grieving old man who had just come up because he thought Lula had called down to him that she was upstairs. He was no one to fear or scream about. Besides, the farm was crawling with police. Shouldn't they have stopped Sullivan, though? Or did the father of the victim have some freedom in roaming the scene of the crime?

"I took the shortcut," he said.

Jane nodded. Nellie had said not to tell

the Sullivans about Fuzzy. Jane didn't bother at the time to inform her mother that the Sullivans, strange birds or not, were the grieving parents who had hired Jane to find out who killed their son, Johnny. If she happened to see them, she didn't tell her mother that she might feel some obligation to offer them something.

"Take the corn path to the property line. When you hit Fuzzy's land, you walk through the soybeans right up alongside the flower garden. Lula's got a path in there through the roses that you can't see from the yard. Takes you right alongside the house, then boom, you're at the porch steps."

"Can I make you a cup of coffee?" asked Jane. His explanation of getting into the house, unseen by everyone, made her want to be on the first floor — the well-lit, well-patrolled first floor of the house.

"Regular or decaf?"

"I can make decaf," said Jane. She realized it was almost nine. Had anyone eaten dinner today? Where had the hours gone? "I need to see if my . . ." Jane stopped herself from saying the word "son." "Would you like some decaf?"

"I'm eighty something," said Sullivan. "What the heck do I want to sleep for? Regular."

Jane laughed and walked toward him standing at the door. She felt some relief, but she still didn't like being trapped in the room. She had never liked being in a room with someone blocking the door. It awakened all of her latent claustrophobia. She could stand crowded spaces as long as the exit was open and available. Time to take the lead on this one.

Jane hooked her hand through Sullivan's left arm and gently turned him and walked with him into the hall. Feeling how frail his arm felt under his cotton, zip-up jacket, she was ashamed of her own anxiety. How could this man hurt her?

"I brought my gun," he said, pulling some kind of pistol out of his pocket with his right hand.

Yes, right, that's how. What was it with guns these days? Did everyone except Jane have one?

"In case the killer was out there," he said, "and knew the shortcut, too."

He put the gun away without Jane having to ask, and they walked downstairs and into the kitchen. Jane checked from the kitchen window and could see Nick through the lit window of the shed. He was sitting at the high, wooden counter, his head bent over a box of Fuzzy's various finds, his stuff.

Jane opened up the porch door and poked her head out. Never a cop around when you need one. But Jane had an old comfort trick she had invented for herself when she was a latchkey kid. When she used to walk home from St. Pat's and arrive at her empty house, she worried that someone might have followed her. If someone was stalking her all the way to 801 Cobb Boulevard and then saw that she entered a house where no one waited for her, what would stop the bad guy from walking right up to her door? Her trick for fooling this villain in her head was to always unlock the door, throw it wide open, and yell, "Hi Mom, hi Dad, I'm home," and then — and this was the best part of the invention because any bad guy would know that the greeting was only her side of the conversation, easily faked — she answered her imaginary parents' imaginary question. "Yeah, a great day. How about you guys?" and closed the door behind her, locking it once, then twice by snapping the deadbolt into place. Hah! No bad guy would bother with someone who was coming home to not just one parent but two. As she got older, Jane realized that the phantom bad guy would also be unlikely to bother someone crazy enough to be carrying on a conversation with dead air. It was a win-win situation.

"Bostick and Miles?" Jane said to the empty porch. "I'm making coffee for Mr. Sullivan here. Would you like a cup?" Jane nodded to the darkness. "Okey-dokey, then. I'll call you when it's ready."

Childhood fears might translate into adult traumas for some, but Jane had become more of a believer in the "use it or lose it" school of neurosis. If you couldn't make sense of your lousy childhood by weaving its trials and tribulations into your adult life, you might as well give up and plop down on the couch. It would be a long bumpy ride through analysis. Jane was beginning, and just beginning, to learn that Nellie's questionable people skills — as applied to her own family anyway — might have been the ideal preparation for adult life. After all, what did a happy, saccharine childhood really prepare you for? The cold cruel world of adulthood? Hardly. Maybe it was time to stop blaming Nellie and Don for not being June and Ward Cleaver and start thanking them. Jane looked over at raisin-faced Jack Sullivan, sitting down at the table unzipping his jacket with the gun in its pocket, and offered up a silent thanks to good old antisocial Nellie. She had prepared Jane to be a private detective as well as anyone could. Expect the worst. Be suspicious. Strike the first blow. Believe no one. Be tough. Figure everyone for a strange bird. Thanks, Mom.

"Mr. Sullivan," said Jane, measuring out the coffee for Lula's ancient percolator, noting that this was one kitchen item that she didn't regard as desirable vintage. This was just an old electric coffeepot that, Jane was pretty sure, would make vile-tasting coffee. "Upstairs I was holding an envelope, and you said you had one like it? What did you mean?"

"Letter from that Joe Dempsey and Mikey Hoover. They're going to make my farm into a fishing ranch."

Jane stopped spooning out the coffee.
"Mikey?"

"He knew Phillip. They were in the service together. Now he's hooked up with Dempsey, and they're going to make a million."

"By making your farm into a fishing ranch?" Jane asked.

"If I let 'em," said Sullivan. "Got some cookies to go with that?"

"Did they offer to buy your farm?" asked Jane.

"Yup. They're making this whole town into a tourist place. And when I told Dempsey that the best part of my farm was the fishing hole, he said that's exactly why they needed it. They wanted to make a kind of fishing dude ranch. Parents and their kids, bringing picnics and fishing, and then we'd have a place where people would clean up their catch and they could bring it home. Or maybe we'd have grills so people could cook 'em up right there. We'd sell bait and rent out poles and such."

Jane had seen that same dreamy look on her dad's face when Dempsey had talked about making the old stove factory into a big-band ballroom. He was good, this Dempsey. He stared into the eyes of these old men, picked up the threads of their young man's dreams, and wove them into a fantasy he could offer them; all they had to do was to sell them their property, and he would turn it into whatever they wanted.

"Elizabeth told Dempsey that we might like to stay on at our farm, and he said we could do that, no problem. We'd sell them the property, then they'd rent back our house to us for as long we wanted."

"Have you already signed the papers? Are you giving them the option?" asked

Jane. She opened up the cupboard from where, this morning, she had glimpsed Lula filling a plate with cookies. Holy Toledo. Lula Neilson's everyday cookie jar was Smiley Pig, made by Shawnee in 1942. It was not the model that was all-over gold and platinum — that could have sold for over eight hundred dollars to a collector. But it was Smiley with a green neckerchief with a hand-painted shamrock, with gold, so it could go up to four hundred dollars at auction. And filled with Lula's fresh oatmeal raisin bars, as the credit card commercial spokesman might intone, *Priceless*.

"Johnny asked us to wait. He wanted us to get the best price, he said, but Elizabeth thought maybe he was thinking about coming back to farm. I knew he wasn't. He's no farmer."

Jane's eyes burned at the present tense.

"Hell, he's too old to change now. I told Elizabeth just 'cause he was our baby boy and we still called him Johnny, he's no spring chicken," said Sullivan. "Elizabeth's just a kid. She's just seventy-five or something like that, so she doesn't really see the world like I do. Still thinks people will change and things'll turn out different every time. But I told her they don't.

Things turn out the same."

Jane set out their coffee cups and cream and sugar. Jack Sullivan poured in an inch of cream and loaded his coffee with sugar. Then he took three oatmeal bars and set them on the saucer.

"Find out who killed Johnny yet?"

Jane watched the old man dunk the cookie into his coffee and take a big bite. He half closed his eyes as he chewed. She thought he looked so content and lost in the sweetness of his snack that she might not have to answer his question.

"I came over to tell you all that I know you found the guns out at the shooting range. And I was wondering if it was one of those guns that killed my boy."

"The police don't know yet."

"What do you know different from the police?"

Jane shook her head. "So Johnny knew about the fishing ranch? You discussed it with him?"

"Yes."

"And he asked you not to sell?"

Sullivan nodded.

"Did he tell you why?"

"Said we'd have to read about it in the papers like everybody else," said Sullivan. "But he said we'd be thanking him. I thought he was being ornery not telling us; but Elizabeth was so happy he was coming home every weekend, she said we had to do whatever he said. He'd been to college, he worked at the paper, she said he knew more than we did."

Jane got up to pour more coffee, but Sullivan covered his cup with his hand.

"I had enough, thanks. I just drink it for the cookies anyway," said Sullivan. "Better save the rest for those policemen. You forget their cups?" He stood up and put his jacket on. Jack Sullivan lifted his chin and looked down his nose through his bifocals at her. "You know, those policemen that were supposed to be on the porch?"

Jane nodded. Round one, Sullivan.

"How did you know that the police found the shooting range, Mr. Sullivan?"

"Don't you know the old joke about why you're not supposed to tell secrets in a cornfield?" he asked.

Jane shook her head and Sullivan whispered, "Too many ears."

Chapter 15

Jane filled Tim in over breakfast at Pink's. The diner perched on the Kankakee riverbank was an all-night, greasier-than-your-average greasy spoon. All-night was the operative segment of the description since Pink's was not open twenty-four hours. Instead Old Pink, who had been succeeded in business by Pink Junior, had found the winning strategy for a successful Kankakee restaurant. Open the doors around midnight and serve the over-tipping, after-bar-closing crowd who need the hangover preventative of a full breakfast, heavy on the fried potatoes, before falling into their beds; and, as a secondary market, the under-tipping teenagers who were defiant of and/or unbound by curfews, yet had nowhere in their little old town to go to get their party on. Close and lock those doors around 10:00 a.m., maybe 11:00 if Pink had a full pot of coffee he didn't want to waste, wash the dishes, sweep the floor, go home, and sleep in front of a baseball game until it was time to come back and scrape the grease off the grill and start over. In the winter Pink Junior disappeared altogether for two or three months, and the restaurant had a CLOSED UNTIL? sign in the window. Then one day in early April, to herald spring, the first robin appeared, and a small grease fire broke out when Pink Junior started cooking again.

"So Fuzzy was officially arrested?" asked Tim.

Jane shook her head. "At least not yet. The lawyer said that if they matched the gun that killed Johnny to one of the twenty-twos that Fuzzy had in his possession, he'd likely be charged. They just questioned him to death. When Dad and Oh brought him home, I asked Fuzzy if he remembered being outside that night, if he remembered that he spoke to me from the outhouse."

Jane accepted more toast from Pink and nodded that she also wanted more coffee. Lots more. Pink brought over the thermal carafe and set it on the table.

"Fuzzy's answer was that he never used the outhouse. Outhouses were a crime against nature, he said. He was exhausted, couldn't focus at all, and when he looked around and couldn't find Lula, he became so agitated, I thought" — Jane broke off for a moment and put more strawberry jam on her toast — "I thought it was a good thing Munson wasn't there to see it."

"Where was Lula?"

"Pacing the floor at my mom and dad's house. Nellie couldn't get Lula to sit or sleep, but Fuzzy said he didn't want her to come to the police station, said it wasn't any place for a woman. But when he got home . . . he went a little crazy. He walked from room to room looking for her, wouldn't listen to where she was, wouldn't accept the phone to talk to her. In fact he looked at the phone like he had never seen one before. Oh helped me with him while Dad went and picked Lula up and brought her back home. She walked in, went directly to the refrigerator, and whipped up a plate of food and sat Fuzzy down with it and a glass of buttermilk and he was a lamb. It's like she puts something in it," said Jane.

"Come on," said Tim, unwinding the spiral dough of a homemade cinnamon bun and eating it piece by doughy piece. "All Lula has to put in her food is food. I mean she's a wonderful cook, but basically she just soothes him with the familiar. Like we're doing for ourselves right now. Nobody comes to Pink's for the haute cuisine." Tim lowered his voice to a whisper.

"This food is terrible, but it's our personal and intimate terrible, so it does the trick."

"I hoped you'd still be here," said Bruce Oh, whom neither Tim nor Jane had seen or heard come in.

Pink brought over a cup, a tea bag, and a pot of hot water and set it down between Jane and Tim.

Neither one of them had seen Oh order anything.

"Claire told me she was meeting you at your floral shop at noon, Mr. Lowry. She said the garage-sale plans are going well," said Oh, sitting and removing the tea bag from its package.

"And Jane tells me that you were Fuzzy's best friend last night," said Tim.

"Mr. Neilson had a terrible night," said Oh.

"Tim, can I have your BlackBerry?" asked Jane, remembering that she had meant to check the names of the drugs prescribed to Fuzzy first thing this morning. Tim assured her she could "Google" on his tiny electronic "assistant" and once again Jane felt at least four incarnations removed from the "very latest in technology." It didn't matter. While she was typing on this current miraculous machine, something newer had probably been invented, test marketed, sold, reviewed, and been declared obsolete.

"I've done some checking at Mr. Johnny Sullivan's newspaper to find out if he was well liked, if he had enemies there," said Oh. He waited while Jane typed a name into the BlackBerry. "It was unusual. There's really not much of an office associated with his work on the paper. He works for the edition of the paper that serves the south suburban communities of Chicago, and most people who work for it are freelance reporters. No office culture. In fact, no office at all. His editor had only met him in person three times. Very little salary. Mr. Sullivan lived in a very small and cheap apartment. According to his landlord, he was behind on his rent."

"Maybe the landlord's a tough guy, wanted to teach him a lesson?" said Tim.

"Some lesson," said Jane. "He can't pay, so he gets killed? What kind of business savvy is that — kill somebody because they can't pay?"

"Yeah, I guess all those stories about bookies and gambling bosses putting out hits on guys who don't pay up are ugly rumors," said Tim. "Memo to the mob: Stop hurting people; it's not good business."

Jane turned her attention back to the BlackBerry.

"Hey, look, it's Mr. Hyde," said Tim.

Dr. Jaekel, the acting coroner, was at the counter trying to get Pink's attention. Jane knew he would be unable to attract it — everyone in Kankakee knew that Pink ignored customers who wanted to order food or drinks to go.

"They come in to take out? Oxymoron. If they want coffee to go, let them find a Starfucks," said Pink, according to Tim, who loved to quote Pink Junior on most subjects and, Jane guessed, embellish his words to feed the man's legend.

Whenever someone pointed out to Pink that there was no Starbucks in Kankakee, he would smile and nod, suggesting that it was his point exactly; if you're too busy to sit down and eat a Pink's breakfast, you belong in another town.

"Dr. Jaekel," Jane called out, "won't you join us?"

The doctor approached the table tapping his wristwatch. "I'm just getting coffee to go. Due at a meeting."

"You're not going to get any coffee until you sit down anyway," said Tim. "If you take a seat, Pink will serve it to you in a paper cup if you ask, but he doesn't do a 'to-go' business."

"I don't understand this town," Jaekel said, through pursed lips. "People complain about no work, they complain about no business, but when you offer someone work, try to give them business, they complain that it's not the right kind of business."

"I am not sure that would be peculiar to this town," said Oh. "It sounds more like the contradictory nature of human beings. I am Bruce Oh."

Jaekel shook hands with Oh. "In town for the hometown investors' meeting?"

Jane studied Oh's face and rejoiced at her mentor's talent. His expressions were so slight, so subtle. She knew all about the stereotype of the inscrutable Oriental and, of course, deplored it. Deplored the stereotype part anyway. But the hard fact about Bruce Oh was that his face was, at times, well . . . inscrutable. It was a painting whose eyes followed you around the room, whose color changed with the light, whose minutely raised eyebrow conveyed whatever the person looking at it wanted it to convey. Jane thought she was getting better at reading the expressionless expressions, but now realized they were not designed to be without meaning; they were valuable because they were infused with any and all meanings. They allowed Oh to be whomever one wanted him to be. Right now, to Jaekel, who had made an assumption that a stranger in town, an Asian man wearing an expensive suit, with a distinctive vintage tie, must be a foreign investor. Oh, in his wisdom, allowed his eyes to be mildly curious, relaxed his mouth into an almost smile, that seemed to agree with Jaekel's assumption. All this without one spoken word, without one spoken lie.

Oh had once told Jane that if she listened exactly twice as long as she spoke, she would never have to ask another question. People hated silence so much that they would always fill in the blanks of the conversation.

Jaekel once again proved Oh right.

"I'm not going to make it to Dempsey's meeting. Police want me over at the station to discuss my report on Sullivan."

"You are an investor?" Oh asked.

Jane noticed another trick. She knew Bruce Oh had grown up in Ohio with one Eastern parent and one Western parent. She knew that although his language sometimes sounded formal, it was a reflection of the man's character — not any confusion with the English tongue. However, when he wanted to trade on his own foreignness to bring out something in another, he dropped contractions. It was a simple ploy, and it worked. He sounded as if he might stand and bow at any minute.

"Considering the proposition. Sounded interesting the first time I heard it. Of course the more I have to be in this town, the more I think Dempsey's going to have nothing but trouble getting anyone to cooperate with him. People will say it's a good idea; but as soon as anything happens, they'll do anything they can to mess it up."

"Can you tell us about the autopsy?" asked Jane.

"No," said Jaekel, standing up as Pink approached the table with his paper cup.

"Can you tell us about the bones of Otto the cat?" asked Jane.

"What about them?" Jaekel asked, as he threw a dollar on the table to cover his coffee. "I can tell you the same thing your husband can tell you. A huge waste of time. I have to drive over here when I'm filling in as Kankakee County coroner and what is normally a boring fifty-minute trip is now a frustrating two-hour drive because of road construction. I get here for a look at something that sounds interesting on the phone, and I get treated to a tour of Fuzzy Neilson's pet cemetery," said Jaekel, then straightened a little. In a more professional tone he said, "Male adult cat. Probably died naturally. I didn't really examine it. It was given a decent family burial next to the garden. Been in the ground a while, at least ten years, maybe more. Don't have any idea why they needed me. Damn government red tape."

"Who called you in?"

"Somebody from the police department. They had to determine that it wasn't a crime scene. I might have it somewhere," Jaekel began rummaging in his briefcase. "Why? What's the big deal about that cat anyway?"

"Charley was wondering who called it in and reported it as a possible site, that's all. He couldn't get anyone at the Illinois office over the weekend, and Fuzzy couldn't give him any paperwork. We were just wondering who . . ." Jane stopped when she saw Jaekel pull a small notebook out of his bag.

"I got the call from an Officer Ransford, and he said it was called in by a citizen whose name is . . ." Jaekel strung the sentence out as he squinted at his own handwriting. He held the notebook out at arm's length and then brought it close to his face.

"Rober Grayland?"

Rober Grayland? An unusual name, so why did it sound so familiar to Jane. "Roger Groveland? Could that be Roger Groveland?"

"Yes. Yes, Roger Groveland. According to my notes, he was the one who reported the Neilson property."

"What's the date? When did you get called in?"

"Three weeks ago, minus a day," said Jaekel. "I have to go. Munson will be sending a squad car. Will he give me a lid for this?" Jaekel asked, holding up the flimsy paper cup of coffee.

Jane got up, went behind the counter and picked up a lid for the paper cup. Pink Junior gave her a slight shake of his head, but smiled. Jane knew he figured it was only a matter of time before she came back to Kankakee for good and became Nellie Junior so he thought of her as a colleague. Jane handed the lid to Jaekel and resisted telling him that the lid was superfluous anyway. Pink's coffee would probably eat its way out of that cup if he didn't drink it immediately. If she wasn't going to tell him his cat skeleton case had been instigated by a dead man, she probably shouldn't tell him anything at all. Then she remembered the BlackBerry.

"Dr. Jaekel?"

He looked up from trying to get the lid on the cup with one hand without collapsing the whole mess.

"Do you know anything about a drug called Aricept?"

"Don't worry about your parents, Mrs. Wheel. Don is as sharp as a tack and, from what I've observed of Nellie, she only forgets names and dates when it's convenient for her to do so. She's crazy like a fox, your mother. Nothing wrong with her cognitive skills," said Jaekel.

Jane couldn't stand to see him struggling and put the lid on his coffee herself, wrapped the cup in a napkin and handed it to him. "So its only use is for . . ."

"Alzheimer's. Yes."

At 10:00 a.m., Tim parked in front of Mrs. Schaefer's bungalow. Jane had phoned Charley and spoken with him about Fuzzy, and they agreed to talk to Lula together later. Oh had gone back to his motel, bringing a carryout breakfast that included a Pink's special omelette, fried potatoes, slices of melon, and toast.

Jane had watched Pink Junior prepare it and pack it without a murmur of dissent. It wasn't the first time she had seen people react differently to Oh than they did to other people. Although she was distracted with her own thoughts, Jane wondered if Oh practiced some kind of mass hypnosis.

"Look, honey, this is hard news about Fuzzy, but it means he won't go to jail, so maybe . . . ," Tim began, but he couldn't finish the thought. He knew that she knew that he knew what everybody knew. A diagnosis of Alzheimer's might mean that Fuzzy wouldn't be charged with first-degree murder, but it didn't mean that he wouldn't be in jail. His prison might not be presided over by Munson and his officers, but it was only a matter of time before Fuzzy was behind more and more locked doors. First, he would be confused about why Lula locked him in away from his garden and his fields, then another deadbolt would fall into place and he'd stop finding comfort in Lula's cookies and pies and forget to eat. Then he'd forget Lula altogether.

Jane knew she could talk to Tim about it. They would have that crying and laughing conversation that would end with them pledging loyalty and friendship to each other. Jane would give Tim the *you'll-always-have-a-family-with-us* kind of promise and Tim would give her the *even-if-Charley-is-there-I'll-come-in-and-pick-out-your-clothes* assurance. She just wasn't ready to have that conversation yet.

Suzanne Blum, Mrs. Schaefer's niece, opened the door. She motioned for them to come in. "I was watching you just sitting out there. Did you think I was meeting you outside?"

Since neither of them wanted to explain their vigil in the car, they both nodded.

"I actually ended up sleeping over here last night. I got involved in going through some of the stuff, and I found I couldn't help myself. Once I opened one box in the attic, I couldn't stop. This must be what happens to those people who get addicted to old stuff, right? You know those people who watch the *Antiques Roadshow* and get all starry-eyed over house sales? Their houses must be something, full of other peoples' junk. I hope I've just got the twenty-four-hour version of this disease. Wouldn't it be terrible to be so fixated on all that stuff?"

Three slides flashed before Jane's eyes: one, her living room, an architectural wonder of old suitcases stacked to the ceiling; two, the master bedroom where space for the master or the mistress of the house had long been filled with maps, architectural plans, books, vintage textiles, and souvenir travel pillows; three, the garage-sale interruptus tableau, where Jane's garage was filled with the items she reluctantly agreed to part with — piles and tables of . . . everything . . . . Jane, unable to speak, nodded. It would indeed be terrible to be so fixated on all that stuff.

Tim, however, found his voice.

"Absolutely. But something caught your eye last night, right? Tell me what fascinated you, and I'll see if your symptoms are short-term or if you've caught the chronic form of the illness."

Jane heard Tim's excitement. They had come over to deliver the lists of high school volunteers who were going to help the residents on this block clean out their basements and purge their attics. They hadn't planned on actually going in and sorting through any inventory themselves today.

Jane watched Tim give Suzanne the once-over. If something caught this woman's eye, this woman who was wearing a Calvin Klein lightweight cashmere T-shirt with her designer jeans, Tim was thinking, he and Jane might have to check it out. She had an eye for shoes, too — weren't those Manolo heels? She was wearing distinctive earrings, knots of gold with what appeared, to Jane's quasi-trained eye, to be real diamonds so maybe, Tim was figuring, maybe there was treasure to be found. Looking at the house from the outside, knowing the owner, Mrs. Schaefer's approximate age, and adding that to the fact that she lived alone, had no daughters who would beg the odd side chair for their first apartment, or the extra set of china that no one ever used anyway . . . yes, Jane might have to agree with Tim, there might be something worthwhile in the house.

Jane was always aware that as tragic as it was that some people had too little, it was sad in a different way when people living alone had too much. Not only did they mourn the family they had lost or perhaps never found, they mourned the lives of their objects, the family heirlooms that had been passed down to them. They had dusted the furniture and polished the silver; they had guarded the crystal and wrapped the plates. They had curated the keepsakes and archived the letters and the photographs. When it came time for them to go, where would all of these things find a home?

No one wanted to think about a public sale of their goods, where strangers tracked mud through the house picking up a juice glass here and an old painting there. The strangers didn't care if that glass had been little brother Henry's favorite in 1932, the only glass he would drink milk from, they just cared that it had a small chip in the rim. The owner might remember the day Henry lost his tooth and got so excited that he tipped the glass, spilled his milk, and, if he hadn't just lost a tooth, would have gotten a spanking from Mother.

That's where the chip came from and that's what had made the glass worth saving all these years. To the picker or dealer shopping at the house sale, though, a chip was a chip, and it made the "as-is" item worthless. The little juice glass would sit on the table, unwanted, unsold, and it would be part of the stuff tossed into a box and hauled out to the alley when the sale was over. That's what would happen to it eventually, but not before countless shoppers had picked up the glass with interest, rubbed their fingers around the rim, then put it down with expressions of disgust and disappointment — and no one, not even the most practical and unsentimental, wants to hear his or her possessions, infused with life and meaning, pronounced trash by a collector who might know his Heisey from his Hazel Atlas, but did not know brother Henry from a hole in the ground.

Suzanne led Tim to a box she had carried down from the attic. Jane trailed behind, noting the botanical prints hanging on the wall in the bedroom whose door stood open. There was a pair of dresser lamps in there that also looked good. Dark green pottery arts-and-craft bases . . . yes, Jane wanted to detour off into that room . . . the extra bedroom. It was usually where you found the sewing box with the button tin and the Bakelite needle case . . . Jane stopped and took a breath. She wasn't at a sale. She was in the home of an elderly person who had just moved to a smaller, more manageable place and that woman's niece was showing them a few boxes that might be sold at a yard sale. That was all. Jane had to stop herself from being consumed by sale lust. Was this what hot flashes would feel like?

Suzanne ushered them into the kitchen and told them she had carried down five boxes last night, thinking she could go through them quickly, and they would be closer to the garage for the sale.

"I had no idea Aunt Liv had kept all the family photo albums. Look, she labeled everything . . . I mean I throw all the pictures into a drawer . . . no one would be able to tell . . . Here it is."

She held up a wedding photo. A hopeful bride, a nervous groom. Both of them wide-eyed as if they were asking, "What's next?"

"It's my parents. Look at my beautiful mother," she said, with wonder. "I've never even *seen* this photograph before."

Tim murmured something that sounded appreciative, but Jane knew he was disappointed. This kind of discovery was part of the Jane Wheel school of garage-sale memorabilia, not the Tim Lowry college of collectibles and valuables.

"But what I thought you really might be interested in is this. Maybe you could tell me how this should be priced. I wouldn't want to leave it up to the high school volunteers."

She opened up a second box and Tim's eyes grew to the size of the bridegroom's in the photo. Silver. If Tim had been wearing an eye patch, he couldn't have looked more like a greedy pirate standing over a treasure chest. He lifted out a magnificent tray. Round and heavy with some scrollwork around the handles. Tim began nodding and muttering under his breath. There was a set of individual citrus bowls, sherbets, and fish forks. These were the odd pieces of a magnificent set, and what it told Tim and Jane was that there was more. The pitchers and the serving pieces and the gravy boat? Where were they?

"About eight more boxes in the attic," said Suzanne.

Tim whipped out his BlackBerry. He made a date for later in the week, told her he would come back with a few students so they could do the lifting, and they would set up in the garage. Tim would appraise the silver and other valuables Suzanne did not want for herself or anyone else in the family, and he would try to find her a buyer.

"I was wondering if you have a minute to look at . . . ?"

"Wow," said Jane, looking up from an old piece of card stock, heavily decorated with gold around the edges. She had picked it up out of a small box on the floor that had plastic bags full of matchbooks and swizzle sticks.

"This is a program from the Majestic Inn Night Club," said Jane. "My dad talks about this place. In the thirties it was the

Studio 54 of Kankakee."

"Update your references, honey," said Tim. "Studio 54 hasn't been *the* Studio 54 for twenty years."

"You know what I mean," said Jane. "Look, they had an MC and a comedian and two dancers and a singer . . . this was quite a program. And it played Wednesday through Sunday. Must have been great, you know . . . live music, dancing, people dressing up and going out."

"Uh-oh, you've got the same look on your face that your dad had when Dempsey and Hoover were describing the big-band palace they want to put into Roper Stove," said Tim.

"The Hometown guys? My aunt went to one of their community meetings. She said Roper was going to be a giant bingo hall."

Jane had a feeling that Dempsey and Hoover might be pretty facile at turning any memory into a potential reality. Don and Nellie might long for a place like the Majestic Inn, so poof! Hometown USA would conjure it up from the ashes of the abandoned factory across from the EZ Way Inn. Jane wanted to explain to her father that in all of this created nostalgia — and that's supposing Dempsey and Hoover were on the up-and-up — there would be no room for a real tumbledown bar like the EZ Way Inn. If they were really using Disneyland's Main Street as an example of what they were attempting, they would have to scrub, scour, tear down, and rebuild half the town to make it seem as believably quaint and "authentic" as they wanted it to be. Created nostalgia worked because it was clean and hygienic and brightly lit. It was safe. But it wasn't real.

"How did she hear about the meeting? I thought those guys were just starting to go public?" asked Tim.

"Oh, somebody came to the senior center and talked to her quilting group. Handed out flyers and answered questions, I guess. There's the notice," Suzanne said, pointing to the refrigerator where a few business cards and papers were held fast by magnets advertising plumbing services and the warning signs of diabetes. The flyer announced an informational meeting about a better future for Kankakee, and there was a business card stapled in the corner. It wasn't Dempsey or Hoover's Hometown USA card. It was a K3 Realty business card. The agent's name was Roger Groveland.

Jane took the notice off the refrigerator

and read it a second time.

Jane replaced the Majestic Inn program in the box of memorabilia and told Suzanne Blum that she'd love to go through the entire collection of ephemera and mine it for collectibles. She would put together a package for her to take to her aunt, since there were pieces in there that might prompt some good stories. Suzanne liked the idea, and Tim rolled his eyes. Jane knew he would chide her later for taking on a type of appraisal and conservation that would take hours but never turn a profit.

"Was there something else you wanted us to look at?" asked Jane.

"I just need to know if clothes like these are worth putting out. I'm not sure they fall into the vintage category. My aunt has said I should throw them all away or donate them somewhere, but if you think they're worth anything . . ."

Jane followed her into the second bedroom. "Those lamps are good and so are the prints. Don't let the kids price those," Jane said, opening the closet door. She knew Tim was walking in behind her, and he agreed about the lamps but was lukewarm on the prints. That was odd, since she knew Tim liked botanicals; he had quite a collection in his floral shop, and . . . right. He was lukewarm on them because he wanted to buy them. He wouldn't give Suzanne a completely unfair price, but he would err on the side of underinflation rather than overinflation.

Jane quickly looked through the closets. She liked Olivia Schaefer's taste. Her housedresses were cheery prints and well made. She had a collection of great aprons, clever fabrics from the forties and fifties, trimmed with rickrack and embroidery. And in the back of the closet, a muslin garment bag had a few tailored dressy suits and two exquisite cocktail dresses, one black with sequins, the other, an iridescent dark blue.

"She might have worn one of these to the Majestic Inn," said Jane. "What are these?" she asked, pulling out a fistful of hangers.

There were five colored smocks with the name of Kankakee's hospital stitched over the pocket.

"Aunt Liv worked at the hospital for years; and after she retired, she volunteered three days a week. She worked in the gift shop and delivered flowers and mail. She called herself a professional volunteer. I think these different colors represented the different departments she worked in."

"Perfect," said Jane, taking one of the smocks out of the closet. "These are absolutely perfect for . . ."

"For what?" Suzanne asked.

Jane smiled. "For working at the hospital."

"I hate to interrupt, but I have an appointment back at the shop," said Tim. "My opinion on the clothes is to put everything out. Just throw up a rack and put it out there priced to sell, and it will go. What doesn't can be donated, but you'd be surprised at what sells. Even those hospital smocks will sell for a quarter."

"And I'll buy all the aprons," Jane said. She was still fingering one of the hospital smocks. "Could I have this now?" Jane asked.

"Sure," Suzanne said. "You can have them all."

"You're getting spooky in your old age," said Tim, as they headed for the flower shop.

Jane was looking through one of the phone books that Tim always kept in the backseat of his car. At home in Evanston, Jane used a map she made from the classifieds to shop garage sales efficiently. Tim, though, was an early bird caller. He had a regular phone directory and a reverse directory, the kind a Realtor used, which listed property by addresses and provided names and phone numbers. The night before a promising sale, Tim would call and ask about items that had interested him from the ad and would also offer his professional expertise if the seller needed help pricing. Most people hung up on him, furious that he would presume to dig up the phone number and try to weasel his way in early. But there were always a few who, exhausted from trying to set up a sale and loopy from trying to figure out what was really worth a dollar and what was really worth two dollars, would welcome his offer. All he charged for his services was a first look at the merchandise.

"What are you looking up?" asked Tim. "And why did you want those hospital volunteer smocks?"

"Can I borrow your car?" asked Jane.

Tim pulled up in front of his shop and saw that Claire Oh was already there waiting for him.

"Yeah, I guess. Claire and I can take the truck, but where are you going?"

"I'm going to spend my lunch hour looking at a fine little piece of Kankakee real estate."

Chapter 16

"No good will come of this," said Tim, watching Jane roar off in his Mustang.

"Tim," said Claire, "I hope Jane doesn't feel like I'm overstepping, you know, moving in on her territory?"

"I'm more concerned right now with Jane moving in on your husband's territory," said Tim. "She's starting to go all detectively on me. Did you see the way she drove off in my car?"

"Where is she going?"

Tim shook his head. "I don't know, but she's definitely not going off to look at real estate."

Tim entered the shop to grab another one of his fat notebooks, filled with the names of who was on board for the sale and who wanted to volunteer for other jobs. He had food vendors to contact and a call to make to another bus service for backup. He and Claire would visit some other holdouts, and together they would charm them into cooperating. And the ones they couldn't convince? Jane would get them. He knew no one could resist her. He also knew that she didn't know that, and he wanted to keep it that way. Her charm was in her own self-effacing innocence. Besides, keeping her in the dark about her own talent allowed him to be the boss.

He knew what Jane was thinking about this latest plan. She figured he wanted first crack at whatever was left here in Kankakee, whatever he could find hidden away, the objects he hadn't pried out of people's basements and cupboards already.

But Tim Lowry had a higher purpose this time. Well, he still wanted to pry loose a few pieces of crystal and silver from some of these old fogies who kept everything wrapped in newspapers from the forties and sealed in cartons in a crawl space, but that wasn't the only goal, the main purpose. This time, Tim Lowry wanted to do something for the town. If some ridiculous ratings organization wanted to name Kankakee the worst of the worst, let them go ahead. He would take those lemons and sell lemonade. Another phone call to make. He was going to call the mayor and make sure those two gazebos were front and center on the courthouse lawn. Maybe he ought to get the Brown sisters over there to take pictures of people at the gazebos. Maybe Letterman would put that on the show. Hey, maybe if he could get word to his staff, they would send Biff to attend the sale and do a comedy piece on it.

"Claire, I've got to send an e-mail and then . . ." Tim stopped. Someone was sitting in his desk chair. "Oh?"

Bruce Oh looked up from Tim's computer.

"I hope you don't mind?" said Oh. "I was waiting with Claire, and it occurred to me that I might investigate Hometown USA."

"That's a great idea — anything come up? Those two been tarred and feathered and run out of some town on a rail?"

Tim took out his BlackBerry, resisted the impulse to plant a kiss on this perfect little wonder, and wrote himself an e-mail about his ideas for Letterman. He crossed the shop to peer over the shoulder of a young protégé who was arranging Gerbera daisies in a vintage green bowl. He opened up the cooler and selected some baby irises and sweetheart roses and laid them down on the table next to the bowl. "Don't be afraid of contrast, Sarah, experiment a little."

Oh had not found anything online about Hometown USA. He had found a few political groups that used a variation of that name, but nothing about an amusement park or company that dealt in nostalgic recreations. He did find that ten years ago, a J. Milton Dempsey had been named in a complaint about selling phony oil and gas leases. The ages didn't quite match up though. He'd also found a newspaper article from an Indiana paper dated two years ago about a company called Make-Happy, whose president was listed as Dempsey Josephson. It was under investigation for fraud. Apparently, MakeHappy was a large event/party-planning service. A woman named Judy Iacuzzi, who had hired MakeHappy to plan a conference for a Young Presidents' Association, had arrived at the site of the conference to find that not one of the high-end services she had contracted for had been performed. The space had been booked but not paid for, although she had authorized them to use a line of credit from the association. By the time she had driven to their office, MakeHappy had vanished. The suite full of stunning office furniture and sample books, phones, secretaries, even the coffee-maker in the conference room — all gone.

The superintendent of the building had said that all the furnishings had been rented for thirty days. The office had only been occupied two days that month — the two days Judy Iacuzzi had come to meetings there.

MakeHappy had made themselves about fifty thousand dollars. And their entire operation, offices and furnishings, had been paid for with the line of credit from the Young Presidents' Association, making Judy Iacuzzi not only unhappy but also unemployed.

"I would like to hunt that man down like a dog and kill him," she was quoted as saying. Apparently her lawyer was present during the interview and advised her not to say that, but she insisted that the reporter print it. "Please quote me. I will kill Dempsey 'Joe' Josephson with my bare hands."

"If this is our Mr. Dempsey, his references are less than what one would hope for," said Oh.

Claire smiled at her husband. She had been examining Tim's exquisite collection of American arts-and-crafts pottery while listening to Oh recount the MakeHappy story. The best examples here were the ones with the simplest, cleanest lines, the strongest shapes, the purest colors. Honest understatement. That was what made these pieces valuable. It was also what made her husband unique.

"Where is Mrs. Wheel?" asked Oh.

Tim shook his head.

He wasn't sure what Jane was doing right now. He just wished she wasn't doing it in his car.

Chapter 17

Jane's first phone call was to the Riverview Real Estate office. If one could judge the size and staff of an office by the size of its display ad in the phone book, it was at least as large as K3 Realty. Jane hoped that meant there would be an agent waiting by the phone who could arrange an immediate viewing of a property. Jane described the house she wanted to see and told the agent that she only had thirty minutes on her lunch hour and she hoped they would be able to accommodate her.

"I know it's crazy, but my husband and I have driven past it a million times and I just have to get in there before he leaves on his business trip tomorrow. He'll be gone for a month, and he said if I can make up my mind today . . . well, we can just go ahead with it, so . . ." Jane let her voice trail off and hoped that all Realtors in town were as desperate as those she had met at the K3 office.

"I can meet you there in five minutes," said the agent, whose name was Ted

Burke. "I have the house up on the computer, yes, and there's a lock box, so there should be no . . . hmmm . . . Well, there are renters there."

"What does that mean?" asked Jane, who had just pulled up in front of the late Roger Groveland's house.

"The owner's note says it can be shown; but if the renters are there, they can refuse to admit us. . . . We're supposed to give them notice," said Burke. "But don't worry, we'll just knock on the door, and if they're home, I'm sure they'll cooperate. If they're not home, no problem. I'll put in a call right now and just check. You go over there."

"I will," said Jane, getting out of the car and stepping onto the lawn.

She slipped on one of the hospital smocks and buttoned it over her T-shirt and jeans. She stepped up on the porch and knocked at the front door. No answer. She tried the door, but it was locked. She walked around to the attached garage and peeked in the window.

The scene inside the garage was reminiscent of her own stop-and-start garage sale, but this one was not abandoned as much as closed for business. Boxes had been packed and were labeled for Salvation

Army pickup. There was a collapsible clothes rack still hung with men's clothing. A bowling ball sat on the one table that was still set up. There were some bags of what might have been books.

"Hello?"

Jane turned to see a large man in a suit and tie, smiling the smile of a man with something to sell. "I'm Ted Burke and you must be Mrs. Schaefer," the Realtor said, reading her name tag.

"I must be," said Jane, extending her hand.

It had been one of those two-for-one brainstorms. When she saw the hospital smocks, complete with official hospital name badges, Jane immediately thought of Johnny Sullivan wearing the K3 Realty blazer with Groveland's name tag, Roger Groveland's blazer. The person who had reported the discovery of bones on Fuzzy's property had given the name Roger Groveland. The flyer and business card on the refrigerator was handed out by someone using the name Roger Groveland.

Everyone had asked why Johnny Sullivan had been wearing Roger Groveland's jacket on the night he was killed. Jane knew Munson initially had concentrated on finding a link between the two men, but what if the only link was the one forged between seller and buyer at a garage sale? When Henry Bennett had failed to identify the body as Roger Groveland, he had mentioned that after Roger died, some family member had come and run a house sale. He had also said the house was still up for sale.

House sales, name tags. Name tags, house sales. When Jane saw those hospital smocks, with the ID badges still clipped on, it had crossed her mind that perhaps the tags should be taken off before a sale. Otherwise, couldn't someone buy them, slip one on, and walk into the hospital and have access to authorized areas? Once Jane had been at a Chicago house sale and seen a Lincoln Park Zoo volunteer shirt, complete with employee ID clipped to the shirt. She had worried about it all night.

"I should have bought it," she told Charley around midnight, when he opened his eyes and saw her wide awake staring at the ceiling. "What if someone buys it and wears it to get in someplace they don't belong?"

Charley had laughed it off and told her she had been reading too many mysteries, but Jane was not mollified. First of all, she never read mysteries — too contrived —

and second, she knew that her first thought when she saw the uniform — and she was a law-abiding citizen — was that she could buy the shirt and use it like a backstage pass at the zoo.

Jane wasn't sure why one might desire backstage access to the Lincoln Park Zoo. Did animal tranquilizers have a street value? And was it realistic to envision a drug lord sending out his minions to scour every garage sale in the city to see if they could round up some bogus name tags to get them into the private areas of public places?

Jane tried to picture a dangerous street punk waving an ID badge from the Field Museum. "Hey, boss, now we can get behind one of them Great Plains prairie dog dioramas and score us some taxidermy!"

Maybe Charley was right about this one particular anxiety not being worth the sleepless night. On the other hand, Olivia Schaefer's hospital smock had easily allowed Jane to assume an alternative identity. Had Roger Groveland's blazer allowed Johnny Sullivan access to a scam he was about to expose? Or given him an alternative identity so he could participate in it?

"Looks like they moved out in a hurry and left things behind. Unless those boxes are the renter's things," said Jane.

Burke scanned the paper he was holding. "We're not the listing agent on this, so I have to see if the notes . . . here. Oh, sad, this was Roger's house." Burke stopped reading and looked up at the house. "Of course, I should have known that. I've been in here before," he said. "The owner died. No immediate family in the area. And I assure you, it was natural causes, in the hospital, not in the house."

He waited for someone to answer the bell, then punched in a code on the lockbox and removed the front door key. "I called the tenants from the car and there was no answer; but I always like to ring the bell, don't want to scare anyone coming out of the shower or . . ."

The front door swung open at his touch. The house was dark because every curtain was closed, every shade pulled. Burke immediately went for light switches and drapery cords. Jane walked through the living room, making what she hoped were appropriate interested buyer noises. She wanted to go through the house as quickly as possible and get to the garage. She wasn't sure why she felt the leftovers from Roger Groveland's house sale held one of the keys to Sullivan's death. Perhaps it was the simple reason that she wasn't ready to assume that Fuzzy, in his dementia, had wandered out to his cornfield in the middle of the night and shot Johnny Sullivan. Case closed. Even if Fuzzy did wander around at night and even if he did carry his rifle with him, there had to be some reason Johnny Sullivan was out there wearing that stupid blazer. Besides, Nick had said something she couldn't forget. No matter how much of his memory he was losing every day, Fuzzy would find a way to tell them that something had happened. Fuzzy was a storyteller.

"Mr. Burke, this is going to sound a little nutty, but my husband is a stickler for the details on the furnace and hot water heater. Could you go down to the basement and jot down the particulars while I measure the garage?" Jane said. "And I mean every fact and figure, please, and also note the serial numbers on the utility meters, please. Also any appliance serial numbers you can get to. He's a nut for checking recall lists." Jane had no idea what she was talking about, but she thought it sounded like the kind of nit-picking details that might keep him occupied for ten minutes.

"My husband is a collector of vintage

cars," Jane said, "so I'll check out the garage," she added, not knowing if antique cars would require more or less space, but waving her key ring with a flashlight, magnifier, and tape measure, essential for a picker and, it seemed, handy for a detective pretending to be a home buyer. She'd have to remember to tell Tim — it was the kind of Nancy Drew lore he loved.

She didn't wait for an answer and stepped down into the two-car garage and closed the door behind her. The garage-sale tables had been pushed back toward the walls to allow space for at least one car. The overhead light was burned out, but enough sun came in from the high windows on either side to allow her to see the sale leftovers. A lot of kitchen plastic, some old burned pans, an encrusted waffle iron with a frayed cord. Roger's relatives must not have read one of the garage-sale guides that suggested that merchandise be cleaned before it was offered for sale. One table held a few boxes that were packed with books, but additional volumes were piled on the table. One was a yearbook, the Herscher Hi-Reminder. Roger had gone to Herscher High School and Jane to Bishop Mac; but they were the same year and Jane paged through the annual, trying to remember who else she knew to look up besides Roger. A flash of green on the clothing rack caught her eye and she walked over to it. The rack was shoved up against the wall opposite the garage door, and Jane could see by some of the marks on the clothes that whoever had been parking the car was not being careful about keeping a distance. Jane thought the clothes were the saddest remnants of this man's life. Inexpensive white shirts, slightly frayed at the cuffs and gray at the collars, were hung with pieces of masking tape on the hangers offering them for a quarter. The green Jane had noticed was a K3 Realty blazer. So perhaps Johnny Sullivan had done a little shopping here?

There was a small ink stain at the pocket. The name badge was still pinned in place. Jane touched the badge and pictured her childhood friend, now a grown man, struggling alone every day to make a life. She pictured him looking in the mirror, seeing the ink stain, and hoped that he would realize he could pin the badge a little lower to cover it. Roger had always had good ideas when they were kids. He invented the game "adventure bike rides" where one of them had to plan ahead some secret destination and plant a picnic or a snack there, then lead the other one to it. Remembering that, Jane stuck the yearbook under her arm and, using two hands to unpin the badge, began to repin it to cover the stain. It wasn't much reparation for not mourning him properly when she'd heard about his death, but it was something.

A loud grinding noise surprised her. Light began moving from the ground up over the contents of the garage, and it was one of those unexpected moments that causes lost bearings and small screams until one realizes that a perfectly normal event is occurring. After all, to Jane a garage might mean the appendage to a house that allows for goods to be bought and sold, and an area where the overstock of items purchased could be stored; but to most people a garage meant a safe enclosure in which to park a car.

The garage door continued grinding open and Jane, finally realizing what was happening, flattened herself against the wall. The car was coming in too fast and too carelessly and Jane, too late, remembered that she had just seen dirt on the clothes where the car would have kissed up against them. She jump stepped over the bottom of the rack, ducking under the hanging clothes; and from the other side, pushed as hard as she could. The rack moved forward and tipped, falling on the hood of the car with a crash. When the brakes squealed and held, the front of the car was four inches from the yearbook Jane had instinctively held in front of her.

"Oh man, oh man, what the hell am I going to tell Joe?" The driver lifted the rack and ran his hand over the dent in the hood. "Goddamn it!"

Jane was, of course, familiar with the expression *caught like a deer in the headlights;* however, she had never been so acutely aware of what the deer actually felt like. Since she was not sure she had the ability to speak and since she could think of nothing relevant to say at the moment, except perhaps a thank you to whatever angel, saint, and/or survival instinct had helped her to move and think as quickly as she had, she remained still. The driver, illustrating that rule of illusion that says one seldom sees what one is not expecting to see, was completely unaware of her presence. And illustrating a different kind of rule, the rule of male drivers who are really pissed off at something and therefore need to punish an inanimate object, this one flung the rack back off the car where it hit the wall, framing Jane with the bars but covering her with the clothes that had miraculously remained on their hangers. Jane, peeking out from behind polyester and acrylic, saw the driver clearly, Michael Hoover. He walked over to a large cardboard box by the side door, clicked the automatic trunk opener, and lifted the box into the trunk. She could tell it was heavy, watching him struggle getting it over the side of the car. A piece of paper that had been stuck under the box flap fluttered unnoticed to the floor. From her spot behind the clothes, Jane could make out a large *B* written in marker on the side. Hoover then reached up and pulled a flat box from a stack of what looked like old board games on the metal shelf shoved against the side and threw it in on top and slammed the trunk lid. He pulled a cell phone out of his pocket, punched in a number, and waited.

"Yeah, it's me. I got them and I'm leaving right now. Come on, Joe, what's done is done. Nah. Why? Not if they lock up that crazy sonofabitch."

He then got into his car and backed out of the garage as fast as he had pulled in. The garage door went down with the same painful grinding noise, and Jane was left standing there against the wall, still covered with clothes.

A few minutes later, when Ted Burke opened the door to the garage from the small mudroom and asked if she was done measuring, Jane was standing in front of the metal shelves, facing the stack of boxes. She was writing something down in a large notebook, which she stuck back into a file folder. Looking down, she tsked-tsked at a piece of paper she had apparently dropped and picked it up and stuffed it, too, in the folder. Tucking it under her arm, she stepped back into the house, accepted the notes Burke had written down for her, and told him she would be in touch. She tore a piece of paper off the business notepad that was by the phone in order to write down Burke's cell phone number, but he handed her a card. She kept the piece of paper and the card and slipped them both into the bulging folder. She hurried out of the house into Tim's red Mustang and drove off, leaving Burke staring after her, looking like a man who still had some questions. Why didn't she want to see the bedrooms or the dining room? Didn't she care about the steam shower and the Jacuzzi?

Was she carrying that file folder when she entered the house?

Chapter 18

When Jane realized how hand-shaking hungry she was, she laughed out loud. She always got hungry when she was excited and that little bit of work in her newly chosen field was pretty darn thrilling. It was a fine line, she had to admit, between scary and thrilling. But when it was possible that one might be pinned up against a wall like a bug and one escaped the pinning . . . well, that was thrilling. And walking out of there with Roger Groveland's Hometown files, K3 stationery, and business cards was pretty high on the thrill-o-meter, too. And as for the Herscher Hi-Reminder she had also tucked into the cardboard file jacket? Perhaps not really part of the case, but she could never resist a yearbook and this one she would keep in honor of Roger. The five-dollar bill she had left on the table in the garage more than covered her shopping spree.

The only thing she wanted but couldn't get away with taking out of there was one of those boxes. There were six of them left on the shelf, and none of them were games

371

like she'd originally thought. They were all commercially labeled rock collections, the kind of hobby kits that one bought for a child who wanted to jump-start his or her own collection. *Professor Geology Junior* and *Mr. Stone's Rock Shop — Genuine Samples from All Over the World*. Rocks were glued to cardboard squares listing the relevant facts about each sample. Jane was familiar with them — Nick had always received a fair share of these kinds of hobby sets every birthday since friends and family assumed they were the perfect gift for the son of a geologist.

In fact at Jane's own garage sale — when was that? Two, three days, twenty years ago? She remembered that Claire Oh had lined up a few cigar boxes full of those rocks that five-year-old Nick had, of course, pulled off the cardboard backing and mixed up into containers so he could carry them around like they were his own discovery . . . his buried treasure, he had called them.

Jane grinned like an idiot. Not only was she alive after a close call, she was pretty sure she had found a source of Fuzzy Neilson's buried treasure. She could remember that stone she had examined at Fuzzy and Lula's — the Austinite. She recalled that she had seen a small speck of green on the sample and was going to ask Charley about it but had gotten distracted. Now she knew exactly what it was. Not a part of the rock or a speck of moss or a streak of some other mineral, it was one of those stubborn bits of green felted cardboard that these rocks were always fixed on inside of the boxes. She remembered finding Nick, when he was six years old, scrubbing away at some of his rocks with his toothbrush. When she had asked him what he was doing, he told her he was cleaning his treasure. Jane helped him finish scraping off the gluey green bits before they went to the drugstore for a new toothbrush.

What did Michael Hoover want with one of these rock collections? All it took was one expert like Charley — heck, in this case, all it took was an amateur rockhound like Nick — to identify a piece of Austinite, to prove the interesting find was phony. Maybe that was just an accident, planting the more exotic stones. Most of the boxes contained dinosaur teeth, fossils, and genuine arrowheads as well as rocks. Maybe it was those kinds of artifacts they were using to salt the farmland around Kankakee.

Jane's thoughts zoomed and raced as she

headed for the only food she appreciated in Kankakee besides that of her mother's at the EZ Way Inn, the Root Beer Stand. It might not have the character of Pink's, but it had food she loved. She needed a frosty mug and a sauce bun with onions right now. She drove a little faster, trying to keep up with her mind, she told herself. Contributing to her feeling of reckless detective joy was this car . . . this magnificent red Mustang. No wonder Tim drove like a maniac. Jane finally got it. She now understood Tim's abandon when it came to driving. In fact she was feeling so giddy and in tune with Tim, it took her three blocks to realize that the red flashing light in her rearview mirror was not some kind of exuberant aura, but a police car that had been following her and now was using the bullhorn to tell her to pull over.

Jane had no idea where Tim kept the registration and was about to go fishing in her bag for both her cell phone to call him and her driver's license when the policeman stood in front of her window.

"License and registration, please," he said, looking into the car.

"I am so sorry," said Jane. She stopped digging in her purse for a moment and looked him in the eye. He looked to be about a year older than Nick. "I have no excuse here. I am just so hungry that all I was thinking of was a root beer and a . . . you know," she said, looking up and hoping she sounded apologetic and dangerously hungry, "from the drive-through up ahead."

"Well, Mrs. Schaefer, you're right. That's not such a good excuse. On your lunch hour?" he asked.

"Yes," said Jane, wondering if answering his question without correcting his assumption about her name would compound her speeding ticket. "I am on my lunch hour."

"My mom works at the hospital. She's an ER nurse."

"What's her name?" asked Jane, wanting for some reason to prolong this conversation with such an obviously doting son. No matter that it wasn't Jane's doting son, and that there was no chance at all that she would know his mother.

"Phyllis Brenner."

"I know your mom," said Jane, her relief making her sound absolutely joyous. "She was a few years ahead of me in high school. President of the French Club her senior year," said Jane. "I didn't even know she worked at the hospital." She smiled as she realized she had completed two truthful statements in a row.

"Well," he said, sighing, "I guess you'd better go get your lunch." He looked pleased with himself. "I'll tell my mom I met you, Mrs. —"

"I'll bet she's proud of you," Jane said, interrupting him before he could repeat that name again. Could she lay it on any thicker? If she didn't pull away quickly, he might have to write her up a warning for excessive bullshit.

Jane read over Roger's files in the car, eating her sandwich and drinking a giant mug of root beer. She had fished two fat manila envelopes out of the box of old papers and notebooks — one was labeled *SENIORS/COPY* and the other, *AIRPORT/ COPY.* They had been at the bottom of a box that had held old notebooks and paper clips, pens, COMPLIMENTS OF K3 REALTORS calendar datebooks from five years ago. Jane hadn't looked at the inside of the house very thoroughly, but when she did her normal house-sale scan, she noticed that the tenants were using a folding card table with a laptop on it for a desk. Niece Groveland must have sold her uncle's desk at the estate sale, which was why its contents had been dumped into the boxes that were now just sitting open in the garage.

Jane patted her smock. Two families, two sales. Two nieces disposing of households for their relatives, but with a major difference. Suzanne Blum was falling in love with her aunt's life and learning from her history, and Niece Groveland was all business and fast turnaround.

The envelope marked seniors was stuffed with photocopies of newspaper articles, membership lists of every seniors' organization in town, lists of names from churches and groups who received Meals On Wheels, and home visits from nurses. How had Roger accumulated so much private information? Jane stopped herself from pursuing that line of thought — hadn't she just lifted these files from a dead man's closed-for-business garage sale?

The *AIRPORT* envelope had copies of newspaper articles and various proposals for sites for the new Chicago-area airport. Jane had read a few of these pieces already, the ones that carried Johnny Sullivan's byline. A quick scan reminded her that Johnny always slanted the pieces just a bit in favor of the airport. It wasn't that overt, but the people he quoted were usually upbeat on the proposal, and the facts and figures he cited were geared toward the economic advantages of the plan. Jane skimmed the rest of the articles and noticed that some of the documents had been printed from Internet sources. Twelve pages were stapled together, the cover sheet titled *Planning for Projects Involving Historic Resources,* and it detailed two Illinois laws. One, the Archaeological and Paleontological Resources Protection Act, covered the sanctions and fines imposed for disturbing burial mounds, human remains, shipwrecks, or other archaeological resources on public lands.

The second law outlined in the pages was the Human Grave Protection Act. Jane had heard Charley quote this law, chapter and verse, many times. Most recently, she had heard him talk about it to Munson. Someone — Jane presumed Roger Groveland — had underlined the words "private property" and had highlighted in yellow marker ". . . makes it unlawful for anyone to disturb skeletal remains, artifacts, and grave markers . . ."

Jane pulled out the paper that had fallen out of the box Hoover had hoisted into his trunk. GRS. It was a handwritten receipt. She put it away for the moment in favor of a newspaper article photocopied from the

Chicago Tribune where the phrase "Human Skeletal Remains Protection Act" was highlighted. The story itself concerned a real estate developer in the Chicago suburbs who'd bought an old farmstead at a foreclosure sale and had planned to fix up the house that was there and build two new houses, selling them for a profit. All work was halted, however, when a construction crew began digging and found bones buried near the original house. When the bones were found to be Native American remains over one hundred years old, all work was stopped. The developer now had the burden of having an archaeological survey done, and he had to assume all cost for the research.

Jane skipped to the end of the piece and read that many such "finds" are relocated and buried. However, all construction on the original site is completely stopped while the property is researched and the artifacts are being catalogued and assessed.

"Poor guy thinks he's getting a good deal, then ends up tying all his money up with specialists and lawyers," Jane said aloud, reading the last paragraph of the piece. The property owner was quoted as saying, "I own all the headaches and expenses and trouble of the property, but the land itself is not really mine to build on, live on, or sell."

The lament sounded familiar. It had been Fuzzy's battle cry since she and Charley and Nick had arrived at the farm. All Fuzzy had wanted to do was sell some topsoil to someone who had admired his vegetable garden. Once he turned over the dirt, and someone had reported his "find" — bones that looked like they belonged to a small animal and did not look to be very old, even to an untrained eye like Jane's — Fuzzy's claim to be lord of his own manor was completely ignored.

Jane believed from the beginning that whoever had reported those bones to the police and to the state might be someone who wanted to take over the manor for himself. Those official-looking contracts to buy the Neilson and the Sullivan farms? It looked like Hometown USA — Dempsey and Hoover — were poised to be the new owners of Fuzzy's land, topsoil, bones, and all.

At the EZ Way Inn, listening to Dempsey describe his fantasyland for Don and Nellie, Jane had been suspicious. If he and Hoover were running a con, it was reasonable to believe that a journalist like

Johnny Sullivan might be getting ready to expose them. She had been ready to call the police then and there but had held back. Why? Because she watched Hoover eat a cupcake and decided that they didn't seem like a murderous pair?

Johnny was writing articles about the airport, nosing around the town, and stirring up excitement among the property owners. If people believed they were going to be able to sell their land to developers who were banking on the airport, why should they let it go to Dempsey and Hoover — unless they believed no developer would come near it because of the Human Skeletal Remains Protection Act? And maybe some of the farmers thought they could unload the land and the headaches of hiring a geology crew and get Hometown to absorb the "relocation costs" of any artifacts. Then, after Hometown bought the property, all of the "remains" would be dismissed as unimportant, and the rollercoasters and fishing ponds could be built. Or, as Jane was beginning to suspect . . . the runways and terminals. Of course, in order to really stop development of the land around Kankakee, they'd have to do better than Otto the cat. It didn't take a genius to . . .

Jane took a deep breath and tried to still the ricocheting thoughts. If Johnny Sullivan knew about Otto, all he had to do was write a story and expose the hoax. But it looked like Johnny was taking the bones the night he was killed. Did he want them for a photo or some kind of proof?

He had been at the farm earlier — Jane thought she had seen him during the picnic. Charley had been introduced all around as the expert, the one who was going to get to the bottom of whatever it was Fuzzy had found that the government might have a say-so over. And it was that night that Johnny had shown up to steal the bones. Interesting timing.

Jane put all the papers back into the envelopes and wiped her hands on the wad of napkins she had been given with her drive-through lunch. Unfortunately, no matter how many napkins they gave you it was never enough. She tried to clean up the sauce that in her excitement she had spilled all over Tim's immaculate front seat and realized that it was a lost cause. Tim would have her head if she didn't get this mopped up.

Jane put the envelopes on the floor, gathered up the garbage, talking to herself the whole time about how foolish she was to eat a sauce bun in Tim's car. Tim never allowed food in his car, particularly not Root Beer Stand food. She dropped the napkins and wrappers in the garbage and went inside the drive-in where there were tables, a waitress who had been there since Jane was in high school, and a bar for condiments. She helped herself to about thirty napkins and checked out the bulletin board. Teenage girls still posted their numbers for babysitting, townspeople still advertised free kittens, and local businesses still stuck up their cards. Jane wondered if any potential client had ever chosen an insurance agent based on the fact that they ate the same fast food for lunch.

Hello. This was a familiar handout. *HOMETOWN USA.* Jane unpinned the card and held it at a better reading angle. This one had Michael Hoover's name at the bottom instead of Dempsey's, but it was the same business card. *Pretty flimsy.* It was the kind of business card anyone could get made up in a hurry at the local copy shop.

"You know that bum?" Lucille, the waitress, asked.

"I've met him," said Jane.

"You can tell him I'm gunning for him," said Lucille, with a grim smile. "And it ain't going to be pretty."

Jane shook her head and smiled her best Olivia Schaefer, hospital-worker-at-large smile. "I guess I don't know him as well as you do."

"Him and that loser, Johnny Sullivan, were in here Saturday night, drunk as skunks. I must have brought them about ten sandwiches apiece. They were so obnoxious that everyone else cleared out," said Lucille, narrowing her eyes. "And when the place was empty, they dumped out a sack of rocks or something. Dirt and shit all over the table. Made a total mess."

"Why? What did they say they were doing?" asked Jane.

"Hoover asked me if I'd ever heard of grave robbers. Tells me they're grave planters. Then that Sullivan, who is a sloppy ass drunk, says, no, we're grave traders, and gets all weepy about a cat and says he's taking him home with him and Hoover can put in anything he wants.

"So I says, 'Get them cat bones off the table.' I mean this place serves food, you know? And Hoover starts laughing and says that these bones aren't a cat and that they were worth more than my old bones and I told them to get the hell out."

"What time was this?"

"We're open real late on weekends now.

Boss is in some kind of pissing match with Pink and wants us to take some of his crowd of drunks, I guess. Must have been around three or three-thirty," said Lucille.

"Do you work that late and then work days, too?" asked Jane, momentarily off the case and stunned by Lucille's apparent schedule. She had to be nearly sixty-five years old. What was it with Kankakee women? Were they putting something in the water here?

"Got nothing better to do. When I'm off, I'm taking care of my mother, so I figure I might as well be working here. But not Saturday all-nighters anymore. Not if the drunks can't tip better than they've been doing."

"Hoover didn't tip well?" asked Jane.

"Bastard left me this," said Lucille, pulling out a tiny bone fragment. "I was going to throw it away, now I'm glad I didn't. I think I'll put it in his sandwich today. Maybe he'll break his damn tooth."

Jane took the piece of bone and tried to remember what she had heard Charley say about bones. This was hollow, like a bird's, which meant something. Then she realized what Lucille had just said.

"How do you know he's coming in today?"

"He's here. I just saw him duck into the can."

Jane grabbed more napkins and walked around the corner to the restrooms. The door to the unisex was closed. She knocked, knowing what she'd hear from the other side of the door.

"Ocupado."

Jane wet some napkins in the drinking fountain to bring out to clean Tim's front seat and hung back by the jukebox, waiting for Hoover to come out. When he did, he was talking on his cell phone.

"One with cheese and one with onions, right? Oh yeah, forgot you were the ladies' man. No onions," Hoover said, laughing.

"Joe, let it go. They arrested the old man, didn't they? He can't hurt anybody. I'll be fine. I can plant the duckbill today or I've got some nice arrowheads. Hey, it wasn't our fault. Yeah, I know. Nobody's ever supposed to get hurt."

Jane waited until Hoover went around the corner to brave Lucille's wrath and place his take-out order. She went back out to Tim's car and reparked it so she could watch the door. She dumped the napkins on the sauce stain spreading on the uphol-stery and went back into the folder she had taken from Groveland's garage. Where was that receipt? GRS. She smoothed it out and read that an order had been overnighted to Roger Groveland at his Kankakee home address two weeks after Roger had died. The company's full name was Rapid City GRS. That name had sounded vaguely familiar and now, reading the small print under the initials, she knew why. Geological Research and Supply. Charley had an account there. A reputable South Dakota business — some amateur paleontologists who supplied museum-quality specimens, led collecting tours, and supervised educational digs. Rapid City GRS had sold the late Roger Groveland quite an assortment of bones, arrowheads, and plant fossils, including the partial remains of a duck-billed dinosaur.

Hoover came out with a bag of food and let himself into his car a few rows ahead of Jane. She pulled out after him, easing onto the street, careful to stay at least one car length behind. She made a mental note to always drive a less noticeable car. If someone was being followed by a red Mustang, he or she would probably notice. It was a remarkable car. Right now it was a remarkable car that reeked of Root Beer Stand special sauce and she rolled her window all the way down, hoping that the air would help.

Jane glanced down at the passenger seat where the napkins started blowing around. She slammed her hand down on the pile, but they were already flying. Distracted for just an instant, she allowed Hoover to pull through a yellow light and found herself stuck at the intersection as he disappeared into traffic.

All the way to Fuzzy's she swore at herself for losing him, sure that she could have caught him red-handed planting fossils and bones and God knows what all on the land of some unsuspecting old farmer.

When she had exhausted her last string of swear words — and she knew a lot, since the EZ Way Inn had been great training ground for learning to wash glasses until they sparkled, playing sharp gutsy euchre, and learning how to swear like a drunken sailor — she was almost at the farm. That was Fuzzy's cornfield that bordered the side of the highway. And there, pulled over on the side of the highway, was Hoover's sedan, dented hood and all. More precisely, dented hood and none, since no one was in the car.

Chapter 19

"Why'd you stop at the Root Beer Stand?" asked Nellie, looking her daughter up and down. "Lula's got a wagonload of sandwiches in there that she's been force-feeding everybody who gets within hollering distance."

Jane almost asked how her mother knew where she had been, but she stopped herself in time. Where did Jane think her masterful detection skills had come from anyway? Besides, it probably did not take a Marple, a Drew, or a Bond to link the bright orange sauce stain on her smock to the only place in town that managed to make food that color. Mothers had been trying to get it out of their teenagers' clothes for the fifty years the place had been in business. The secret in their sauce? Probably permanent dye.

Jane was unhappy that one of her new lucky smocks had been stained, but she at least rested easy knowing she had the rest of the collection. One more detail of Nellie's odd workings — she noted and discussed what Jane had likely eaten for lunch, but seemed curiously uncurious about why Jane might be wearing a work uniform of a total stranger.

Jane stopped herself from tumbling into Nellie World and getting lost in that maze of funhouse mirrors by seeking out Charley, who said he had spent the morning going back and forth between Munson and Alan Bishop, who wanted to represent Fuzzy but was already having trouble getting information from Lula about Fuzzy's recent medical history.

He did want to know why she was now a cafeteria employee at the hospital, so she took off the smock and shared her morning adventures. She had been so invigorated by working this case — and didn't she love that term, "working the case" — that she told the story with abandon, totally forgetting that Charley might not be as energized by her near miss in Roger Groveland's garage.

When Jane realized Charley looked sick and was about to say something, she felt her defenses rise. The old Jane rebelled every time she thought Charley was going to be protective, every time Charley was going to correct her. In fact, Jane knew that the old Jane got defensive even when

Charley said nothing or was totally supportive. And, in wrestling with all this internal sorting out of possible reactions, Jane realized she had to ask herself a big question — when exactly had she become the *new* Jane?

"In that garage, Charley, I was scared, but I knew what to do," Jane said. "I don't know how to explain it better than that. It was like passing a test I didn't even know I was taking."

Charley nodded and pointed behind her. She turned and saw Fuzzy returning from the flower garden in the front of the house. In one hand he was clutching a bunch of zinnias and cosmos and in the other, he held two large, dirty bones.

"Hey, kids," he called to them, "I got some more."

While they waited for Munson to arrive, Charley reassured everyone that they were looking at the leg bones of a large dog. Everyone except Lula was sitting out on the side porch — Don and Nellie, Fuzzy. Jane saw her through the window staring into a kitchen cabinet. Jane thought maybe she was trying to figure out what to cook next, then she saw her take out a bottle and shake a few pills into her hand. Lula looked at them, poured herself a glass of water, then Jane watched her let the pills slide from her hand into the sink. Lula poured the water down after them, reached into another cabinet and got out a pitcher. "I'm making lemonade," she called out.

"Jeez," said Nellie, "she's driving me crazy with her make-work." She stood and walked over to pull a few stray dandelions that had dared sprout by the porch steps.

"Welcome to my world," said Don softly.

Jane had called Munson back, after Bostick had made a frantic call about more bones, and reassured him that they had not found a human skeleton, but if he could round up Dempsey and Hoover, who were likely somewhere on the property, it might be a good time for a little show-and-tell session.

Tim and Claire had arrived just in time to see Fuzzy waving the bones over his head in the front yard when they drove up.

"Where's Bruce?" asked Claire, and Jane realized she had not seen or heard from her partner since the morning.

"He and Nick walked the shortcut over to the Sullivans'," said Charley. "He thought he might see something interesting on the way. And Nick was going to take him past the shooting range and back here by the corn path."

"Sullivan's a nut, you know," said Nellie. "Always has been."

Don gave her one of those looks that in the hands of a less-practiced husband might have shouted for her to be quiet. But since Don had been smoothing out the rough edges of Nellie for over forty years, he had his look down to a slight incline of the head toward Fuzzy, a tight, almost straight smile, and the barest of head shakes.

Jane thought it eloquent and subtle. Lula, carrying out a tray with pitcher and glasses, saw it differently.

"No need to coddle us, Don," she said. "Fuzzy's got the Alzheimer's, and we all know what that means, don't we, Fuzz?"

Fuzzy stared straight ahead. After his excitement over finding the bones, he had gone quiet. Lula hadn't wanted to be so forthcoming about Fuzzy last night, but something in her this afternoon seemed different. She had softened somehow. She had not gotten kinder or warmer exactly, she had just blurred a bit around the edges. Jane thought it was as if she had been holding her breath, standing up straighter than necessary, and now she exhaled. She looked like a woman who had made up her mind. *Or had it made up for her*, thought Jane.

"My car smells like a Coney Island hot dog shop," Tim hissed into Jane's ear. He had thrown his notebooks and bags into the backseat. "Did you solve the mystery of what the Root Beer Stand puts in its Italian sausage?"

Jane saw Oh and Nick walking single file along the corn path, still out of voice range. Oh was waving Nick ahead of him. It must be a narrow stretch on the path. She waved, then noticed Jack Sullivan walking along behind them carrying a fishing pole. Maybe the Hometown boys had been over there to discuss the trout pond.

Munson came around the back and walked up the porch steps. Dempsey and Hoover were not with him, but he held the door for Elizabeth Sullivan, who stepped up and took a seat, nodding to everyone. Dempsey and Hoover could have cut through the cornfield and be over at the Sullivans' farm right now sneaking arrowheads into the front lawn.

"I was over at the Sullivans' when I got your call, and Mrs. Sullivan insisted on accompanying me," Munson said. He wasn't happy. "Mrs. Wheel, you've had a productive day?"

Jane gave an uneven nod. Yes and no. Until her conversation with Lucille and her eavesdropping on Hoover, she had felt strongly that there was a case to be made against the Hometown USA partners. If Johnny Sullivan had been about to expose them as charlatans, they might want him dead. If Johnny himself had been trying to pull a little hoax, they might have wanted to cut him out. And there was the mysterious man unmasked — Michael *"Ocupado"* Hoover. But she had heard Hoover on the phone talking to Dempsey about Fuzzy as the shooter. If she told Munson about that, he would be even more certain Fuzzy had done it. Case closed. And Jane knew that wasn't the way it was supposed to end.

Jane was sure that Hoover had been out here on Saturday night with Sullivan. They had probably been planning on leaving a more convincing bone display somewhere that night. They didn't want Charley to sign off on the site as the innocent burial ground of Otto the cat. Jane wanted to talk this through with Oh or Charley or even Tim, who was still glaring at her for eating in his car. She was not quite ready to intone the lugubrious *"and the reason I've called you all here today."*

Jane was thinking maybe she'd run out

to meet Oh when Fuzzy stood up and began moaning. He was not saying anything intelligible but was just staring ahead and making a mournful cry. It might have been the sound of a person's heart breaking.

"I'm telling you, Don, if that happens to me, you get a gun and shoot me," whispered Nellie. Jane winced. Nellie saw her and whispered loudly to Jane, "I mean it. You kill me if I get like that. And then you remember I . . ."

"Oh no," said Jane, seeing Lula's face go slack watching Fuzzy. "Oh, no."

"Yes, Nellie, you want to be cremated," Don said, stopping her. "I know. We all know. Maybe we could cut out the middleman and I could just set you on fire."

An unusual speech for Don, but Jane realized that Fuzzy's wailing was affecting everyone. What must that effect have been on Lula, who had been hearing it alone for so long? When Jane had checked Fuzzy's prescription bottle, she noted that the original date of issue had been over a year ago. Lula had been doing the heavy lifting for a long time. Jane watched Lula cross over to Fuzzy, take his arm, and begin stroking it. Lula saw Jane watching her, nodded, then turned all of her attention to Fuzzy. He quieted the sound but continued to cry.

A popping sound made them all pay attention. Jane recognized it. "That's it. The noise I heard that night. It wasn't like thunder, it was more like that, a car backfiring, or a tractor . . ." She looked toward the cornfield and was momentarily confused. Why was Jack Sullivan pointing his fishing pole into the air?

The entire group on the porch stood and faced the trio who stood at the end of the path. Nick stood in front of Oh who stood in front of Jack Sullivan who was pointing a rifle at them. Jane realized that it wasn't a fishing pole, had never been a fishing pole in this landlocked Illinois farmland. Nor had it been about a narrowing of the path before, it was Oh trying to keep himself between Nick and Sullivan.

Even in her panic, Jane noticed that Munson was scanning the entire yard. He had called off the officers he had stationed in the field's perimeter. But Bostick and a few others should be somewhere on the property.

"Hey," yelled Sullivan, "Fuzzy up there? Damn sun's so bright, I can't see you all so good. Is that you, Fuzzy?"

Fuzzy had stopped crying and had come back to them. He squinted back at Sullivan and nodded. As an afterthought, he yelled, "Yeah?"

"I hear that you killed my boy. That true?"

"Nope," said Fuzzy. He looked at Lula and shook his head. She shook her head back. "Nope, I sure didn't," he yelled back stronger.

"I heard in town that the police think so because you have that senile Alzheimer's."

"I haven't been myself, that's true, but I didn't shoot anybody. You let those two come up here, Jack. You come, too," said Fuzzy, starting to walk forward.

"Stop right there."

Oh had been whispering to Nick at every exchange between the two old men. Jane could see his mouth move and saw Nick nod. She hadn't seen any steps taken, but she could tell that Oh was telling Nick to move slightly ahead and over. Oh was cheating sideways so he could watch Sullivan's face and see where he was pointing the rifle.

Claire had not taken a breath.

Charley, Jane noticed, was breathing heavily, almost choking. He was edging closer to the edge of the porch.

"Let go, Lula. I'm going to go talk to him," said Fuzzy.

Munson said no, but Fuzzy didn't pay any attention. He walked down the porch steps and stood in front of the assembled group.

"I did not kill your boy, Jack."

Sullivan seemed to weave a little back and forth, but he held the gun, now pointed at Fuzzy, steady.

Oh must have given Nick the word because Nick, quickly, but without breaking into a run, disappeared down the first row of corn. Oh had blocked him from Sullivan's line of vision so that Sullivan did not even see that he was gone. Oh himself stood perfectly still.

"What I did," said Fuzzy, "was kill your boy's cat."

"Oh man," said Tim, "I'd love to see this one get torn from the headlines."

"Shut up, Lowry," said Nellie, "this I want to hear."

Charley had backed off the porch by the side steps, and Jane could see him cutting over into the stand of trees and heading toward the cornfield, out of Sullivan's sight. Jane knew that he'd reach Nick in a matter of seconds. They'd both be safe as long as they were out of sight. And Fuzzy was now commanding Sullivan's entire attention.

"I should have told you ten years ago. I

ran over Otto with my tractor," said Fuzzy, warming up to telling the story. "I mean the cat was a senile bastard by then, and he just didn't move. I think he was sleeping under the tractor for the shade. I felt real bad, but Elizabeth told Lula that she thought he was going off to die somewhere every night when he limped away from the house, so I just buried him and figured you didn't need to know the end had been like that for him.

"I'm sorry, Jack. I forgot all about it and burying him and everything. Then at the pig roast I was talking to Johnny about something — he was asking me all about the bones and I said it wasn't going to amount to anything — I just called in Don and Nellie's girl and her husband to go along with a good story. I knew it wasn't anything big here. Been planting treasure rocks for the grandkids for years and this was just an old pile of cat bones. That's what I told Johnny. He laughed at me and asked how I could be so sure about it. So I told him it was Otto."

"So Johnny came back that night," Jane said, "to take home the family pet."

They all heard another rustle in the cornfield, a thud like something was being dropped.

"Who's there?" said Sullivan. "Come out and show yourself or I'll shoot you."

Jane held her breath. Had Nick and Charley gotten turned around and circled back to where Sullivan was standing with the gun?

Oh spoke softly, but loud enough for them all to hear. "Mr. Sullivan? Let's go up on the porch now and talk about this. Mr. Neilson would like to make his apologies."

Jane didn't take her eyes off Sullivan, who was looking more and more confused.

"Mrs. Sullivan," said Jane, "can you call to your husband? Will he drop the gun and come up here if he knows you're here?"

"I'm telling you, come out and show yourself," said Sullivan, into the seemingly endless rows of corn.

"I don't know," she said. "I don't know what anybody will do. I thought Johnny would never come back here. He was a college boy; he didn't need to be a farmer. But he always wanted the farm, said he'd sell it and make us all enough money. Said he was going to make sure all the land around here went for top dollar."

"Call your husband before he hurts somebody or kills himself," said Nellie.

Sullivan fired a shot in the air.

Dempsey and Hoover came out from the

corn a few rows back.

"Thank God," said Jane.

They all heard the cars on the road. No sirens, but they all knew that in a matter of minutes police would pile out of cars and surround the house and yard, all the way down to the corn path. If old Sullivan didn't drop that rifle, they would shoot him down.

"Too bad you police took all my guns," said Fuzzy. "I could shoot old Jack from here."

"Don't, Lula," said Don, who was the only one to notice that Lula had returned to the porch from inside the house. She was standing a few steps higher than all of them, framed by the kitchen door.

"I can get him, Fuzzy."

Lula aimed and lowered her twenty-two — they all knew it was hers by the loopy cursive *Lula* written on the stock — and fired.

Jack Sullivan crumpled to the ground, clutching his leg and swearing. His wife walked out toward him, more slowly than Jane had thought she might. Bruce Oh, who was right there, took off his tie to use as a bandage on the leg. Jane could hear Claire mutter under her breath that it was a particularly rare vintage tie and perhaps he could have used Sullivan's own sleeve, but Jane was sure she was the only one who could hear this complaint.

"Is that where you were aiming, Lu? The leg?" asked Fuzzy.

Lula nodded.

She carried her rifle over to Munson, who was on the phone ordering the ambulance and reporting to whoever was in charge of the backup that had just arrived out front. Lula handed the gun to him.

"Here you go, Franklin," said Lula. "You'll be needing this to test for your investigation, I suppose. You can give back all the others now."

Munson nodded.

"This doesn't change anything, though, Lula," said Munson. "Just because Fuzzy claims to have killed the cat doesn't mean he didn't come out here and see Johnny, grab a gun from the barn . . ."

"Franklin, I swear I am going to call your mother and tell her to start giving you some smart pills," said Lula.

Jane felt sorry for Munson. He wasn't even trying to figure out what Lula was talking about. Jane went over to him and said softly, "This is the gun that you're going to have to test." He still looked blank. Jane thought she could picture little

Franklin sitting with Will at the table, eating Lula's homemade doughnuts. "This is the gun that killed Johnny Sullivan," Jane said, almost whispering. Now Munson would really be sorry he came back to work in Kankakee.

"Why didn't you tell everybody right away, Lula? You shot Johnny because you thought he was a trespasser . . . it was an accident," said Jane. But she knew the answer. Lula couldn't admit anything because that would mean she'd have to leave Fuzzy alone.

Charley and Nick came out on the porch, and Jane swept them both up in a hug. Nick had such a familiar look, a kind of giddy sparkle around his eyes. *This is bad,* Jane thought. *He has that thrill thing going.* Any minute he would announce that he wanted to be a detective, too.

"Mom? I know this is going to sound weird, but I'm starving. Can I go in and . . ."

Jane hugged him as hard as she could. Thank God the hungry part came first. Maybe she could head off that adrenaline rush, that thrill, for a few more years. She didn't trust her voice with him yet, so she nodded and gestured toward the kitchen.

Munson stood there holding Lula's rifle

and said nothing. She turned her eyes from him to Fuzzy, standing in the yard. He had gone ramrod straight, staring out into the cornfield.

"He'll stay like that all night if I don't go get him," said Lula. "Last couple of years, he's been about the same, not really getting any worse. A few months ago, though, he started going downhill fast. I stopped letting him drive. I'd say I had to go to the store or something and drop him off at the EZ Way every morning so he could stay in his routine; but it was getting harder to know when he'd just shut down like he's doing now. And that crying, that crying is new. Doctor said things'll probably be getting worse and worse, faster and faster.

"When he told everybody he'd found those bones, that's when the trouble started. The fool knew it was a cat, but he liked telling the story. Somebody called us and said the government would have to come in and . . . he got so agitated about it all. I couldn't make him understand. Truth, I don't know if that was the Alzheimer's or not because I couldn't understand it either. That's why he thought it'd be good if Charley was here to help explain everything."

"And you knew he went outside every

night?" asked Jane softly.

"Yeah, he'd go out there and wander around. Plant things. I thought maybe one night he'd disappear into the cornfield and we'd never find him. He liked to eat though so I could keep getting him to come home by offering food. I planned to do this, finish it," said Lula.

Munson opened his mouth to stop her from saying anything further, but Jane saw that no words would come. Jane said, "Lula, maybe . . ." But Lula would not be stopped.

"Thought out how it would all go, but would have never done the shooting when you all were here," Lula said, looking at Jane and Charley, "if I'd been thinking straight. But that night, after the barbecue, he'd been so bad in the house, and time was just running out . . ."

Munson reached out his hand and put it on her arm. "Lula, maybe you might want to have a lawyer before you . . ." Munson's voice cracked, he cleared his throat, and a bit louder said, "Would you like to call your lawyer?"

"Nope," said Lula.

They all watched Nick come out the kitchen door and walk over to Fuzzy. He patted his arm, then took it gently in his two hands and led him back to the kitchen, talking softly all the way. Jane could hear him promising some great chocolate chip cookies.

"Night was bright enough for me to see a man out there, and I sure didn't expect anybody else but Fuzzy to be there. It was where he always went to, you know, relieve himself. Didn't expect Jane to be up watching. I've got some pills and I was going to do it, you know, shoot him, then go in the house and take the pills and in the morning we'd both be gone." Lula looked at Charley and Jane. "I am sorry because of your boy. I didn't want to do that with him here, but I had no choice and you two seemed like you'd handle things as good as anybody. I couldn't wait; I couldn't take a chance." Lula took a breath. Didn't want your boy to be scarred for life. I never thought there'd be somebody else's boy out there." She looked at them as if she hoped they had something for her. "Who could have known that?"

"Your kids, Lula?" Don said. "They would have helped you. Nellie and I would have helped."

"Who's Dr. Paulson?" asked Jane. The antidepressants in the medicine cabinet were prescribed by a Dr. Paulson, not by

Fuzzy's doctor. "What kind of doctor have you been going to, Lula?"

"That's right, Jane," said Lula. She smiled and nodded at Nellie. "She is good at snooping around and figuring things out," and then Lula turned back to Jane. "I've got cancer and there's nothing to be done. If they had found it earlier, maybe. I could have had the chemo, but now it wouldn't help enough. Not for long enough. And I'd be too sick to take care of Fuzzy. I was running out of time as it was."

Oh had come up on the porch and whispered something to Munson, who nodded.

"Jack Sullivan's going to be fine."

"Of course he is," said Lula. "I didn't want to kill him."

Dempsey and Hoover had approached the porch, but had hung back, not knowing exactly what they were going to have to admit. Hoover was holding the cardboard box Jane had seen him take from Roger Groveland's garage.

"What do you have there?" asked Munson.

Hoover opened his mouth, but found nothing to say.

Dempsey, however, welcomed the question. Clearly, it was the one he wanted to be asked. Raising one arm for effect, he practically shouted in his best Prof. Harold Hill baritone, "Eureka! We have found more bones on Fuzzy Neilson's land."

Hoover dropped the box and ran back into the cornfield.

Chapter 20

It was a truly amazing feat of garage-sale magic. Up and down Rosewood and Wildwood, Tanner and Cannon, Yates and Hawkins — from the east to the west and the north to the south, in every street and every alley, people came out of their houses, sat at folding tables large and small, and sold their stuff. There were those who brought out two tea towels and an old frying pan, just to say they participated, and there were those who decided to empty out their house to see who liked their stuff and what they could get for it.

Some folks saw it as a chance to start over, begin fresh. Others claimed it was time that they got out of the house and met their neighbors. The busing system worked, and those who drove in from Chicago and other surrounding communities and parked on the outskirts of Kankakee were whisked into town and provided with maps and complimentary shopping bags. Snack carts drove around the neighborhoods doing a brisk business. Private cars were strongly discouraged and severely limited as to where they could be driven or parked. The streets were empty except for the buses, strollers, browsers, and shoppers, and the kids who were riding their bikes with their parents' blessings all over town.

Jane and Charley and Nick had driven down a day early, parked the car at Don and Nellie's, and taken the buses into every corner of Kankakee. Charley had actually found some amazing mineral specimens at the home of a former University of Illinois professor who had retired and taken over his deceased parents' home. Nick had found enough baseball cards and soccer paraphernalia to last him a lifetime. His real find had been an old German erector set. It was huge and he and Charley couldn't wait to start a project with it. Jane was puzzled that she hadn't found anything. It worried her that she could barely feign interest in the tables, in the boxes of books and vanity cases full of costume jewelry. The Pyrex bowls and the mason jars full of buttons were not calling out her name. In two days she hadn't found one thing to buy.

Jane watched the crowds of people shiny-eyed and expectant, all hoping to find exactly what they wanted as soon as they saw whatever that was. She found herself envying them. Even Bruce Oh, walking slightly behind Claire, who was carrying a Vuitton tote bag and a list of addresses where she had to return to pick up furniture, was carrying his own *HOME OF THE TWIN GAZEBOS* shopping bag. When she asked him, he showed her a tie. It was purple with tiny gold skyscrapers on it.

"I knew it would make Claire happy if I replaced the one I ruined that day on the farm," he said. Then he whispered to her, "You are too tired to hear this now, but you did a wonderful job on this case."

"We have one more thing," said Jane. "I promised Munson."

Hoover and Dempsey were participating in the garage sale. Dempsey had met Roger Groveland at some business seminar and Groveland had offered to help launch Hometown USA in Kankakee just before he had his fatal heart attack. Groveland's niece, when she rented the house to Dempsey and Hoover, had told them they could have anything they wanted in the garage. Jane had been sure they would be going to jail for something, but no one had come up with exactly the right formula to send them there. Jane kept trying to accuse them of fraud or intent to commit fraud, but it was a tricky proposition.

Fuzzy had told everyone he planted rocks and arrowheads on his property, so no one could accuse Dempsey and Hoover of trying to trick the Neilsons by salting their land with phony artifacts. The box of bones that Hoover had dropped before he ran into the arms of Bostick at the farm were old animal bones. Jane was sure it was the box that she had seen Hoover put in the car in Groveland's garage, but she couldn't swear to it, and besides, who cared? That duck-billed dinosaur listed on the receipt she had found was going to turn up somewhere, but it hadn't yet. Hoover admitted to being in the outhouse the night of the shooting. He claimed that he and Johnny Sullivan had done a little too much drinking and Johnny had gotten all sentimental and weepy about his cat, Otto. He made Hoover park on the side of the road, and they walked the corn path in. Johnny came up to the shed and scooped up Otto and headed back to the path while Hoover was in the outhouse. When Hoover came out and saw the commotion, he ran back through the field to the highway. He had no idea then that anyone had been shot.

The mighty plans for Hometown USA? No money had changed hands. Were

Dempsey and Hoover planning a swindle of mammoth proportions? Or were Joe Dempsey and Michael Hoover the Don Quixote and Sancho Panza that Kankakee needed to raise itself from the ashes? Munson told Jane that he wasn't even sure he had enough to get them to leave town. Roger Groveland had collected all the information on property owners and seniors who might be tapped for investments. Johnny Sullivan, using the name Roger Groveland, made the phony call reporting the historic find on Neilson's farm. Apparently, Johnny had lifted the blazer from the garage and found that wearing it gave him access to people when he asked questions about their property. He never identified himself as a Realtor, but people assumed he was and confided plans to sell or not sell. Told him how they felt about the airport. Henry Bennett from K3 Realty told Munson, when questioned, that there were a lot of older people who didn't want the airport coming to town, but loved the idea of Hometown USA. People who had said they'd never sell, ever, were flocking to these informational meetings held by Dempsey and Hoover. Johnny Sullivan was a silent partner.

"Pretty damn sneaky," Munson had said

to Jane, "using a dead man's name badge to make people believe you're something you're not."

Jane agreed. Did he have much of a rapport with uniformed officers who stopped people for traffic violations?

"I've got to get them out of town before they leave with somebody's money," said Munson.

That was when she promised Munson that she and Oh would take care of it.

Dempsey and Hoover hadn't had a crowd at their garage. Groveland's belongings had been pretty picked over and they looked it. No effort had been made to spruce up the merchandise.

"When are you planning on leaving town?" Jane asked, stepping up to their card table.

"We're staying for a while. Business is going to be booming here. Tim Lowry has given Kankakee hope, optimism," said Dempsey. "This is a town ready for something good to happen."

Bruce Oh handed Jane a letter, which she held in front of her as she spoke. Oh then took out a small digital camera and asked if they minded being photographed and they smiled broadly and shook their heads. It seemed to amuse them that this Japanese detective, or whatever he was, wanted to photograph them at the world's largest garage sale.

"Going to send this back home to your family?" asked Hoover.

Jane thought Oh smiled.

"I have no idea if you are legitimate, gentlemen, or even if you are who you say you are," said Jane. "If you can convince the citizens of Kankakee that their town needs to be the next Disney World and," she paused, "you deliver the next Disney World, I applaud you."

Dempsey and Hoover both nodded, still smiling and posing.

"And if you are who you say you are and your business is on the up and up, this letter I am mailing today will have no effect," she said, holding it up but out of reach. "It is addressed to Judy Iacuzzi, whom I have been in contact with, and it gives your names, Kankakee addresses, business cards, all the contact numbers on your stationery."

"And I will e-mail your current photographs," said Oh.

Hoover groaned, but Joe Dempsey continued smiling, opening his eyes even wider than usual.

"If this makes no sense to you, great," said Jane. "But if you ever used the name Dempsey Josephson, Ms. Iacuzzi is very anxious to talk over old times."

When Jane's path intersected with Tim's later that day, he hugged her, and without one trace of cynicism told her the garage sale was everything he'd thought it could be.

"People are talking to each other and happy. . . . I can't remember the last time Kankakee was this alive," said Tim.

"That's from *The Music Man*, right? Marian the librarian says that's what the town is like because of Harold Hill and the excitement he brought to town," said Jane.

"If I'm Marian, who's Harold?"

"You, honey. You're the whole damn band," said Jane.

Tim told Jane it would all be perfect if he got 100 percent participation by the end of the two weekends. Jane assured him he would. Everywhere she went, people were talking about how great it would be to make the *Guinness Book of World Records*.

"There's one holdout I'm worried about. Would you give it a try?"

Jane was exhausted from the whole

month. She had helped Lula hire someone to take care of Fuzzy. Lula had been allowed to stay at home until the arraignment — she would be charged with manslaughter and everyone assured her she would not have to go to jail. But Jane knew that it didn't matter what happened at a trial, if there ever was a trial. Lula was declining. Hospice had been called. Dr. Paulson, the oncologist, said Lula wouldn't live more than a month or two. Fuzzy barely knew her now. When Lula saw that was true, that Fuzzy was going, almost gone, she was ready to let go herself. It was as if she had been holding her breath for so long, keeping the illness at bay. As soon as she exhaled, the cancer, poised and ready, reined in for all those months, just thundered through her body.

William Neilson had been here, gone home, and was coming back next week to spend time with his mother. Mary Lee had arrived a week ago to stay until it was over. Lula's children, after the shock and the anger and inevitable questions and unsatisfactory answers, had, to Jane's relief, finally embraced their mother and told her they loved her and would be there for her and do whatever was necessary for their father. It was all the permission she needed to let her body begin to slide away.

When Jane told her what she'd learned about Johnny Sullivan, how he had drunkenly come over with Hoover to steal Otto's bones and plant something else for Charley to find — all to make them think their land was tied up by the government so they'd sign the agreement with Hometown — Lula had just shaken her head. She said she was too tired to think much about it.

"It was Johnny who reported Otto's bones — I mean he didn't know they were Otto's, but he knew they weren't anything significant. He had a friend of his ask to buy the topsoil. He and Roger Groveland were working with Dempsey and Hoover. They were working to get the airport sited here and by then, they'd have the option on your land and they'd resell it and . . ."

Jane had stopped talking when she realized that Lula was asleep.

Now Tim was asking her to do him just this one little favor, to talk to the last woman in Kankakee who refused his pleading, who would not succumb to his charm.

"I am on my knees," said Tim, standing with his hands on her shoulders. "Metaphorically, of course. Please won't you try to talk to her?"

Jane wanted to plead exhaustion. She had earned the right. But Tim had worked too hard and was too close to being completely happy. Maybe a successful mission was just what she needed to get back her own energy. Maybe she would find exactly what she was looking for when she got this stubborn holdout to open her door. Maybe Jane would begin to want something again.

But Nellie was adamant. "I've got nothing I want to sell. I don't keep stuff I don't want," said Nellie. "You know that."

Every time Jane had come home to one of her mother's cleaning binges, things had disappeared. Her stuffed animals. Her Nancy Drew books. Her paint-by-number pictures. Her rock collection. Her plastic gumball machine charms.

Yes, Jane knew it. That's why she didn't have her childhood toys or school papers or scrapbooks or . . . Jane stopped. She had been through this before. They had plowed that ground and uncovered way too many bones. Jane herself was ready to declare a moratorium. Stop the excavation. Declare it a sacred site. Bury it.

It hadn't stopped with childhood. One college vacation, her precisely ripped and fringed bell-bottoms, the ones that fit her perfectly, disappeared. Nellie had acted like she didn't even know what Jane was talking about.

"I haven't seen any jeans like that," said Nellie, "but if I did, I probably would throw them away. Sounds like hobo clothes."

The most irritating part was that Nellie would never own up to getting rid of any of it. She'd say the room looked better without whatever it was Jane was crying for, and then she'd buy her something new to replace the tattered stuffed animal or offer a new outfit to replace the jeans. Jane always refused at first, but eventually came around to the new item and then hated herself for being bought off. It was one of Bartender Nellie's double-whammy doses of neurosis. A cocktail mixed of two parts abandonment and deprivation to one part self-loathing. Shake over cold-as-cracked-ice-lack-of-emotional-support and strain into a shaky relationship.

Oh yes, Jane was ready to bury it.

"Mom, you must have some old pans or dishes in the basement you don't want? Cauldrons? Brooms?" she muttered under her breath. "For Tim's sake."

On Sunday, the last day of the sale, Don stepped in.

He had some worn decks of cards and euchre scoreboards. Some glasses from the tavern. He told her to bring up the boxes from the basement and do whatever she wanted with them. She could set up a table and sell it all.

"Don't buy the junk yourself," Don said, patting her shoulder. "And don't tell your mother."

Don and Nellie were leaving for the EZ Way Inn. Nellie had made soup every day of the sale and sold it out. Don said business was almost as good as when Roper was still there. Everybody in town was already lobbying Tim to make this an annual event.

Charley and Tim were catching a bus to the neighborhood set up as "book city." The four-block area promised everything from vintage *Archie and Veronica* comic books to Shakespeare. They knew Jane planned to put out a few things so Tim could document the 100-percent participation. Nick had set up a card table, and Charley had offered her a cup of coffee from the pot Nellie had left for her.

"I haven't bought anything, Charley," said Jane.

Charley didn't answer right away. He opened one of Nellie's immaculate drawers, revealing the compartment that held spoons, that would always hold spoons, and most important, would only hold spoons. Beware errant fork, loner knife, lest you end up in a compartment where you do not belong, are not wanted. Nellie would take it as a personal blow if someone ever wantonly messed up her silverware drawer. Charley looked at his wife. He placed a fork in with the spoons and closed the drawer.

"Need any help carrying Don's stuff up here? Before I leave with Nick?"

Jane shook her head and allowed him to hold her, to wrap her up in his arms. She said she wanted to want something. Well . . . there was Charley. She smiled into his jacket.

"Are you crying?"

"No," said Jane. "I'm ready to go home, though."

"Yes, tonight, dear one. Now get a table set up for an hour or so and let somebody take a picture so we've done our duty for Tim. Then," he said, holding her out at arm's length, "I am taking you home."

Jane nodded.

"And Nick and I are going to make you look at all of our stuff, each and every little thing that we found."

Jane got out the glasses and decks of cards that Don had packed away. She set them on the front porch and went back downstairs for a final check. Was there anything else her father had to sell? The basement was eerily clean. When Don and Nellie had moved into this house, Jane was a senior in high school. She had never really formed an attachment here, but she remembered liking the idea of having a finished basement. "Finished," of course, was a relative term. The previous owners left their "party room" furniture, which consisted of a large, round Formica table with uncomfortable metal chairs and two couches that were so characterless that no one could call them vintage. They were just old sofas that Jane couldn't imagine anyone ever buying new.

There was knotty pine paneling behind the built-in bar and netting hung behind it, lit with tiny Christmas tree lights. Don's boxes had been stacked under the bar, which was probably how they had remained hidden from Nellie's eagle eye. Jane dragged out the last one and turned to look at the twinkling lights. So odd that Nellie hadn't ripped down all that netting. Even Jane could see that it was a dust catcher. And God knows, Nellie didn't like dust catchers. Jane lifted it, just to see where the lights were plugged in. Maybe she would unplug them and dust. That would shake the Nellster up a little bit.

Lifting the net revealed something much more surprising than an electrical outlet. There was a handle and below it, a spring-loaded latch. The knotty pine paneling had a door cut out of it. It made perfect sense since this wall was actually against the stairs and Jane realized this was just a way to use the wasted space as a closet. The bar had been built and the previous owners had walled off the under-stairs area with the paneling so it wasn't noticeable. Did Don and Nellie even know about this?

Jane tugged on the handle, squeezing down on the latch. It gave and the door opened to reveal a space about three by eight, the height correlating with the stairs that formed the closet ceiling. Jane ducked her head and stepped into the cramped cupboard. Too dark to see. She stepped out and turned on all of the basement lights. Nellie, with her almost batlike fear of bright light, had screwed fifteen-watt lightbulbs in all of the basement fixtures. Jane found one floor lamp that had a forty-watt bulb and dragged it closer to the bar. In flipping one of the light switches, Jane had turned on a radio that her father had set on a low table by the couch and another set of Christmas lights now twinkled above the bar. The music was some kind of elevator arrangement, an instrumental of something familiar. Jane could hum it, but it was so off base that she was having trouble wrapping her mind around the lyrics. "When I'm driving" . . . oh, no. "Satisfaction"? The Rolling Stones would turn over in their graves if they ever allowed themselves to be pronounced dead.

Jane went back to the cupboard. Stacks of boxes. Neatly packed and sealed with masking tape. What was this feeling rising up in Jane Wheel? The exhaustion and the ennui, the sadness and despair she had felt with Lula and Fuzzy felt fainter. The feelings were not completely gone. They were just medicated. Jane knew that. But it felt so good to feel the old familiar itch. She dragged out a stack of two boxes and put them next to the light. Then, greedy, she went in for two more. There were at least six left inside, but she decided to open these up to see what she was getting herself into. She couldn't remember from whom her parents had bought the house. Senior year in high school, she had one foot out the door and had barely spent any time at all in this basement.

Around the other side of the stairs, where the washer and dryer were located, she had done some laundry, although Nellie usually took care of that. She told Jane she didn't like the way she added the soap. Her mother also told Jane that she didn't understand the shaking out of wet clothes. If they weren't shaken properly, Nellie told her, they would dry with more wrinkles. Jane had half wanted to know where these laws were made, but she was seventeen and she also half wanted to get the hell out of this house.

Jane remembered having friends over once and coming down here to the basement, but Nellie kept opening the door up in the kitchen and asking if Jane had called her.

"No, Mom, I didn't call you," Jane would answer.

"Huh. I thought I heard you call me," Nellie would answer back.

The third or fourth time, Jane's friends got the message and gave up. There would be no cigarettes sneaked, no bottles sipped, no kisses stolen, not on Nellie's watch.

"So what have we here?" Jane asked herself out loud. Whatever this hidden treasure turned out to be, someone had thought whatever was in these boxes was precious. The cartons were carefully sealed and Jane had noticed that the ones on the bottom were set on bricks inside the closet to guard against any dampness.

Jane carefully pulled off the tape and opened the first box.

The smell of mothballs rolled out like a wave. Jane lifted off a layer of tissue paper and held up a blue wool coat with a princess collar trimmed in green leather. It would fit a little girl, maybe three or four years old. It was a perfect Sunday coat from the midfifties and Jane found herself grinning and oohing and aahing over it. Who did she know who had a little girl she could dress in vintage? Or maybe she should contact a costume designer? If all these boxes contained clothes in such mint condition, they could be worth something. The next item was a matching hat that tied under the chin. Also on a knitted string, a pair of mittens and a blue fur muff. Jane kept pulling out clothes, one item more adorable than the next. When she got to the bottom of the box, she pulled out a navy blue wool jumper.

"They must have had a girl at St. Pat's," said Jane. "This has got to be a St. Pat's jumper."

"They did," said Nellie.

"Jeez!" Jane screamed and jumped to her feet. "When did you come in?"

"I been watching you dance around and talk to yourself for about five minutes," said Nellie. "What do you think you're doing down here?"

"Dad said . . ."

"Yeah, he told me. He's sitting at that stupid card table right now selling worn-out decks of cards for a dime."

"Did you know about this closet?"

Nellie stared at her. Jane looked into her mother's blue eyes, as pale as Jane's were dark. Nellie's mouth twitched as if she had the greatest secret, but she just didn't know which was sweeter, keeping it or revealing it.

Then Jane knew.

It was her coat, her hat, and mittens. Her St. Pat's jumper.

Nellie nodded. She walked over and poked her head into the closet.

"Yeah, it's all yours except for the two boxes in the corner. That's all Michael's report cards and schoolwork. Some books, I think. Maybe his baseball glove."

"You've had this stuff all along?"

"What's the big deal? That coat isn't going to fit you, is it? Nick sure as hell wasn't going to wear it. Figured I might have a granddaughter someday. Or a great-granddaughter," Nellie said, sniffing and tidying up the tissue paper that Jane had thrown on the floor.

"What else?"

Nellie shrugged.

Jane tore into the next box and pulled out an old friend. She had thought her bear Mortimer was gone forever. Smaller than she remembered, raggedy, and with one eye missing. But it was Mortimer.

"You told me you got rid of him."

"Never. Never told you I threw anything away. You just thought I did. I told you I had cleaned up your room. And after a while, when you had new stuff, you stopped asking. I just wanted you to have nice things. Who knew you were going to grow up into somebody who wanted junk?" Nellie said. "God knows that isn't my fault. I put you around nice things."

By the time Nick and Charley got back, Jane had unpacked the treasures of the hidden closet and discovered her favorite old toys, her old school notebooks, religious statues she had won as school prizes, pictures of Tim and her playing in their old backyard. She had called her brother, Michael, in California and made him cry when she told him she was holding his baseball cards.

Nellie kept shaking her head and shrugging, circling her finger around her temple and making the cuckoo sign to Nick.

"Why'd you hide it all, Grandma?"

"Wasn't hiding it. Just keeping it from getting all dusty."

"But you never told anybody, Nellie," said Charley, "you kept it all buried down here."

"Who cared about it?" asked Nellie. "Jane figured I'd thrown it away, and she never asked me for it. I had forgotten it until I saw Jane down here messing around. Besides, people need to move on and not sit around with their memories. Jeez, where does that get you?"

Jane was leafing through an old notebook from her junior high English class. She had been exchanging notes with her best friend, Peggy Sandwell, the entire year, it seemed. She wondered if they had ever written down anything from the class.

"So why did you keep it, Mom?"

"I had the closet for it. It all fit," said Nellie, seriously trying to answer the question. She hadn't thought about it before. "You were leaving. Michael was going to leave, too. So I thought I'd keep it for you.

In case you ever came back, I guess," Nellie said. "You really never asked about this stuff."

Jane considered the objects scattered around the basement. She had never asked. She had assumed her mother had thrown them all away. And she had been trying to replace so much for such a long time. Looking for love in all the wrong places? When had her dad switched the radio station to Country Western?

"What about my jeans from college? What box are they in?"

"I threw them rags away," said Nellie.

Charley stood up and started up the stairs.

"Where are you going?" asked Nellie. "Hungry? I'll get you all some supper before you drive back."

"No, not hungry. I just remembered a fork I have to put away."

Jane had decided to let her mother repack all the boxes and put them back into the closet. Nellie was visibly relieved, telling Jane that they'd just get lost in the shuffle at Jane's house. Jane had to try one more time.

"Mom, you know I collect all this kind of stuff, so why didn't you ever think I'd

432

want to know . . . ? You know, that you had my childhood packed away in there?"

"Because I didn't. It wasn't yours. It was mine. You didn't even remember that coat, but I know the day we went to the Fair Store and bought it. You put it on and spun around in the mirror, and we couldn't afford it. There was no way I could spend that money on a coat you'd wear a few Sundays for one year. But you liked it and I bought it; that's all there is to it. You didn't even remember it was yours. That was my memory, not yours," said Nellie. "What do you save that's Nick's? Because I'm telling you right now, it won't be the right stuff. It'll be your stuff of Nick's childhood, not his."

Jane thought of the carefully packed away Brio train that Nick had never played with that she wouldn't let Claire Oh sell at the garage sale.

Nellie was right. The buried stuff Jane mourned were things that her mother couldn't possibly have recognized as important, as vital, as precious. What was it Nellie had said before? Jane didn't take what her mother offered; she just kept asking for things she thought her mother had. She thought about Fuzzy burying those pennies, leaving his treasures behind.

Would the person who found them recognize their value?

"Sew his eye back on, okay?" Nellie said, shoving something into her arms and ducking away when Jane tried to kiss her good-bye. "Clean your house. Fix the bear."

Jane nodded, hugging Mortimer to her. Fragile and temporary . . . she and Nellie had finally come to an agreement on at least one memory.

About the Author

Sharon Fiffer collects buttons, Bakelite pottery, vintage potholders, keys, locks, and other killer stuff. She is coeditor of the anthologies *Home: American Writers Remember Rooms of Their Own*; *Body*; and *Family: American Writers Remember Their Own*. She is the author of three previous Jane Wheel mysteries and *Imagining America*. She lives near Chicago.

Visit her Web site at
www.sharonfiffer.com.

The employees of Thorndike Press hope you have enjoyed this Large Print book. All our Thorndike and Wheeler Large Print titles are designed for easy reading, and all our books are made to last. Other Thorndike Press Large Print books are available at your library, through selected bookstores, or directly from us.

For information about titles, please call:

(800) 223-1244

or visit our Web site at:

www.gale.com/thorndike
www.gale.com/wheeler

To share your comments, please write:

Publisher
Thorndike Press
295 Kennedy Memorial Drive
Waterville, ME   04901